S C O T T   T I E N K E N

The Remove

Cartophile

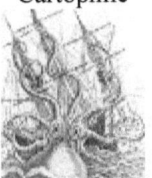

Imprint

THE REMOVE. by Scott Tienken.
ISBN: 978-0692570203
Copywright © 2015 by Scott Tienken
A Cartophile Imprint, Portland, OR.
thecartophileimprint.com
Cover illustration by Kimberly Patton

For our Papa, The Captain

You know more than you think you do.
—*Dr. Benjamin Spock, Baby and Child Care*

I am the wisest man alive, for I know one thing,
and that is that I know nothing.
—*Plato, The Republic*

Plato says that the unexamined life is not worth
living. But what if the examined life turns out to
be a clunker as well.
 —*Kurt Vonnegut, Wampeters, Foma and
    Granfalloons*

—Go ahead, baby.

    The car Warren gave her knows she cannot drive. Twice already it has seized to a halt in protest and slammed her daughter into the back of the passenger seat. But until she gets another bicycle this is how they will get around.

    —Big girls cry, too.

    And the spring rains keep boiling and traffic sizzles on by.

At the last red light she had re-secured the bandage on her stomach and tightened the chest restraint around her poncho, but the child is already slumped over again. Outings make her crumble like this. Likely, too, she knows they are headed to another socialization.

    —Maybe we can get some ice cream after?

    Bribery. God, how cliché. She'll need to be more creative if she is ever going to persuade her daughter that the other children's poking and prodding is useful somehow, even enjoyable.

    —Your sister likes ice cream.

    But they will keep showing up. Otherwise, the membership would come knocking, remind her how beloved they are. . .*especially now*. . .and drag them out of the bungalow. And, who knows, if this morning they install her on a swing to see how high she can fly and she somehow manages to not fall to pieces then maybe all this suffering will have been worth it for that tiny bit of progress.

    —Not that you have to be like your sister, though.

    Yes, she will cooperate even if their counselors keep insisting she and her daughter *both* need to become more independent, *both* need to begin evolving separate identities. There was just no point in telling them anymore that she will never let this child out of her sight, that she would rather turn into some drooling goony bird and become trapped inside the same marble-walled silence as her daughter than risk being separated from her.

    —Everyone has their own likes and dislikes.

Just don't ask her to be like the other parents calmly watching their children flee to the distant corners of the playground, bragging about how trusting or outgoing their little so-and-so's are, cooing and pshawing like there wasn't this kernel of utter terror inside requiring a serious form of mania to ignore. No, not until her daughter can cry out at her tormentor or wriggle free from their clutches will she allow herself to begin reconstructing that intricate complex of delusions known as 'confidence' and not panic when she is more than an arm's reach away.

—Everyone is different.

At the next light she stops short, leaps backward, and throws her arm across her daughter's chest harder than intended. But the fragile child only goes on staring out the melting window, looking in that way of not seeing, her poncho ticking back into shape.

—Your mother loves her children equally, Sweetheart.

She listens to the echo of her lie for a moment, huddles under its flimsy dome, feels like a fraud and failure, stares into the whitewash sky spitting tears, the presumptuous bulk of the surrounding city's machinery, the skeins of traffic mercifully delaying their destination, the flood of private citizens commuting to the public lives which distract or console them—If these relatively fortunate souls equipped with leverage and language still sometimes become lost while navigating their divided lives then how will it be for a child stranded solely at a remove and beyond the reach of even her mother?

—You believe me don't you?

Two days ago Belladonna Mabuse called the Co-op caterer to remind him not to shave the boar. When he barked back reassurances and hung up without once addressing her as 'Sister' she gaped at the receiver and snorted in delight. Here was a kindred spirit, a non-doctrinaire brother she might steady her nerves with in Grand muh-Ma's four-poster before her Seventh Annual. Plus, having such a brute serve dinner would make her personal transformation appear all the more extraordinary in contrast. Yes, it looked as though Belladonna Mabuse was finally beginning to make her own luck.

So when the knock finally comes in the early afternoon before the soiree, Belladonna sends her chair clattering to the floor, nearly upends muh-Ma's vanity, lunges down the rickety staircase, gallops across the dining room's wailing floorboards, leaps into the sunken, dry-rotted vestibule and whips open the water-warped front door to feast her eyes on this monstrous confederate. But what she finds horrifies her. Stooping good-naturedly under the door frame, then looming over her in his crisply laundered Co-op blacks is a tauntingly pretty young thing with obvious grace and immaculate *toilette*. This wasn't just another of The Co-op's endlessly recycling *suaves* but a being so physically magnificent as to be not only stylistically and dogmatically opposed to Belladonna Mabuse but almost *chemically* repulsed by her! O god where was her beast from the phone?! What kind of conspiracy was this?!

Slouching, struggling against the suck of one of her miasmatic little depressions, she watches him cheerfully lift the dome from the platter to reveal that one bristly creature capable of truly understanding her. There are, she silently confides to the hirsute boar, too many potential tragedies in life to mourn for long. A woman of discipline should know better than to expect instant results. She must concentrate only on what she can control. Yes, and only very occasionally bare her fangs at ridiculous fate.

So and thus, Belladonna Mabuse overcomes the first little crisis of her Seventh Annual Co-op Soiree.

—Very good, Brother. The kitchen is through there.

o   o   o   o   o   o   o   o   o

Later that afternoon her guests are enjoying the caterer's predictably perfect hors d'oeuvres while standing by the dining room's rain-strewn windows. Since this is the first Co-op Soiree which she has opened the curtains for, each new arrival has the rare opportunity of viewing *The Mabuse Ravine*—a steep canyon choked with tangled oak and bathed in the devious red glow of the footlights twisting up the ancient staircase to the street. Nervously clutching her wrists behind her back, steaming up the window she gazes through, Belladonna explains that the Mabuses were an ultra-orthodox Huguenot clan who fled their persecutors, ventured west long after it was fashionable, bought the unclaimed slash of jungly trench before us, hacked out just enough room for this simple oak house, and went about the dogged business of becoming oak barons. Reciting and occasionally embellishing the tale of those self-righteous and spiritually masochistic forebears of hers she experiences genuine emotion. Strange. Maybe some un-killable ancestral urge has traveled through all that dense wood, mystically penetrated the window and briefly possessed her. It is a quaint notion easily dismissed. More of *moment* is that her guests appear stimulated and this phase of the soiree can be rated a success. She may now allow them a brief interval for talking about their children, jobs, and whatever other enthusiasms they share while she sips her wine and pretends to listen. Before long it will be time to close the curtains.

   —There are name cards, brothers and sisters. Please be seated.

The worn oak tabletop is crowded with dilapidated Huguenot heirlooms; chipped china with a wheat threshing scene in faded royal blue, fat-faceted scratched crystal, dented and un-varnished silver, threadbare serviettes. If not for the caterer who knew to arrive two hours early to sort through the Boschian scene in Sister Belladonna's kitchen, many of these place settings would be incomplete.

   —As you can see our guest list is a bit more selective this year.

   Before entering with the side dishes the caterer turns up the electric moose antler candelabra. This dust-draped contraption (purchased by her grandmother's brief, fraudulent, and absconding husband) does little to illuminate this oak dungeon smeared with 154 years of eating and recriminations. No, there are only degrees of begloomment here. And since Belladonna is afraid she might burst through the bottom of her 154 year-old oak chair if she tried to replace the dead bulbs, her soirees get darker, her table setting becomes more lurid, and the membership (all dressed as instructed in their formal Co-op blacks but one) seep deeper into the background.

In order to conserve light, she has eaten upstairs for the last six months crammed into muh-Ma's teetering oak vanity. Staring into the mirror bisected by a NW—NE crack, counting each chew of the bland dietary meals delivered thrice daily, she has repeatedly told herself that each small austerity would add up to the triumph of her Seventh Annual. . .*I only need enough light for just this one more*. . .But her guests' are more obscure than ever, their ramrod postures superimposed onto the black walls, their heads static except when their shadowy faces contort into a caricature mask of delight or distaste or, most frequently, intense concern. If not for the yellow C∞P pendants attached to their lapels they might be mistaken for a gathering of disembodied and decapitated ghouls. [Except of course that one scofflaw, the guest of honor seated next to her who Belladonna is doing her best to ignore.]

After serving the side dishes the caterer returns carrying a scuffed silver platter. With the dignity and deference of someone expert at disguising his inner-rebellion, he sets it down to await Belladonna's cue. Undoubtedly, he has shaved the boar on the instructions of someone in his work group. . .*Ignore Sister Belladonna. . .She's completely undoctrinaire*. . .and has prepared some excuse for not following her instructions. But when he removes the dome a gasp goes up. The boar for The Seventh Annual Co-op Soiree is not some sleek and glistening pig but a leather-skinned beast covered with singed and curling hairs! Belladonna covers her mouth with her serviette to muffle her snorting.

—Ahem. . .yes. . .er. . .*oui*.

Her heart is racing and her palms itch and she thinks this must be what optimism feels like. Yes, her delicious little mascot has heralded her rebirth. Just see how as the caterer slices into him his flesh falls. . .no *surrenders* from the bone in gentle, almost worshipful hushes. It is as though her sacrificial pig wants to demonstrate for her guests just how easy it is to relinquish old grudges.

3

—Voilà the traditional Huguenot recipe, brothers and sisters. An homage to my forebears. Please. . .*enjoy.*

Her guests skeptically consider the meat placed on their plates. Belladonna cannot blame them for thinking this aggressively ugly centerpiece is nothing but a prelude to her annual offensive. O but that was the old Belladonna Mabuse, brothers and sisters. Haven't they noticed how much she has changed? Didn't she allow each of them to give her a good long look in the vestibule? (She *can* reach the vestibule light, thankfully.) Didn't they notice the weight loss? The new teeth? The austere little black bob replacing her witch's tangle? The swapping out of her black and blue make-up scheme for what the Co-op cosmetician called *Azure and Violet Dawn*? How her signature black leather dress was no longer wrinkled and stained but tight and sleek? And, most of all, isn't it obvious that in addition to no longer *resembling* the tusked centerpiece, she has ditched her boorish *behavior* as well? Yes, brothers and sisters, she has taken all the appropriate modules, traded in her honorary status for regular membership and learned all the secrets to becoming the perfect little Co-op sister. Just notice how as the evening progresses she. . .*honors each person's right to their own intellectual space. . .allows for others' personal journeys. . .takes her turn at driving the pack forward.* . .all while nodding respectfully at even their most outrageous bits of preachy drivel. O couldn't they see how pleasurable it was for her to be this mild little hostess drinking unhurriedly, pecking at her boar, blending in with all the warm and tinkling Co-operative talk? And don't her darling guests know by now that her massive annual donation, while not contingent on their attendance, should encourage them to not only take their hostess more seriously once a year but. . .*embrace her personal journey*?. . . And this year above all others?! Couldn't they concede that while she was still no beauty. . .nor pretty. . .nor even sturdily handsome. . .that her nose still resembled a turtle's beak. . .her grey eyes remained hopelessly bloodshot. . .that she was only slightly less morbidly obese. . .would never be considered intelligent or witty. . .or remotely attuned to what is considered humorous these days. . .or perceptive or winning or uncalculatingly kind or good in any obvious way. . .that despite these many stubborn shortcomings she was still well on her way to becoming far more *palatable*? Yes, given her exemplary behavior so far they should be much further along in realizing that she deserves a freaking *reassessment* here, okay? Yet no one so much as compliments or even addresses her. They only go on excluding her by talking about those infinitely adorable little protégés and projects of theirs—their children. And when she tries to gently insert herself into their conversations she begins to notice, unmistakable even in this dark light, a collective after-aspect of *rejection*. Yes, look close! You can see it in an over-rigid jaw, a pulsing vein in the temple, a pair of eyes rolled heaven-ward; a seemingly prearranged refusal to enter any zone which their hostess might project herself into, however doctrinally. Yes, their secret selves give her brothers and sisters away! If Sister Belladonna Mabuse is to express herself at all tonight she must limit herself to crude and horrible talk. That way they can talk to her like they do the rest of the year—like she is nothing but a stupid, lost little child. . .*What's become of our old Sister Belladonna?. . .What happened to that idealistic young woman we used to know?. . . She bled for this Co-op. . .Was practically a radical. . .God, how we loved her. . .But now she's become so self-seeking. . . So non-doctrinaire. . .We don't keep saying this just because it's good doctrine. . .We say it because we want the old Sister Belladonna back.*

Obviously, they thought the new woman in front of them was a sham. And O but weren't they perceptive. For only by pulverizing each bite of boar into fine cud instead of speaking can she remain doctrinally disciplined enough to appear worthy of their unrestricted love again. But with each moment that passes without someone giving her the smallest encouraging look or the most minor bit of kudos she becomes increasingly unable to not think back to last year's soiree. (What with the diet pills clashing with the bottomless glass of wine and her then still recent rejection by a new age monastery compelling her to drink straight through her dizziness and fully depart the sweet little cloister she had carved out in her mind to blurt out Warren's sexual tendencies for the benefit of his fiancée, last year's guest of honor.) And why else but for the diminishing likelihood of ever being loved unreservedly by her brothers and sisters again would she now be sipping so immoderately from her wine after so many months of relative discipline and reconstructing all the traumatic childhood years which all the oppressive oak and

5

Huguenot heirlooms so easily summon. . .*Remember your waistline Belladonna, dear. . .No dessertsies for ma petite ce soir. . .Votre muh-Ma is très sérieuse, completemente et too-too.* . .reinventorying the savageries she experienced at this table as a vulgar teen with a drunken swinger of a mother. . . *Sweetsie-Belle! Do not sin against your Grand muh-Ma! Perform the dinner grace, maintenant!.* . .and a holy-holy flagellant of a grandmother. . .*Non, granddaughter, stop! I will pray to our Lord for all of us since I am the one responsible for bringing all of our sin into this rotten world.* . . thinking if only she had built herself up a little more in college, had more time to shed her old self in that distant city before being called back to become caretaker of this brooding manse of the historical register at a highly immature 25. . . *Amen already. Now, Sweetsie-Belle, listen. Your grand martyr is right. Never have children. Let your grand martyr and I be the last Mabuses to bring another one of us monsters into the world.* . .well then she might not have so swiftly gone from being a budding young Co-op reformer intent on tithing her fortune away to an even more disgusting version of that vulgar little teen she thought she had been well on the way to erad-icating. And O but *non*, her guests wouldn't care to notice that her soul is gradually departing her body to hide in the same buzzing black corner of the ceiling she hid in during her mother's own soirees, and that in the space separating that soul from the shell left at the table remains not only her past selves but the many after-aspects of the horrible women who continue to haunt her. muh-Ma butchering her French to needle grand muh-Ma. Grand muh-Ma only ever addressing the ceiling and that sole tolerable Companion of hers housed far above. Teenage Belladonna entering a fugue-state while they sneered and spat at one another. Yes, all those cloyingly recurring lives separating the soul from the body now tran-sport Belladonna further back to the night she was promoted from eating in the kitchen with the maid to this same oak table. . .*Now that you are a young woman, Sweetsie-Belle (primp of Belladonna's undersized bosom, squeeze of the already over-flowing hips, theft of the serviette in her daughter's lap to tent over the boar remains on her plate), let's try not to rely too much on this tumsy-wumsy of yours keeping up your chastities. . .After all, your muh-Ma could fill her chastities when she was barely 12. . .(grand muh-Ma*

*sneering past the candelabra to address the ceiling, throwing
her serviette down at the untouched boar on her plate) O lord,
my sinful daughter neglects to mention she was too busy*
removing *the chastities to have any idea how well they fit her.
Your filthy lambs are all doomed liars, O Lord. . .(muh-Ma
shouting up into a different zone of the ceiling) Oh tell your
lord to take a drink now and then. That'll help him swallow
us. . .*No, her guests cannot see the child now re-inhabiting the
adult as she squints into that same shadowy ceiling remove
where she practiced being just as much of a bitch as that dear
sweet bitch of a muh-Ma of hers and just as capable a shrew
as that regal ole shrew of a grand muh-Ma of hers so she
could at least feel closer to the two women who were too busy
tormenting one another to spend much time loving her. Yes,
The Remove, that invisible cloud which follows us everywhere, steals over us when we are tired or confused or too
alone, that inexorable chemistry which recycles our memories,
reduces our existence to hopes and fears, then persuades us to
believe there is a coherent narrative or even just a figure of
speech which might make a lick of sense out of our lives,
where our shortage of understanding allows our imagination
to run amok and our hungry reason to grasp at straws and so
leaves us vulnerable to the various forms of possession we
sometimes mistake for our identities. Belladonna, caught in
this vicious circle and whirlpooling downwards, slurps her
wine and starts gathering up her after-aspects, only pausing
over the Novice-Bitch-as-Teenager and the Idealistic-Post-
Collegiate to conclude that the moral distance between them
and her 32-year old self is negligible. Yes, she has always
been just another awful Mabuse woman. And since The
Remove encourages just these sorts of syllogistic and melodramatic thoughts, Belladonna can further conclude that there
is a certain nobility in being the last in a long line of loveless
bitches.

    —Ahem. a-HEM! Excusez moi.

    So, bon. It is time to raise the same serviette that
drunken but somehow always elegant muh-Ma of hers raised
during that most memorable of soirees when she dabbed the
air with wild embellishments while telling the stock tale about
their oaken forebears and grand muh-Ma was forced to push
herself up from her place setting, throttle the same serviette
now lying in the lap of tonight's guest of honor, and

frantically polish the air her daughter had. . .*befouled with fabulations, O lord*. . .while muh-Ma smugly folded her ser-viette into quarters with that magnificent slowness of hers (O god how Belladonna remembers. . .the slowness of a goddamn geologic epoch. . . . . .*fold*. . .*fold*. . . . . .*smoooooth),* tucked it under the rim of her china, pincered the glass of wine which would always be sea-tossed but never quite mount the sur-rounding quay, curled her sinfully provocative figure side-ways to interrupt her gaunt, tiny, and gesticulating muh-Ma, tossed aside the peroxide-scorched hair away from the smirk-ingly lovely face which tormented her mug ugly muh-Ma so . . .*(Belladonna, years later, looking down on the pale marble planes of her mother's forehead glowing up from her booze-built death bier, wondering if those cold nullities betokened an ultimately far preferable remove. . .Belladonna crying for the final time then, knowing she was inheriting far too soon). . .* leered deliciously as grand muh-Ma shouted her own em-bellishments about the intense temporal hardships those Huguenots had endured only so her rebuke of a daughter could defame their memory by sharing too-rich meals and bottles of un-cheap wine with the Godless. . .*(grand muh-Ma finally brandishing her silverware at the candelabra then pleadingly upturning her palms). . .Another husbandless mother, O Lord!. . .But this one a fallen woman with a ruined womb!. . .*in sum providing this dooming influence to a 16 year-old child (Belladonna) whose own intensely non-exemplary performance across a range of early indicators. . . *My granddaughter should know our forebears practiced diligence. . .humilité. . .chastité. . .Ils mangeaient et dorm-aient ces choses pour Dieu. . .*was undoubtedly the legacy of her mother's unrelenting waywardness. . .*Sweetsie-Belle, votre grand martyr despises our weakness. . .(Swallow). . . Voilà, mon chou, have une autre petite tartlet. . .*Yes, after this relatively programmatic mutual assault, the guests (muh-Ma's usual roster of libertines) indulged in their typically contra-puntal wiseacre and insisted Belladonna's mother merely acted as their circle's promiscuous angel. . .*Now Madame Mabuse. Esther. Honey. Listen. Your Hortense is one of our New Women. . .a sex-positive NOWer. . .a feminist revolution-ary. . .And her precious Belladonna will carry the tradition on after her. . .and then her daughter will after her. . .and so on and so on and so on. . .*Then muh-Ma took one long swallow of wine, veered to her left to cup the cheek of her howlingly ugly yet already competitively promiscuous daughter, smiled so languorously it seemed like she might tip over, and stunned not only her guests but even her muh-Ma by adding. . .*Yes, and while it may be true that Belladonna takes after me spiritually, muh-Ma. . .(swig, swig) (gulp). . .at this rate mon pouvre pouvre dear darling looks like she is going to be just as ugly as her dear ole grand muh-Ma. . . (gulp). . .just more fully formed. . .(primp of Belladonna's hips). . .(squeeze of her belly). . .and, hopefully, as barren as winter on your precious Quebecois plain.*

So as Belladonna lowers the very same serviette to shakingly dab her mouth, she wishes she could be a fraction as demure as her boozo knockout of a mother or have a single shred of her imperturbable sense of dramatic *moment* instead of having to hear herself shrilly corral her guests' attention by blurting what she wants to purr. If only she could look as magnificent as muh-Ma did once she embraced her duties and started to get *ugly*.

—You know I was just realizing that Sister Ronette is the only one here who hasn't tried yet.

Given the confused looks on their faces the new invitees must be unaware that this 154-year old oak table has sat countless holy-holy's and a priest short-listed for saint-hood (gulp of wine), not to mention those same zealous acti-vists who parlayed hustle and poverty into the fortune from which their hostess has tithed massive quarterly checks to The Co-op since she more or less endowed the sucker seven years ago. Oui, *that* Belladonna Mabuse, you sanctimonious twerps.

—That is besides me, of course.

You see, even if she is just the minor splinter of muh-Ma's Total Rejection of the Family Faith she still shares her line's reform-minded fervor in spades. Ah, bon, the ugliness was beginning to flow now. She will use the alcohol to galvanize her hurt and sloppily shepherd her disparate souls for the pell-mell flagellations to come. And while her highly non-doctrinaire behavior will delay her Co-op rehabilitation this may yet turn out to be a productive evening.

—You know! Une petite *bébé*!?

In the past six months, while Belladonna rehearsed her new manners in muh-Ma's vanity, off to the side she had reserved a small spot in The Remove for scrumptiously inventorying resentments, fabricating grievances, and deciding what was the most damning thing she could say to tonight's guest of honor. And however pathetic it feels to be on the brink of doing just what she had hoped she would not *have* to do, she is also finding herself pretty turned on by breaking down and doing it anyway.

—Well, you're all babying up now, right? Just recently there was Anna and Celia. . .and oh The Jennifers are expecting again. Then there is Courtney and oh Lou and Manuel, that counts too. I mean even Warren and that *teenager* are talking adoption!

Belladonna re-dabs her mouth with the serviette, looks at her old black lipstick stains, then the fresh purple ones, then her mother's faded red ones, and begins to experience the perverse pleasure of maintaining an awful reputation. Yes, she will go about the dogged business of attacking a blameless woman and appearing every bit the monster she has worked so hard to forget. Though with a victim like Ronette Okampo—what with all her spring-summer aura, the freckles and strawberry blond braids, the serenity of her emerald pools, the limber lips prone to smiling in lieu of speech, the non-cosmetic straightforwardness she is always beaming back—sometimes the best that can be done is to remind her how she used to be different.

—I mean there are things to cuddle besides cycling trophies, Ronette.

But, Christ, it's demoralizing to even *look* at a woman like this. She was someone who could arrive late to The Seventh Annual wearing nothing but a tight yellow bike messenger outfit, plead 'late deliveries,' and still appear chic. Just see how the woman's intense personal wattage glows back from her grand muh-Ma's seat like some bountifully judgmental harvest moon. No, absolutely no one objects when a woman like *this* breaks dress code. *No* one.

—There was life *before* cycling and there will be life *after* cycling.

Belladonna dabs her mouth, looks away from the lovely woman placidly smiling back at her, and suddenly remembers when muh-Ma stationed her next to grand muh-Ma's oak four-poster to disinfect the cancer-riddled flagellant's wounds and how even as the last of her release pains racked that desiccated body she went on joyfully gasping about the consolation of everyone's spoilage. . .*Life is nothing but sinning and suffering, child. . .But if you wrap yourself in the swaddling clothes—Aaaaagh!—of the good lord's graces—Oh! OOOO!—you will not have to die as alone as your mother will. . .It's not too late. . .even for you, child. . .* But surveying the severe masks of sympathy and concern her guests wear for Ronette, Belladonna concludes that there are only two types of people in this world: Those who know they will die alone and those, like Ronette Okampo and her idolaters, who have happily forgotten.

　　—You've never been a hard-core Cooper, Sister Ronette. No one will expect your baby to join *The Cause.*

　　Yes, grand muh-Ma failed to realize that the living gods are everywhere among us. They build monuments to themselves with self-righteousness and personal pronouns. . .*All lines wither and die, Child. . .It's never too late to begin mortifying your flesh. . .*This world she whipped herself raw in is now teeming with The Uni-gods of Self-Love whose lives are arranged to be one long pageant, a relentless display of private holdings, shouted from rooftops to reach ever more fresh ears, whispered to the sky in defiance. And when the wretched among us are barred from their ever-triangulating orgies, our new gods wonder what essential quality, what littlest bit of luck us untouchables lack. Then the well-intentioned among them throw us benefits which feel more obligatory than loving, and we only become more certain of our isolation.

　　—I mean, the trophies will dry up and then suddenly, voilà, so will you.

　　Belladonna sprawls over the boar's backside to indict The Co-op's precious little athletic champion's womb with her blunt heirloom knife.

　　—Your oven has its limits, Sister Ronette. What are you now? *28?!*

　　Of course her brothers and sisters had been right. She was incapable of making it through her soiree without committing some atrocity. What's more, this was the preferred order of things. For without her once again humiliating herself, they would be deprived of the opportunity to smile down from their own, better-hidden removes, pity her, feel grateful for how different they appear and smugly pronounce judgment on her life.

—Isn't it selfish of you to keep another little Co-op all-star out of the world?

And so. . .*pouvre pouvre.* . .Belladonna Mabuse is caught out between The Remove and her desperate need for care, boxed from all sides by after-aspects and perceived slights, jerking between the stations of her unwieldy emotions, gradually resembling the seized, imagining herself plunging through the mental thicket of *The Mabuse Ravine* but never finding the staircase, sneeringly reminding herself that whatever kind of new woman she thought she had become she remains incapable of slowing her descent into cruelty, plummeting down the depths of her accursedness as she is without any sign of a bottom to reemerge from. No, she will plummet and plummet, irresistibly drawn towards her unfathomable baseness.

So voilà le performance: A dab of the mouth while staring through the chest of Ronette Okampo, her chin caved deep into her neck in skepticism, eyes and mouth thinned in worried appraisal, lips pinched between thumb and forefinger in mock doubt as she slowly assesses Ronette's toned figure to return to the waist which (in an inspired touch) Belladonna starts circling her blade tip at. Yes, she is feeling pretty turned on again what with all the disapproving eyes passing over her face and the sweat collecting in her armpits and crotch while the latency of the knife melts into the curvature of her palm and gradually acquires such a pleasurable heft relative to the tensile force of her hand as to exist in extension with her hand her arm her body until the dull heirloom becomes proboscis and antenna, tooth and claw as it scents the now blood-beclouded air of her Seventh Annual like an aspergillum as she stares bug-eyed into The Remove and thrusts the knife into the boar's flank in an ecstasy.

—You can't rip them all out, Sister Ronette!

There are a few groans but no gasps. It is just the sort of lukewarm reaction which always incites her to new heights of baroque nastiness. Yes, all the Miss Manners crap holds little truck against a lifetime store of lovelessness.

—Well can she, everybody?! *Can* she?!

Belladonna tries to look triumphant but her face fractures into a series of grimaces. When she removes the knife from the boar she becomes queasy. No. . .not queasy. . . *regretful*. This performance has been nothing but cruelty for cruelty's sake. There is nothing traditional or fateful about it—just habit. And, my god, she's not sure she even *means* any of it anymore. She then realizes she *has* become a new woman. . .a *weaker* woman. . .one who now understands that kindness is necessary if she is ever to receive any in return but who also feels no uncomplicated kindness for *anyone*, least of all herself. And while she has taught herself to *behave* better, how long will it be before her *insides* follow suit? When will all the accumulated hurt choking her thoughts begin to evaporate and allow more useful and genuine feelings to prevail? Or will she forever be baling water like this, wondering if it would just be easier to scuttle herself and everyone else. Yes, she is caught in between and flailing in the deep. Sweat pushes through the many layers of her white foundation and gathers purple mascara from her eye corners. Then her mouth goes dry and she starts manically licking her lips which, in turn, smears her lipstick all over her mouth and makes her teeth appear to retreat into the depths of something more maw than mouth as each spitted and choked syllable swirls what's left of her *Azure and Violet Dawn* into a luridly streaming and premature midnight.

—I meeeean, SHIT. It's not 'ike (cough, hack) it's not 'ike it's privwedged INF-fo.

The boar stuck in her teeth makes her tongue catch as the tantrum worsens.

—We owe rember thutff olt days, Ron-it. Orf ad weast Behwo-doan-uh Ma-boofta doze.

She could clear her mouth with some wine or wipe the clay collecting in its corners with her serviette or ask to be forgiven but that would only slow her fall. Heaving inside, pleading with herself to stop, she only loses control more quickly. The words, or what passes for words, come unbidden and she cannot help but degrade herself.

—Dintcha say it was the moeft naturow thingff in the wo-ed?

Grand muh-Ma's face contorts in excruciating disapproval from the four-poster while muh-Ma smirks from the kitchen between un-repentant chugs from the decanter and lascivious looks at the caterer. Later, when Belladonna is alone at the table and drinking herself fully into The Remove, she will wonder what those unkillable women thought about after another evening of cruelty and conclude they never gave their behavior much of a second thought.

—You know, Ron-it! Abfthortion?! Huhm? *Huhm?!* Abfthortion?! Abfthortion-Abfthortion-*Abfthortion*!!!

2.

Sympathetic glances are passed around the table to land on Ronette. Our sister can take this. She's one of our trans-cendent Co-op women. Nothing can touch her. No more mod-ules are necessary. Wasn't she like *constantly* in training now? Yes, Brother, and constantly *winning*. Gosh, to have *that* much time on your hands. Likely Brother Sid begged her to come. Yes, even Sid Doe knows a little bit of good doctrine once a year keeps you in good standing. But remember, Brother Sid, we are the same ole old schoolers with the same ole proselytizing hearts and just because we want to see you and Sister Ronette become more involved members doesn't mean that we will judge you if you choose to be nothing but bike messengers. Yes, our Co-op is about liberation and you guys are *totally* liberated. . .of responsibilities. . .from the community. . .from all of us. But, hey, your late-life date with a non-Co-op affiliated group home is your business.

—Now-now, brothers and sisters, remember your modules.

Forgive us, it's just that faced with her braids, tan and musculature, the sculptural elegance of her posture, her steel trap jaws only becoming more relaxed as the inevitable Mabuse attack intensifies, flanked by her adoring Brother Sid, slouching under all that hair of his, fidgeting in his wrinkly formal blacks, rubbing against her edifice like some faithful and adoring dog-mate, what with this united front of unde-niably attractive otherness it becomes difficult for us to not feel a little left out. Some of us remember our two-wheel days . . .doing time as messengers. . .or waiters. . .or customer service reps. . .good days. . .romantic days. . .plenty of party-ing. . .And what were we?. . .Hippies? Progs? Punks? Mods? New wave? No wave? Indie?. . .Whatever it was it felt urgent . . .But then we somehow stumbled into careers and financial stability, could afford four wheels, baby-sitters and Co-op school, became happily befuddled by how cliché–. . . er. . . how comfortable that felt. . .still reform-minded of course but

. . .well. . .even that has been co-opted at this point . . .And so, yeah, maybe we are a bit more prone to feel defensive over Ronette's still-fresh outsiderness, how she abruptly extracted herself from our tight-knit. . .okay. . .somewhat claustrophobic circles, cleaned up that little drug habit, started training, sheltered under that once so timorous bike-dude at our periphery, banished her destructive behaviors without taking a single module or retrain, turned down Warren's offers to kick upstairs and became the cycling champion wearing the C∞P symbol on her back.

And so as Brother Sid shoulders into Sister Ronette to give her a 'whatever' grin and forward our poorly modulated Sister Belladonna's words to the doctrinal hinterlands we wish we could step in and perform some service, prove our value to the invaluable Sister Ronette, apologize for not knowing how to help her when she set out to destroy herself, even scold her into reminding her we are still worthy of her love. Like for starters? We totally have your back here. I mean woman-wise and these days? The Co-op has sister clinics across state lines and we're sure Sid is eyes-wide-open about Ronette's pre-life. The Wild Child? The Co-op Salome of Yore? Anyway, all that matters is that he got Ronette on the back end of all that and she was a different woman now and that was that. Period.

—But, bro, isn't it natural to briefly indulge ourselves and reminisce about The Old Ronette for a sec.

Yeah, sis, she was an entirely different force of nature back then wasn't she? Heedless of physics. Reckless of body. Aggressively un-encumbered by circumstance or membership. Hair down, flesh everywhere. You wanted to stand close and get little contact hits off her, however unstable the chemistry. You wanted to be in the pit exploding into life instead of just killing time. You wanted to skip the modules and learn how to be so darn free. Become a true original just like her even if it wasn't sustainable. But now you see how all her freedom has been braided to such awesome effect and suspect something passed you by while you went to all those experimental modules and retrains. You think of all the bargaining with death called 'choices' you do, all the potential draining out of you by the second, how the death of heroes is always an indictment of the followers. Then you doubt the purity of your intentions, call your compromises living and resign yourself to the low-stakes victories of the lateral life. You'll drink less. Be a better mate. Demonstrate nothing but laudatory and super-cool behavior to your children. Pursue some undiscovered passion on the side. You remember passion, dontcha?

—And oh but Jesus did you miss the old days, The Old Ronette.

Yeah, she was freaking *boisterous*, bro. But this new one. . .well. . .she's pure slow burn. Practically unengagable. But whatever. Life is lived. Past tense and all that. As long as she's happy we're happy. Truly. And shame on ugly ole Sister Belladonna for bringing up dead issues anyway. Let's just get past this and drive home. A few laughs can be followed by a swig or two more and that's it. We're all more doctrinaire than this. This evening can still end righteously.

So when Ronette's Sid pulls the hair away from his eyes to show us his fallen face, fixes us with his shy and soulful browns, twists and struggles against his formal blacks, fails to disguise his dislike for most of us, coughs softly, sputters a few indistinct syllables, stews, then finally just sits there looking stunned and bashful like some little lost lamb, he accidentally endears himself to the brothers and sisters quickly formulating reassuring words and recalibrating body language to convince him he isn't a failure for having chosen to attend this year's jerk's quorum. No, he should understand that what Sister Belladonna Mabuse has instigated is not of a part with our overarching and sometimes tediously dull kindness and definitely not of a part with Co-op doctrine. He should just slough off our brief fang-baring and relegate the bitch hostess' pot-stirring to memory. This perfectly mediocre evening can end without incident if he takes a deep breath. . .relaxes. . .feels himself floating into the inner-orbit of his precious Ronette. . .that's it, Brother. . .just relax. . .and lets her reflected glory wash over him while we regroup and try to understand what has become of us that we would allow our blameless Sister Ronette to be attacked by that heretic Mabuse.

—But wait. That's it. Now we see.

Tonight is the doctrinal synod! *The Reconsideration of Ronette Okampo*! Yes, this is what we can decide our hostess is after. Some of us did Catholicism as kids, right? In confession there is liberation. And when will there be another

opportunity to shame Ronette back into the fold? Belladonna
Mabuse may be the fallen angel but tonight she wields her
silverware and napkin for us like sword and standard. Yes, she
has accidentally bellowed our sadness. We want The Old
Ronette back gosh-darnit and we'll take whichever version's
on offer. A small redemption can occur on both sides. A new
better union formed. Yes, maybe Sister Belladonna's annual
boorishness has finally served a purpose. Let's just let this
play out for a sec. This can still be a productive evening.

Belladonna wipes her face with her serviette and clears her
mouth with some wine. She is calm now that she has finally
humiliated herself. A pleasant aimlessness settles over her
thoughts and allows her to start talking without thinking.
During such moments she is capable of both accidental kindness as well as a particularly dangerous form of cruelty. For
her part, she is just letting herself run off at the mouth.
        —I'm just saying that some of us don't have the
luxury of choosing anymore, okay.
        A new stillness rises from the table. Someone hisses
her name in warning. Faces try not to turn to the woman two
chairs to her left who has spent much of the evening staring
off into one the room's dark corners.
        —What? Aren't I supposed to be straightforward? I
mean that's what I was told in the *Open Road* module.
        She takes a brisk sip of wine, notices one of her
breasts has nearly spurted out of her dress, tucks it back in,
fans herself with her serviette, and spins to address the air-
space of the woman two seats over. These seemingly casual
movements, unnaturally graceful for Belladonna, give the
false impression that cruelty comes naturally to her.
        —I'm sorry, Exene, I'm not speaking for you of
course but, well, best laid plans and all. . .
        The man seated between them throws his serviette
onto his plate.
        —Are you done now, you nasty old bitch?
        Typically, this man who intimidates even longtime
acquaintances would try to add some warmth to his tone then
smile to reassure them that he was not about to tear their
throats out. But there is only so much a man can take sometimes. Virgil Gibson hates his hostess and disrespects almost
everyone else here. What a mistake to don the Co-op blacks

on again, to think he could make nice. Exene was naive to accept the invitation. He loved her for it, but naive. This was no way to start socializing again. This shitty dinner, just like the last two years, has been nothing but an exercise in not tearing someone's throat out.

—Now look, Virgil. *Look*. . .

Instead of looking at Virgil the hostess calmly asks each of her heirlooms to see reason. The befouled serviettes. The flickering candelabra. The creaking oak chairs obscured by the vague forms of her guests. All her dead forebears interred in these soul-heavy objects, judgmentally groaning, forced to accept their inheritor for the new brand of bitch she was.

—. . .we still consider you and Exene family.

—*Family*?!

Virgil laughs ruefully into his plate, tries to control himself for Exene's sake.

—My family is this woman here. . .

When he grasps Exene by the thigh her shoulders fall, making the back brace she is wearing creak slightly. She stiffly turns to him, indicates with a slow and fatigued nod that she has heard him, and looks back into her corner.

—. . .and the two poor motherfuckers over there who are the only reason we came to this bullshit in the first place.

Virgil raises two fists to Sid and Ronette and Sid raises two fists in reply. Virgil then looks back at his wife who has become frustrated by her fruitless search of the corner and begun to cry. Two tears race down her cheek, plummet, and finally plink onto the china—a heartbreaking sound. No one but Belladonna seems to know what to say.

—Now Virgil, I know The Co-op failed you and Exene.

Belladonna places both palms on the table with her fingers splayed in the direction of her guests.

—Believe me, I know. I—

—You don't know shit, lady.

Three years ago Virgil had tried to unionize The Co-op Bike Messenger Service. The owner, Warren Renshaw, a former professional cyclist, broke the union with promises of improved healthcare benefits. The plans wound up being piss poor with premiums no bike messenger could afford. Exene was still delivering at five months when she crashed. The miscarriage almost killed her. Her back was broken. She was in the hospital for three months. They would be in debt for decades. Warren offered to help with their bills and had cried apologies in their home. Instead of yelling at a crying man, Virgil turned down the money, quit The Co-op and showed that hypocritical dick the door. Since then, Warren, with the help of those steady checks this Mabuse bitch is always cutting, has extrapolated the unwritten rules of the professional *peloton* into a socio-spiritual ethos and The Co-op has become not only an economic force in town but an especially well-respected cult. Healthcare has been marginally upgraded. Warren appears at their door every few months to ask them to kick upstairs and help run one of The Co-op's many explosively successful new enterprises at some absurd salary. They politely refuse and Virgil continues to deliver for a rival messenger service.

—Tell me, where's your precious COO tonight?

He cranes his neck to look down the long table of nervous looking tools.

—I can't seem to find him.

—Brother Warren doesn't do meat since he met the teenager.

Belladonna morosely stares into her serviette and sighs.

—And the traditional meal is boar, of course.

—Don't you mean to say that your old boyfriend, Saint Warren himself even hates your guts now, too? Huh?

Exene leans into Virgil to make him stop, wipes her face with her serviette, tries to say something lighthearted, but trails off after the first few inaudible words. She then smiles weakly, sniffles, and looks back into her corner. The Seventh Annual Co-op Soiree is silent for ten seconds or so.

3.

Sid has put his hand on Ronette's thigh. Ronette has put her hand on top of his hand. They lean into one another. Little charges of reassurance circulate through their arms and into their chests. Both want the other to know that despite what the hostess has said everything will be alright. Their battered souls have endured far worse and both are internally organized so as to avoid undergoing anything like that ever again.

Sid hadn't known about the abortion and doesn't care. Or of course he *does* care insofar as an abortion must be traumatic for a woman and he hopes Ronette did not suffer too much. . .*I mean, my god, what a process. . .Just think about it* . . .But just to confirm his initial reaction? No, he's not hurt she never told him and supports her ongoing attempts to relegate the Old Ronette to ye olde dustbin. No, nothing as good as Ronette Okampo has happened to him before so why not just lop off their entire timeline prior and cling like holy hell to the one stretching forward.

So, yeah, he would only care about the abortion to the extent that she did and likely find that she didn't care to think too much about it anyway. But just to be thorough he should provide her with some tenderness and acknowledge-ment when they get home even if she acts as though she requires neither. Yeah, this is roughly how they work, right? He enacts one of the pre-established iterations of behavior which has proven acceptable to, if not pleasant for her. An accrual of successes—or at the very least his ongoing adher-ence to the pre-established iterations—more deeply stakes the tent of her wind-buffeted soul before some rogue gust can tear her from his grasp and send her kiting away for good— Ronette still being prone to long saucer-eyed séances with invisible others in the stucco sky of the bungalow's ceiling whenever conversations get too heavy or remotely threaten portage into her mucky old sloughs. So, yeah, definitely. Screw the old modes. We're happier with the new ones. We get by fine with short sentences, soft touches, secret notes, and zero reminiscing. Screw everyone and everything else.

And Ronette will observe Sid's behavior as though he were a member of a tribe untouched by civilization, concentrate on the good and simple motives he evinces between all the babbled words and stunted gestures, and isolate The Core Sid whose slumping person she has chosen to prop up and cling to, the one who has repeatedly performed the sort of anchor-ing duty she is continually surprised to learn her sea-tossed soul. . .*freaking still!*. . .requires even if his diverse efforts are usually a little to a lot off the mark to almost totally not what she wants at the time but executed in such an eager Noble Protector way as to make it impossible to feel or show dis-appointment, especially to this one man among the many iterations of men she has known through the many iterations of her relatively early life who has earned her long-term tolerance—The gift of her devotion to this sweet dork being a flag-planting for their iterations to come. So. A squeeze of the hand. Another organizing charge of warmth. The peace radiating through her poised body. This sleepy pleasure in the face of the hostess' inquisitorial b.s. Yes, this was sweet and hard won shit, sister. Screw all those dirty old ghosts.

Sid imagines him and Virgil punching out all these hypocritical Coopers who did nothing for Ronette back when she was slowly killing herself. Then he feels petty, tries to forgive, fails, then realizes he should instead be concentrating on the tensile qualities of Ronette's hand on his knee (something more twist and cling than cup and fold) and how tonight might be one of those wonderful and rare occasions when she becomes emotionally *vulnerable*. Seeing her best friend cry. . . *God, poor Exene*. . .might just do the trick. It's terrible, he knows, but he can't help but picture swallowing her in his arms while she bawls herself silly. Yes, the feeling of power complicating this ignoble little vignette (and undeniably beginning to arouse him) may necessitate a biting self-critique as to ultimate motivations later but tastes tartly sweet nonetheless.

Up until Belladonna's attack Ronette had heard little of what had been said tonight because she had engaged the failsafe which allows her conscious mind to opt out under unpleasant circumstances; the ability to melt into this emotional fugue state being, as far as she can tell, both a three-year hangover from those long months spent staring into the bottomless white walls at the rehab facility and a side effect of the mental and physical discipline required of the serious athletic training she initiated soon after her release. A ruthless prioritization possesses her. Excess thought washes away. She is encased by a second skin of non-listening and soon finds herself hidden deep inside what Sid the Latin and Classics dropout jokingly refers to as her labyrinth, unaware of the redundant sounds coming over the walls and waiting things out with that mute minotaur pal of hers while her body goes through the motions on the other side. But when Sid's hand twitches during the Mabuse attack what's left of the failsafe melts away and she finds herself wondering how poor Belladonna Mabuse can keep on being such a bitch. Doesn't the habit exhaust her? Maybe she just needs to laugh at Belladonna inside, make a silent retaliation by palming one of her dessert spoons and tapping Sid's knuckles with it before sliding it into her riding pants. Yes, not taking anything too seriously is one of the tricks to reengaging the failsafe. Remain calm, say little, smile a lot. Allow a series of clichés to do the talking for you.

But Belladonna really has it in for her. Instead of just giving her the usual boilerplate shit about bike delivery or winning trophies she has implied that Ronette is a massive failure for not having had children yet. And then she had shouted something about the abortion. And, yes, it was true that The Old Ronette had told The Old Belladonna that termination was a natural process. Those were in fact the words which had so effortlessly rolled out of her mouth in those bellicose days of frontal assault when she carelessly described the vast planes of null she had felt after the procedure to not only Belladonna but other women who had experienced abortion quite differently; the inconsiderate bitch she was back then being far more interested in convincing herself of what she was trying to believe that month or week or day than being cognizant of others' feelings. . .*The Removal?. . .I felt nothing but inevitability. . .Death or life? Sides of the same coin, sisters. . .All part of the universal rhythm. . .Nothing special either way. . .*And even if she still felt pretty much the same on that score the image of the person who had spoken those words disgusted her.

Thank god she had trained herself into being a better person before Exene had miscarried. She had been able to say all the right things, mean them, and do no further harm to someone who deserved so little. Still, as the weeks passed following the accident and Exene seemed increasingly engulfed by her loss, Ronette had struggled not to become angry. There was introductory anthropology concepts to cite, feminist bromides to chant, all this vague b.s. she only half-believed but struggled not to yell, screaming inside to keep the encroaching waves of pain she felt for her friend at bay, gradually being sucked down the whirlpool of memory returning her to the harrowing old days of being a serial foster teen, hurting anyone who got close, distrusting stability, running away, half-heartedly cutting and once almost accidentally killing herself, the group homes and counselors, the prescriptions and self-medication which followed, then the fruitless days of intentional community college flunkdom and the strict regimen of slow self-destruction which followed— All this unstanchable pain had bubbled back to the surface and made her so intensely empathetic to Exene's loss that she had frequently found herself superimposing the visceralness of Exene's miscarriage onto her own insides and re-experiencing the abortion she thought she had felt so philosophical about. She had experienced all these queasy, residual tug-pulls which plummeted her down ever broader paths of self-doubt which no failsafe can silence. . .*The Curse. . .The Mandate. . .The Condition. . . Motherhood. . .The Procedure. . .The Removal* . . .all the bio-logistical pain that accompanies the heart tears afterward, the mourning of nullities, losses real and imagined, wanted and unwanted, all the empty wonder dogging you after your pregnancy fails or ends, all this shit she thought she had dodged by claiming to not give a fuck. For months she had found herself crying privately, unable to quite shake those little possessions of her insides. And this had infuriated her not only because it put the lie to this supposedly super-center-ed New Ronette, but because emotional pain reminded her of the bitch she had tried to bury with the famously long penance jag which had followed the flunkdom. Not just the drug abuse but the near-total sexual availability. The choreographed humiliations. The blasting to bits of her stubborn ego. . .*I mean fuck me. Fuck this. I suck. . .*Stepping on her glasses and wearing the ugly ones from high school with the dangerously outdated prescription. The helmetless crash outs. The accumulation of concussions. Her total extrication from anyone foolish enough to tolerate her except for her fiercely loyal, undaunted Exene. Then finally the full-on drug dirge. Shit, hadn't she done all the self-annulling housecleaning necessary to rid herself of that self-righteous twat yet? Tamed herself with self-discipline? Made a bonfire of all her possessions but her glasses and textbooks? Slowly erected a labyrinth, allowed Sid to work the drawbridge, and installed the minotaur as night watchman? Weren't the three of them at peace with how useless her past was yet?

So with most of the eyes at the table fixing on Ronette and then on Exene then back on Ronette, she feels her body slipping backward again and becoming diffuse, as though her disparate cells are overlapping with Exene's and causing her empathy to carve a dry, nauseous void from her gut which will set up housekeeping to wait for some chance word or scene to trigger the whole shebang and throw open the floodgates while the failsafe chugs and wheezes and sputters. No, she must not even think about crying. Exene will instantly pick up on her bio-vibes and cry all the harder and officially make this a terrible night, one which will spur a variety of speculations as to exactly why *Ronette* got so upset when Belladonna trivialized Exene and Virgil's tragedy. She tries to breathe steadily but cannot control the spiking heart rate which causes the tips of her braids to trace small counterclockwise circles on either side of her face—one of her few 'tells' according to Sid. God, even if she somehow manages to not break down, Sid will still want to have a serious talk at home about her stupid fucking feelings. The failsafe will engage and she will try to fight it while he lovingly pounds away at her with all that sensitivity and kindness of his.

o   o   o   o   o   o   o   o

—I'm sorry, Exene, honey. Truly. Virgil, you too.

What Belladonna is sorry about exactly she couldn't say but she feels sure she means it. Other people need care, especially this wounded woman. *Pouvre pouvre* Exene and her little lost baby. Yes, she is sure she feels this way. Maybe if she humiliates herself a little more she can make Exene feel better and it will be construed as charity or kindness.

—I mean it's not like I'm going to have one of those little stinkers either and definitely not at the rate I'm going. Virgil'll vouch. . .Huh? Virgil? Oui?

Belladonna slaps Virgil on the shoulder then throws herself across his lap to force Exene to meet her eyes. Yes, she is willing to completely annihilate herself on behalf of this poor woman staring into the corner the same way she stares into her Remove. Belladonna gives her a soft touch on the arm and Exene looks into the grotesquely solicitous face of her hostess staring up from her lap, bites her lip, sniffles once, and grits her teeth into a smile and nods while the other guests blink, say nothing, and wonder if Sister Belladonna's tithing is worth all this.

　　—I mean . . .*bleh*. . .just look at me!

She half-heartedly points her knife at herself. The latency cries inward for a moment. She wants someone to shout 'Belladonna, don't' just before she collapses into their arms. O to take one's self so seriously. O to be unsure whether she means it or not. O to be nothing but a melodramatic wretch.

　　—Who'd care about this withered up ole bitch, anyway? Like *yuck*, you know.

She does a long, gut-clutching pantomime of a re-gurgitant. A tendril of pale saliva connects her tongue to the china then snaps. The room goes utterly silent while Bella-donna Mabuse wonders if there is much of a difference between crying and slowly drowning.

　　—No more buns in this oven. I mean it's probably medically impossible at this point anyway!

Later, after her guests have left the table, swore this was their last Soiree, hobbled out onto the warped oak planks and somberly climbed the staircase to lip of the canyon, after she has thrown the curtains open, turned off the candelabra and dismissed the caterer after he declined her offer of a blow job, after she has done her nightly circuit of La Petite Manse, used the 154-year old key to let her into its unused rooms, shined a flashlight into each of their eight corners to check for ghosts, after she has opened the door to her mother's room, sat at the vanity and touched the reflection of her forehead because it is the only part of her face which resembles muh-Ma's, after she has walked into her own room and sat on her childhood bed solely to hear the springs complain at her weight she will stumble, half-heartedly try not to fall down the stairs, throw open the dining room curtains, return to the oak table still crowded with heirlooms and her guests' scraps to digest this latest devastation to her innards, chug from the cracked crystal decanter and finally plead to the bleeding oak jungle, then the slaughtered boar, then her grand muh-Mah, then her muh-Ma, and finally her own soul slowly departing her body for The Remove that she had not wanted to hurt anyone tonight and only wound up doing so because she knew of no other way to reach out to others. Then she will repeatedly replay that loneliest moment of her adult life when, just as she was about to explain how misunderstood she was, her guests had all turned away at the first of Ronette Okampo's un-restrainable sobs.

4.

Night has swallowed dusk and brought a warm spring rain to the city's western hills. Climbing a narrow, twisting road of running gutters they aim the noses of their rigs at the glowing red light on top of a converter station. Standing and pumping, standing and pumping, Ronette's braids whipping her neck, Sid's hair plastered across his face, they scrawl and re-scrawl red ∞'s onto their vision. As they crest to start the steep descent this image will be briefly superimposed onto the wide slash of darkness beyond which is the river separating the west side from the east. An intervening skyline crosshatched by cranes and gated all round by trapezoidal spires will close in on itself as the ∞ disappears and they pedal into the streaming flats of an abandoned downtown.

This unfamiliar western approach quickly estranges them from the city they cycle for a trade. Nothing is where it should be. They see all the backsides of things. Their landmarks have either disappeared or been inverted. And though everyone else is long fled to the periphery, it feels as though tiers of eyes usher them through the inner core, even huddle inward to narrow the way. Certain Ronette is not as spooked as he is Sid sets a fast pace anyway.

Eventually, they enter the open air of an old vertical lift bridge. Crosswinds and the slick iron grating force them to slow down. Suddenly Ronette's back wheel starts to squawk. Sid scowls into the black river below thinking he had teched her rig this morning and here it was reminding him how careless he was sometimes; him, Sid, the same schmuck who had somehow lubricated whatever strange mechanism had sucked Ronette into its gears and extracted those whooping sobs at the end of dinner, the tears squirting from her lost eyes like indictments and the memory of which would wrench angry tears from him if he were not concentrating so hard on being 'strong' for her right now, riding a good solid lead through the swollen night, keeping a tempo that was neither funeral procession nor sprint, hoping his jerky cadence doesn't seem impatient or frustrated, just one of the stylistic ticks she had ostensibly signed off on when she had chosen to partner up with such a loser.

Okay, stop that. Ronette hates it when he tears himself down like this. Instead of mentally eviscerating himself for forgetting what the hormones do to her some-times, he should simply remind himself that his intense or quiet or maybe just intensely quiet short-tracker falls prey to the occasional menstrual psychoids now and then, not the bitchy-baby brand, just more. . .well. . .*out there*. . .first haunted by a pretty terrifying anger, then fascinated by how haunted she is, and finally dismissive of the whole process once she has finally nightmared herself clear and yelled awake for the last time in the cycle and indicated by telltale movements of her feet and shoulders that she will submit to being held now.

But just listen to how her regional championship-caliber cadence is being sacrificed to the patching of her labyrinth walls. No, she was not about to toss that sweet alto of hers over his shoulder to blend with the wheel whir and rain and roundaboutly reassure him, shout something like. . .*I'm cool, Sid, really. . .The minotaur's got this one. . .*Nor was she about to sing a cathartic verse of one of their songs and let the last growled syllable trail behind to annihilate the recent past. No, the three bike-length cloud following them contained this like seriously heavy humidity, man, so much so that Sid is afraid he might choke on the fat frog growing in his throat and start sobbing apologies for failing her and basically melt into this like utterly expendable milksop of a boyfriend before finally dissolving into the river below.

—Let's take Evers tonight, Ron.

They bank down the ramp and take an alternative route. This was the long way, a side-street meander through the treeless clutch of bungalows walled in by a dying port and a north-south interstate, an. . .*obviously unattractive neighbor-hood.* . .as immortalized by one realtor; but both of them too fuck-prevailing-notions to do anything but feel defiantly proud when they opted for the decrepit four room bungalow in a. . .*frankly even worse.* . .extension south of Evers, a resi-dential afterthought crammed into a bulldozed parking lot of another departed port industry on the lower banks of the city's east side; the 675 square foot bungalow set crookedly on a sunken foundation unevenly fringed by poisoned fill dirt and chronically yellow crabgrass, a tumble-down with a runny flat roof, wormy beams, dandruffic stucco, crumbling plaster, faulty wiring, and dyspeptic plumbing; its high-walled, abrupt, and draft-whipped rooms seeming like a fitting place for two wounded isolates to bunker down, plunge back into the terrors of close quarters living, and aggressively narrow the gaps in their understandings of one another and themselves; both preferring to make sweet concessions for the other like Ronette getting a new prescription and always wearing a helmet, Sid moderating on the stereo volume for his tinnitus and giving classical a try, both trying not to need the stereo on all the time to cover any awkwardness or creeping suspicion which might surface, both leaving sweet and conciliatory notes for one another when words failed them, both agreeing to finally join The Co-op and get heavily discounted health and home owner's insurance. . .*Wow, I guess we're real-life adults, now*. . .Ronette moving out of her latest exurban shit-hole in the city's far east, Sid leaving his downtown shit-hole near work and forcing himself to cross a bridge twice a day to face down his low-grade vertigo, both agreeing to not kick upstairs at The Co-op unless they had to, Ronette thinking office jobs are traps, Sid becoming anxious any higher than the fifth floor, both promising to ride less recklessly (this being as profound a gesture of sacrifice and love as either was capable of prior to move-in); and so mapping out a shared life of slow improvement together, upping the ante on their relationship from casual-but-constant to bilaterally committed until death or some other whim; choosing an unfixable fixer-upper among the long blocks of lost causes, an underground domicile distant from the Co-op enclaves with a far more manageable mortgage payment; both using bequeathed checks for the down-payment, Sid via his old man's taunt of a paltry trust fund, Ronette from the foster aunt who ignored the objections of her foster parents du jour when she wrote up her will. . .*I want to do something for that girl no one seems to know what to do for*. . .These somewhat sour riches quickly disposed of, so not their scene such jackpots, anything resembling an investment still so anathema, but digging the humble digs, man, laughing at the maintenance Waterloos, wielding duct tape and laying tarp to make the place border-line habitable, toilet-papering the joint to commemorate move-in night, chucking their possessions inside, never unpacking, just *installing*, man, just installing, turning their home into collage, dump, and swap meet, Ronette entombing disposable totems in the crumbling drywall, Sid erecting teetering towers, both kicking and diving onto the hills and sprawls of books and clothing and multifarious *objets*, heaping refuse everywhere, embracing this maximalist-junko esthetic, lining the baseboards with album covers and cycling glossies, draping a fishing net from the bedroom ceiling and filling it with mannequin heads and torsos, creating a sofa and 'easy' chair out of twined phonebooks and mismatched cushions, wallpapering the cracked bedroom and kitchen walls with pages from their underused college textbooks, taping bicycle maps onto the ever-peeling and moldy bathroom walls; quickly becoming bored with any one arrangement but gradually loving their home *in toto*, relentlessly repurposing, curbsiding and re-gifting, insulating themselves from the over-orderly Co-operative world with a rotating hoard of strange-ness, finding bungalow living romantic or their version of punk-rock quaint, both joking about the day when another bonfire would be necessary, turning this phase of their lives, together and individually, into a jam-packed boontide, the stability of situation hard to trust at first but feeling pretty damn good finally, cohabitating but still staking out private domains as they did, Sid for weekend cycling 'centuries' with Virgil, Ronette maintaining a training regimen which had her winning at Velodrome, Sid teching for Ronette, Ronette bouncing race strategy off Sid, their most perfect happinesses occurring in that blessed out-of-body rightness that cyclosport provides, mining occasional sweetnesses from each other between all the legwork, Sid amazed to have lucked into this older, championship woman, Ronette trying to soothe away Sid's over-think and insecurity, inspire him with simplicities, gradually admitting that if she had to live with and love someone it should be someone like Sid whose earnestness and attentiveness made her far happier than not, that she was not so stone-cold after her overhaul as to be incapable of tender-ness; both un-ironically enjoying all the small routines and tributes of domesticity and on most other nights looking forward to returning home, hanging their rigs side-by-side in the closet they had taken the door off of, kicking their way through The Big Room (the only room besides the kitchen, bathroom and bedroom) and throwing their packs at the sofa and chair (a.k.a. the sitting room) to attend to their general tendencies, this reentry into their private domain usually providing long hits of the owner's relish but just not on a night which had ended so shittily, these last retrospective blocks ratcheting up Sid's anxiety as Ronette's tempo becomes jerkier and jerkier, him wanting to tell her her cadence is off without sounding like he is criticizing her but, well, she has another meet next month and would want to know if he thinks she is compromising her training somehow, not that Ronette needs help on the discipline end, Christ no, just that, well, she is prone to losing her focus sometimes—this being perfectly normal in elite athletes, training not providing the otherworldly highs of competition—and Sid definitely not wanting to *extort* a single sweet syllable from her yet fully aware that he is not above pursuing a secret agenda and therefore deserving of another quick round of self-chide, prone as he is to mistaking his neediness for helpfulness, so wrapped up in untangling his motivations and worry like this that he often forgets to say something simple like. . .*You cried, Ron. . .Are you okay?*

Ronette pulls a once-white water-stained curtain aside. Rain slants into the west-facing window's 25 glass squares fogged blue on the inside from their predecessors' cigarette smoke and spackled white on the outside with hardened gull shit. A muddy lawn slopes to a cracked sidewalk pocked with puddles and flanked by tightly parked cars. Across the street a 20-foot high sound barrier tagged with graffiti and more impressive sprawls of gull shit muffle the sporadic rushes of interstate traffic. She counts the working streetlights, then the dripping and sparkling cars, then the gloom-shrouded bungalows. She knows none of her neighbors and has never seen a pedestrian here. Neither fact strikes her as good or bad.

Below the window is a dresser with mannequin arms reaching up from each drawer. Each finger is ringed with secret notes written in tiny letters on the fortunes from the bushelful of cookies Sid salvaged from the back of a Chinese restaurant. . .*To Ronette, The minotaur lost your hairbrush . . .To Sid, Anyway hairbrushes are for dimwits. . .To Ronette, My Track Elite Humanitarian. . .To Sid, Well someone has to come in second. . .To Ronette, On your left. Not your right. Forgive me. . .To Sid, Forget it. You will always be my*

centaur Lead-Out Man. . .To Ronette, Pardon my cadence last
night. Signed, Coach. . .To Sid, Let's blame the vertigo!. . .Ad
Ronetta, Cogito ergo sum. Ergo, I love you. . .To Sid, et tu,
*Siddus. . .*Practicalities abstracted, small arguments diffused,
affections encoded; each written from the remove of private
deliberation, stashed between bicycle spokes, then weighted
down with their few precious objects. She removes the stolen
silver spoon from her riding pants. Its fluting bunches into a
bulbous handle while the action end is thin, shallow, and brief.
Such lopsidedness, she thinks, could only accommodate some
malformed hand or maybe a leprechaun with airs.

—God knows what dessert would have been.

She wedges the spoon between the fingers of a hand
in the bottom drawer, takes off her glasses, places them in
their designated hand in the top drawer, considers the arrangement, nods approval, unstraps her helmet, hangs it from the
palm next to the one holding her glasses, tucks a few dis-
placed notes back between the fingers, reconsiders the
arrangement and nods approval. She then tears out of her
delivery yellows, scans the floor, finds a t-shirt and shorts,
rips them on, kicks a spot clear on the floor in the sitting
room, abstracts into the swirling window and begins breathing heavily and regularly. This will be the prep stretch pre-
ceding the prep proper. With each subsequent bow, pivot and
whirl her eyes abstract deeper into the grey-white clouds
hiding the skyline across the river and to the northwest. She
counts aloud. . .*one. . . two. . .three. . .four.*

The big room has a small benched alcove with a south-facing
view of the condemned bungalow next door. These 25
squares, while also smoke-stained, are entirely unshat upon.
This is Sid's transitional space. Here he likes to undress the
day while staring into the jigsaw of particle board covering the
window opposite. This brief moment of semi-privacy allows
him to collect his thoughts, discard the vast majority of them,
then jerry-rig a game plan for the evening ahead from the
remainder. But tonight, as he twists out of his formal blacks,
then tears off the delivery yellows, he instead scowls at the
glowing lights and black plastic geometries of a stereo performing unsatisfactorily. He leans down to press a button,
turns the volume up, listens, makes a face, then turns it down,
futzes with the equalizer, realizes he is standing there naked,

scans the floor, rifles a few piles, hurries into some clothes, presses another button, then presses it again, listens, pulls away the curtain of wet hair half-covering his eyes, presses the button again, listens to the guitar fuzz coming from the speakers stacked on top of the hi-fi stacked unevenly on top of four milk crates and teetering with each new command, squeezes his chin, shifts his weight to make the floorboards creak, shrugs, stands on a milk crate to turn on the lamp crammed between the speakers and the ceiling, squints, angles the shade downward, steps down, squints, squeezes his chin, runs his fingers through his hair, looks back into the speakers, frowns, pulls the two wings of hair behind his ears, stares at the naked mannequin reclined on the alcove bench and looking out the window, wonders what his opinion might be, forces himself to walk away, snatches up his yellow helmet, tromps over a moist tarp, hangs the helmet from the palm next to the one holding Ronette's, tucks in a few stray notes, and heads for the kitchen.

  —Well, I'm hitting the macaroni and cheese. Dinner sucked. The meal too, I mean.

Ronette is thankful Sid knows when to vacate and let her recompose herself. This proper stretch will do the trick.

20 hamstrings.
10 knees.
20 calves.
10 hips.
Both legs X 4.
In under five minutes.

Yes, training requires an adherence to incrementally more challenging task-work. The maintenance work—like this 4 x 4 she is cranking out—requires the same attention to detail that track work does. The extent to which she adheres to this belief is a measure of her discipline. Repeatability in form and frequency is an organizing force, the bulwark against the bad habits which make the minotaur restless. . .*fifteen*. . .*sixteen*. . . *seventeen.*

  But, heck, it wasn't like the crying at the party was a soul cry or anything, probably just the old chemicals taking hold a bit ahead of schedule, shoving The Mandate down her throat again. . .*four*. . .*five*. . .*six*. . .But that was all over now and there was no Big Message to extract, no internal dodge going on. Best to just stretch the episode out of her body and move on. Girls will be girls, basically. No need to sulk. Boo-hoo and whatever. . .*twelve*. . .*twelve*. . .*no, thirteen*.

Hugging a deep blue bowl, sneering past the bluesy wail coming from the speakers, Sid kicks a path to the dresser, removes a teak salad spoon cradled by two mannequin hands from the bottom drawer and plunges it in into the macaroni. This is Woody. Sid's grandfather had made room for this badminton racket-sized heirloom in the single suitcase he packed for the boat ride over from the old country. Sid's father's sole inheritance, it was only used on the rare occasions his parents had company; that way his old man could interrupt his awkward salad service (out of practicality the spoon had been left in Europe) to breathlessly relate its history to a fresh captive audience and force Sid and his mother to witness the spontaneous warmth and affection their stale and stifling family was implicitly undeserving of. That usually so angrily self-pitying little man would brandish that goddamn spoon under his guests' noses like it was freaking Excalibur while sprinkling in what little German he had left to give his tale authenticity and gravitas. Once the guests had left he would hurry to the kitchen to reverentially wash and dry the spoon then place it in a tie box in a little used bottom drawer. Returned to the dinner table, polishing off the wine. . .*for symmetry sake*. . ., he would anxiously revert to his joyless, life-stifled form. Man, had Sid hated that fucking spoon back then.

　　At family dinner one night his old man had as usual used some minor trespass of 13-year-old Sid's as a pretext for expressing how little he loved them. This, though, was to be one of those especially cruel attacks where his father, a failed philosophy academic turned insurance adjuster, would engage in a rambling *facie ad faciem* with the empty fourth chair at the table as though Sid and his mother were not present. These dialogues, punctuated by slugs of wine and wild gestures, circuitously addressed the unspoken family truth—that each member would be better off if the others didn't exist. . .*Is this even happening?*. . .*I mean why do we even bother?*. . .*Going on I mean*. . .*Do any of us even belong here?*. . .*What I'm* *asking is is this the best that can be done in life?. . .For example, do we know for a fact that this particular child is capable of doing better, my friend?. . .Oh no, no, no, no. . . That is far too generous a premise. . .See, what I'm asking you is is how can a hypothetical father know what is inside his hypothetical son?. . .Not to mention inside the hypothetical mother of a hypothetical son?. . .Not to mention a child to a mother. . .a mother to a child who shall remain nameless. . .a mother to a child who might not have provided this hypothetical son with the most. . .erm. . .shining moral example. . . How can a hypothetical father predict what these hypothetical people are capable of?. . .Much less even know who they are? . . .This, my friend, is my premise. . .*When his morosely drunk mother mumbled her perfunctory objections his father pretended these indistinct sounds emanated from some distant medium and then renewed his conversation with his wooden interlocutor. . .*I simply observe that this latest performance seems demonstrative of a hypothetical child whose hypothetical mother might have. . .well. . .how shall I put it. . . stained him with her illegitimacy. . .What?. . .Do I even care what other husbands and wives are like?. . .Don't you judge me. . .You lost that right long ago, mein freund. . .Now listen, LISSS-en. . .If I have my doubts whether my family exists or not there has to be a pretty good reason I feel that way doesn't there?. . .Or am I talking over your head here?. . . Listen, sometimes a man just wants to give up. . .Sometimes a man just wants out. . .*Timid and frightened Sid imagined himself becoming small enough to shelter under a plate ledge and tried to drown out his father's words by thinking. . .*blah-blah-blah. . .blah-blah-blah. . .blah-blah-blah. . .*From this remove his presence might not be so destructive, so painful. But his father's hatred pursued him to every corner and niche of the table's landscape until Sid finally had to imagine his tiny self leaping from the table so it could float far and irrevocably away. . .*I mean, is this supposed to be our legacy?!. . .Ha!. . . Normal?. . .'Normal' isn't even in play here, mein freund. . . No, 'normal' is a word for people with low stand—. . .Whuh? Wh—. . .Oh no-no-no-no, this supposed 'norrr-malll' not only seems AAAB-norrrmalll but absolutely id. ee. AH-tic. . .hid. eee. US. . .STOOPifying. . .What?. . .Hey, I'm just calling 'em like I see 'em. . .Like it or not I'm still judge, jury, and executioner around here. . .They can love it or leave it. . .What?. . .*

*Disown?. . .Disown, you say?. . .Ah, that'd be too easy don't you think. . .*His mother kept on staring down the bottomless pit of her plate while Sid's consciousness floated back to his bedroom to hide under the blankets. Taken together, even just peripherally, their emptiness incited Sid's old man to burst from his chair and furiously loom over the empty one, his histrionics spiraling out of all proportion to his drinking, the man succumbing to genuine emotional extremis and seemingly tormented by some excruciating doubt only his wooden friend could understand. . .*Maybe an exchange of some kind is possible. . .You know, with one of those poorer nations full of high-achieving teenagers and submissive housewives?. . .Yes, that sounds capital. . .bully. . . VUN-derbar. . . ♫ AAAAAA-mennn! ♫ . . .Just think of it. . .To feel proud of your life for once. . .to feel like you are part of something worthwile. . .No, now look. . .You're asking the wrong question, mein freund. . . See, what you should be asking me is—. . .No, STOP it!. . . Now look.. . .What you should be asking me is 'Did I ever really want one?!'. . .The answer is. . .well. . .it seemed like a good idea at the time. . .There were two of us so why not three?. . .No, now, no. . .I'm not making any accusations at this particular moment, okay. . .There is a time and place for certain revelations and this may not be the proper. . .er . . . forum. . .Or at least that it is what I'm given to understand from other parties who shall remain nameless. . .You know, the ones who claim to have a seat at the table as it were. . . parties with dispu(BURP)tatious natures. . .No. No! Now (BELCH) shut up!. . . SHUT UP!. . . Now listen. . .LISSS-sen, mein freund. . .What I'm driving at here. . .what I'm trying to say is. . .well. . .hell . . .what's the point of imagining life any other way. . .The proof is in the pudding. . .The DIE as they say is CASTEROONI. . .we all have our crosses to bear. . . etcetera etcetera. . .dust to dust ♫ A-MENNNNNN ♫. . . What?. . .No, I'm no hero. . .I mean, look, I've played the hand that was dealt the same way you did. . .But could I have done better?. . .Could you and I have done any better than this. . .this. . .well. . .this. . .SHIT?. . .I dunno. . .I'm no fortune teller. . .I mean I did a hell of a lot better than you did. . . Spared the rod. . .or shall I say 'spared the spoon'. . .paid the bills. . .remained faithful in spite of everything. . .No-no-no-no, you are far too generous a spirit. . .This isn't any big achievement. . .This doesn't con(BURP)stitute a fulfilled life*

*. . .No, you withhold certain hard truths. . .Your standards have always been pathetically low. . .Listen, I'm not going to keep sitting by and pretending I don't see what's wrong. . . Just because I'm stuck here doesn't mean I have to accept such?. . .such shit?!. . .*When his mother finally shouted for him to. . .*Shut up!. . .Shut-up-shut-up-shut-up for once!!!. . .*he staggered, flung his wine glass, flailed at whatever had spooked him so badly, then fell to the floor to embrace the legs of the streaming and empty fourth chair. When he finally peaked over the tabletop and recognized the horrified faces of his wife and child, he crooked his bloodied index fingers at them and said. . .*You see?. . .You see what you make me do?*

Early that morning his father was finally snoring off his drunk when Sid snuck into the kitchen and took the spoon from the tie box. He hid it in the sleeve of the communion suit his father had worn as a child and which had always hung in Sid's closet as a sort of monument or threat. Returned to bed, hidden under the covers, Sid curled into a ball, smiled nervously, and felt proud of himself for once.

He had numerous opportunities in the weeks leading up the next dinner party to return the spoon but refused to let go of that small victory. If a search was made of his room and Woody was found the punishment couldn't be worse than having Sidney Johann Dublinski II for a father. So when his old man finally yelled for his mother to come to the kitchen he felt defiant. If confronted he would shout a profanity at his father and probably be struck in reply. Hatred would be branded on his cheek and Sid would never again feel guilty for not loving his father. But when his mother looked into that empty box, she decided to take the blame because she felt like hurting that s.o.b. for once. . .*Do you remember that yard sale? I sold that old piece of shit!. . .*His old man had screamed his head off and Sid had genuinely feared for his mother's life. It was only when he calmed down that he mentioned divorce. This was not unusual but Sid's heart leapt with hope nonetheless. Maybe he would actually follow through this time. Yes, stealing that spoon had been total genius! The chief triumph of his early life. And even though the divorce never materialized Sid considered the spoon a trophy and named him Woody. Throughout his adolescence, hidden safely under his covers, recovering from yet another dinner table reaming, Sid liked to detail for his confidante just what kind of an unparalleled asswipe his father really was. Always a close and compassionate listener, Woody has helped Sid through crises large and small since.

In their third week in the bungalow Sid took Woody out of his hiding place, sat down next to Ronette, bashfully began eating ice cream with him and started to explain why a wooden salad spoon was so important to a supposed adult. But Ronette had interrupted him before he could get very deep into the backstory. . .*Don't worry, Sid. . .I think it's cute. . . Weird but cute*. . .Being told he was anything but implicitly de-ficient in some way still required a fair amount of internal body english for Sid to swallow despite whatever positive reinforcement there was supposed to be in Ronette consenting to buy a house with him. And even if they had had the biggest of Big Talks two weeks prior to move-in and forced themselves to *say* those most reassuring of heart words to one another instead of relying upon a series of notes to imply it, a guy like Sid does not exactly crown himself the Lord God afterward. No, he tends to tear himself apart before anyone else can. But before he had been able to tell her more about his childhood and Woody's sad but ultimately triumphant place in it, there she was telling him he was 'cute.' Like wow. Why bother telling her all the crummy details about a past he wanted to forget? Better to just skip it and wait to find another note with one of her sweetly efficient summaries. . .*I want to live with who you are, not who you think I want to live with. . .* Again like total wow.

So using Woody now is Sid's way of thanking Ronette in advance for her patience with the mistakes they both know he is about to make in the forthcoming Big Talk. Or at least this is how Sid is seeing it, carving gullies and ravines out of the congealed noodles, scoring peeks at Ronette's unbelievable legs while she stretches, feeling incre-dibly grateful, incredulous, awed, everything, man, for how 'together' she is, to the point of seeming invulnerable. . .no. . . impenetrable. . .no. . .practically catatonically *peaceful* some-times. Like how just to look at her counting off the 4 X 4 with that freckled face peeking through her thighs you'd think she was contemplating verities or humming one long *ommmmmm*.

But breaking down crying like she had wasn't something to ignore. No, he will need just the right transition point to start saying just the right things, otherwise he'll have to sit there chomping at the bit, refining his thoughts, shoveling up more squeaky noodles, wondering if this is the right song to engage in talks to. . .or under. . .reminding himself to behave just as his father wouldn't (gentle, thorough, kind) but afraid he will forget somehow. Also, he has to factor in how difficult these sorts of talks are for Ronette, how emotions scare her, how fear angers her, how anger makes her lose control. Yes, Sid is now chomping and gulping, thinking, swallowing, prepping, plotting, pulling his hair aside, wishing he had the discipline to train himself into thinking efficiently, slowly working up his confidence but relentlessly doubting himself and finally becoming so lost he forgets the wisdom of not trying so hard to prove he is capable of productive thought—All this while trying to deny the mounting influence of Ronette's legs on his decision-making process.

      —I meanff weef distussed it, Wahn. Right?

      Sid spumes yellow matter on his shirt, wipes his wrist across his mouth and sends particles flying onto the shag carpet remnants below. Sid and Ronette are both deliberate slobs. They had discovered this in common on their fifth date when Sid was thrilled by what a dump Ronette's place was. . . *(Sid) Objects are better than people in most ways. . .calmer. . . quieter. . .more fair. . .(Ronette) Yeah, and not nearly so full of themselves. . .or maybe just only full of them-selves. . .pure really. . .(Sid) Incapable of taking things personally. . .ergo free. . .(Ronette) unhurtable. . .independent. . .okay with being alone, yet great company. . .*Yes, Sid likes buttressing himself for tough talks by cataloguing what they hold in common like this. Doing so emboldens him to trust his instincts. And his current instinct, most compelling since first, is to dispose of his feelings as freely as he would any object—Yes, the less attached you are to the clutter in your system the more easily you will recognize what is truly important. And since Sid is never really sure what he is feeling anyway and thinks Ronette is pretty similar in this regard might not ad-libbing be the most natural way of disburdening himself of his concerns about what happened at dinner, *ergo ipso facto* the most sincere? And might not some essential Sid-and-Ronette-ness emerge once they start ridding themselves of what neither of them understood? Isn't even a poorly thought out Big Talk a form of personal and relational sculpture? Just look around. Hadn't they collaborated on everything in this ad hoc slob's museum? The bike frame totem pole. The tree of twined together mannequin torsos. The Mystery Mounds of Tarp Valley. Every last bit of glom and accumulation brewed up on the spot and not once regretted. Didn't the dresser full of hands overflowing with notes speak volumes? Hell, this could be the most productive Big Talk ever!

—Like how we are both grossed out by children? Like yuck? Ya remember?

Sid hardly recognizes the casual person he now resembles and wonders if Ronette does. He holds Woody out like he is cheerfully panhandling.

—I just thought that according to what we've said we want no part of them. . .that we would spend the next inheritance on a vasectomy. Heh, ya remember?

Sid questioningly squeezes his shoulders into his neck so hard he accidentally catapults macaroni over his shoulder. Suddenly he feels defensive instead of spontaneous.

—Like who wants the responsibility, ya know?

Ronette is done with the 4 x 4 and massaging the back of her calf in that maddeningly immersed and devastatingly graceful way of hers as though there wasn't something sorta possibly pretty serious being discussed here. The woman is, like, so still in her spirit at moments like this Sid can't help but want to exercise the special privilege of invading her space so she will be forced to either calmly suffer or wonderfully encourage him. So, in order to avoid becoming distracted by some lower, personal motive, and since she has only shrugged in reply from inside her 4 x 4, he decides to leave her alone and go tech that squawk out of her rig instead.

Many deliberate minutes pass as he clears a space in the center of the room to spread out his tool kit and clamp the bike into a stand. Various ratcheting and ticking noises accompany Ronette's loud breathing and snapping ligature. Both become immersed in their fine details as a familiar rhythm issues from the speakers. But when Sid finds a small bit of wear on the threading of a bolt he replaced this morning he becomes annoyed, looks over at Ronette firing off stretches for the back end of her second 4 x 4, thinks there are so many better things to be doing than talking about freaking babies and lowers his voice to flirt.

—But there you go initiating the process again.

He tiptoes through the junk back to the easy chair, picks up the bowl, and reaches the gloop-caked Woody out to touch the back of Ronette's highly vulnerable thigh. During this surreptitious transit Sid thinks there is just enough tension in the volume and spacing of the guitar fuzz in the speakers to pull this off without seeming frivolous or un-sexy, something more pop than punk. Yes, he had really made some strides in the romance department, hadn't he?

—Haaa-cha-cha-CHA. . .

Maybe Ronette would want to screw those championship thighs loose *in studio* of resuming The Big Talk. He could live with that—oh hell yes he could. Also, a relatively soft song was only two tracks away. He would be gentle and then as un-gentle as Ronette preferred. It's not like she would feel objectified or anything, right? That just wasn't her style, thank god.

—'But how are we for prophylactics?' you ask? Ah, a sensible question.

When the spoon touches down Ronette jerks and backhands it clear causing a fan of noodles to arc upwards then slowly descend to land soundlessly in the deep fields of shag. There is a pause. Two gentle people endure a brief moment fraught with relative violence. They scan the noodles and wonder if they have wounded the other by proxy. Neither is cavalier enough to laugh the idea away. Both wait for the other to make things better. More blood flows to their brains. The room becomes hazy. Sid's tinnitus spikes. Ronette's close vision blurs. Sid traces the grain on Woody. Ronette's braids do their slow reverse cycling. Sid slouches so his hair hides his face. Ronette twists the bottom of a braid. They both abstract towards the west-facing window.

And the spring rains boil down and the last strands of the day's traffic invisibly sizzles past.

o   o   o   o   o   o   o   o   o

—I mean I'm right, right? You've said so.

Sid whips the hair away from his face.

—Like, *in summa,* we are not people who should have children.

Sid hears his father in himself and that angers him.

—What with our backgrounds?

He had had the best of intentions prior to broaching the fucky-fuck but would that be entered into the official record, here? Hell no, man. God, this is so stupid and unfair he is prepared to start yelling in service of a conflict he is neither invested in nor knows much about. Yet the words just keep tumbling out of Big Dumb Ole Improvisational Sid like he's some ventriloquist's dummy.

—But maybe part of you *regrets* that abortion.

Ronette scowls at Sid then inflates her stomach only to suck herself thin. This horrifies Sid and Ronette is immediately embarrassed. A vocalist whispers from the speakers while a guitar crackles. Sid's tinnitus attains a humming middle register. Ronette pinches her cheek to remain alert.

—I didn't. . .or don't. . .or couldn't. Whatever.

A guitar drones mock tragedy. Here and there a drum pounds. Ronette suspects this music is part of a collusion of forces—along with the dinner party, the crappy ride home, the noodle incident, her aching eyes—which have made this fight materialize from the bungalow air and put one bike-length after another between her and Sid, her and the room, her and everything else, stranding her in her least favorite place (her thinking self) to listen to this droning ditz who wants to chalk up this pseudo-fight to how her training has been a little off lately or how she probably didn't deserve to medal last week or how her legs have been out of step with her machine and her machine out of step with the ground and the ground out of step with the invisible rampage of the planet beneath or how maybe Sid had teched her rig differently this morning and work had jacked it up or maybe training for competition was just wiping her out or her freaking four eyes needed a new prescription again—Or, yeah, maybe it was that other thing with Exene.

All she knows is that she had not once *belonged* in that chippy of a ride home tonight. Her body had been gypped of the sweet jibe with all the geophysical frequencies, that heightened consciousness which erases thought, the spiritual high which allows her to exist in a mostly instinctive way, whether flowing with the downtown convoys or dancing the dance with the other bike broads at Velodrome—The New Ronette's simple, cyclical life. But tonight she must've entered some inter-zone where the typical unfurling corroborations of momentum and objects just don't *take*. Hell, it felt like part of her might still be out there on Evers somewhere and that the rest was lost in this messy room traveling at an incompatible speed threatening to fall away at any moment and leave her trapped inside a wall doomed to bat away all the boring old whys and wherefores this stupid non-fight had raised while she slowly becomes marooned not only deep inside herself but in a droningly vague way, as though she will be stuck in this flashing moment of non-being forever, her diffuse soul scattered over time.

—And look, Ron, I don't have any qualms with them. Power to the little stinkers. They're going to keep on coming. It's the way of the world. *Fine.*

Ronette stares at the kaleidoscope of shag, tries to latch onto a pattern and settles for a noodle dyed orange. She thinks Sid worries too much and too much of that worry revolves around making her happy and that being the object of such excessive care sometimes makes her wonder what this person he worries on behalf of is all about and what it says about that person that she fails to stem the tide of those worries and so on and so on until her vague selves start multiplying and spinning until they have filled a merry-go-round with anxious, red-faced Sids reaching out for cardboard cutout Ronettes.

—And. . .well. . .never saying 'never'. . .that's probably not our style.

Sid moves to the edge of the easy chair. Tips of his hair touch the food. The hand not holding Woody is upturned and pleading again. How could he hold onto Ronette when she gave him so little to take hold of sometimes?

—But just not now, not when you're still getting better. I mean you could be thinking Nationals in a few years if you want to.

Suddenly the stakes feel incredibly high. Jesus, doesn't she remember he isn't built for this sort of shit, either. What gives her the right to. . .oh but there she goes. . .staring off into the stucco, communing with some more sympathetic other there while he becomes increasingly isolated. So he juts forward another tick in the easy chair, stops, scoots back three ticks, grinds Woody into the macaroni, juts forward a tick, opens his mouth, stops himself from speaking in anger, exhales angrily, gestures in frustration with Woody and jettisons macaroni into his face. . .onto Ronette's lap. . .and all over the shag.

—I mean we *both* had shitty childhoods, Ronette. Period. End of story.

Shit, what a pass. To be brandishing Good Ole Woody at his sweetheart now counting the noodles in her lap in such a sadly unperturbed way it perturbs the hell out of him. Man, their occasional fights? They're like having to die to one another. Like actually *die*. And, well, frankly? One day they *would* die. Just think about that? Bang. POOF. Done. Gone. Over. Gonzo. *Mortuus et sepultus est*. Christ, there was *that* too wasn't there. Like maybe they would luck out and die together in some stroke of elder good fortune, some swift, mutually killing car wreck say. But, more probably, they would perish slowly and well apart timeline-wise and lose the late-life opportunity to fondly look back together at what a laughably colossal waste of time their relatively few but pretty traumatizing fights had been. Jesus, just think how excruciatingly limited there time together is. Was. Will be. Could be. Whatever. And yet here they are failing to deal with whatever the hell is going on when they should just strip down and spit in Time's face by having a thoroughly immortal screw on the shag instead.

—No *way* do we want to repeat *that* cycle.

Sid stabs the spoon back into the noodles and asks himself how he is supposed to navigate all the contradictory and intensely boring b.s. racing around in his head to remember that Ronette has asked him to do just the opposite during arguments and just let it rip for once. But how is that possible when he is busy bottoming down into himself with the certainty of their far too imminent deaths? How is he supposed to just yank Ronette out of her space cadet thing and sort their shit out together a.s.a.p. when their inevitable apartness makes him too distraught to POOF say just the right thing to dissipate the massive wall of static rising up around their individual existences? But oh yeah. . .right. . . shit. . . he's doing it again. . .and by the time he remembers her request to be shouted back into the here and now so they can at least inflict pain on one another more directly and have it over with he has forgotten what he was angry about in the first place and isn't very angry about whatever it was anymore or at her at all really and is feeling somewhat insane, not to mentioned ill-equipped to wade through the vague medium they have immersed themselves in to reach the silent, staring woman less than three feet away.

—Besides, Ron, you've said. . .we've both said that *cycling* is our baby.

Ronette's sightline passes through Sid's general zone of existence, past the tree of mannequin legs near the center of the room, up the stereo, over the speakers, and settles on the orange burn corona on the ceiling above the lampshade. Surrounding this eclipsed zone is an endless stucco fjordland of shadowy harbors and grey-white silence. These abstractions she falls into must be rotten to be around but there you are. She can't help it if she would sometimes rather be a tiny craft exploring this crooked archipelago of uninhabited shores than have to reexamine the rutted planes of her interior. And even if the surrounding sea turns tempest she can always dive down to shelter with the mute and fantastical creatures who spend their lives circulating the lightless and lowering depths of the vastly unexplored ocean bottom.

—So now you're. . .heh. . .you're telling me. . .heh . . .that. . .heh heh. . .

Sid tends to laugh at unforeseen notions and horrors.

—. . . you want uh. . .uh. . .a. . .uh. . .

He hears himself fluster, despises himself, scans his unsettled holdings for some leverage, but can only manage a buffoonish look and an absurdly snide tone.

— . . .a *baaaaaa*-bee?

His emphasis on the most nasal qualities of the word coupled with his pursuit of some elemental pejorativeness in its enunciation fully yanks Ronette out of her fjordlands and has her shouting less at Sid than at some faceless opponent in the stucco above him.

—Well, maybe it'd be nice to take care of something besides you and me for fucking once!

Christ, did she mean this? Hadn't they only just learned how to live together? Remained bunkered down against the world which had damaged them less in romance than out of self-preservation? Clung to this stability even as their insides remained in tumult? No, a baby was all wrong for them, but maybe she wants one in spite of all this or just to prove a point.

—We act like a couple of babies anyway, so maybe having another one around will finally turn us into adults?!

This was nuts. Maybe the bungalow has a carbon monoxide or radon problem which spikes sometimes and turns her slightly bonkers? Or maybe she is a little stressed because her training hasn't just been a little but a *lot* off lately. . .Or maybe it was that other thing with Exene. Regardless, she is suddenly frightened by the lonely and vulnerable life she realizes they have constructed, trapped as they are inside this tiny bungalow with the only person left who can love them, the only person left who can hurt them.

—Maybe she's the only thing which will ever help us feel normal.

Sid rubs his hair into his eyes to hide. He can't believe this shit. Early on she had told him. . .*no children ever*. Fine. Great. Anything to make her happy, basically. Besides, once he slogged through all of society's b.s. pressure around having children he decided he didn't want a third wheel mussing up their mojo. So that was handled. *Quod enim factum est.* But here she is reversing course. . .or at least threatening to. . .or threatening to threaten to. Christ, does she understand the slavish feeling he experiences during moments like this? The apparent ease with which she can, even if inadvertently, upend his inner-life? Doesn't he deserve for his pridelessness to be more sufficiently accounted for here? But, ironically, since he is too proud to ask her these questions and is infuriated by the emotional double-bind he has found himself in, he winds up unconsciously muttering the cruelest thing imaginable.

—Well, I guess there is only *one* reason to wear the rubbers when we fucky-fuck then. . .

Holy shit he had said this. His lax-assed brain had taken some bizarre associative byway and his big fat mouth had made it stick. The hurtfulness of this accidental statement lay in its connectivity to a recent circumstance, a small scare born of a foreboding but ultimately illusory bodily symptom which Ronette had wondered might be some last bit of karma for her ultra-promiscuous days.

—Wait. Whoa. Now, Ron. No, okay? I didn't mean—

Her mouth crinkles then gapes. The freckles on either side of her nose turn from orange to red—another one of her tells. Her body, longer-memoried than her noodle, flash-germinates the seed sunk in her bones during the long wait on the fucking lab work.

—You. . .? What did you say. . .?! How could. . .?!

—No, Ron! No-no-no-no. Okay?! *No*.

Sid jumps to his feet forgetting the bowl in his lap. Their heads turn to follow its trajectory. Both reach for the place they think it will fall. Too late.

Ronette looks down at Sid clinging to her waist with his mouth mashed into her hip.

—Nofe-nofe-nofe. . .I'mff sofe starry, Fwon. . .nofe-nofe-nofe. . .it jufft came out. . .

He looks so pathetic but clutches at her so desperately, so totally un-self-consciously. Yes, her sweet, salvaged loser of a *de facto* husband burrowing his chin into her stomach, displaying himself in this needy form makes all the bone dread bleed out of her and allows an unfamiliar emotional mechanism—one just as malformed as Sid's rash words—to take hold. She finds herself pulling the hair away from the red face smeared with starchy matter and tears wanting to treat his childishness tenderly.

—C'mon ya Silly-Siddy. Mama needs you to get up. Here, let's do some stretches together. That'll make it better.

5.

Thin morning light collects in the black glass of the towers above. Street-level is murky. Traffic lights wink lazily. Virgil's two-way fuzzes. Sid turns his off. They listen to the click and slap of heels against the sidewalk, the complaint of plastic insoles, the drawl of old leather, the rigging of jackets, suits, and dresses buffeted by strides, fabric flapping against fabric and rippling in the cross-drafts, the low languagey mumble joining the surround of muffled traffic and the over-hanging theatre of sound. Yes, the day has begun without anyone's permission and no one knows under whose auspices it will continue. The great mystery is not why we do the legwork but how easily we are seduced by our own hustle.

—You don't finesse this one, dude. You don't write some *note*.

Sid wasn't completely deaf to what Virgil was laying down here. Like always he would big picture the situation like a freaking pro.

—The baby talk was make or break for me and X.

But all his useful words are nothing more than mood music to Sid's slowly organizing plan. Yes, his main home-boy's primary function here was to remind him of a few of his more blatant mistakes so he can like totally transcend them this time around. And after he ignores Virgil's advice on how to true all the fucky juju from last night before it becomes tainty and he winds up half-truing or possibly exacerbating the problem, he will need Virgil to laughingly tear him apart afterwards and help him start rebuilding again like he always does.

—X said 'I want one' and I'm like 'Is it a deal breaker if I don't?' and she was like 'Definitely' and I was like 'Lemme think about it.'

Sid loves Virgil unreservedly, admires him without hesitation and thanks Lord Christ he lucked into this best friend. Wishing he had more of his aplomb when it comes to heavy interpersonal interactions therefore is not jealousy but tribute. He knew long ago he would have no qualms with totally trying to emulate Virgil if doing so didn't seem sorta pathetic, as though, lacking sufficient spine, he could just *decide* to begin acting like someone who had Virgil's brand of neo-noir confidence. But, in addition to this possibly cramping Virgil's style and opening him up to loving ridicule from the only person who notices when Sid is operating on auto-pilot. . .*Do what's in your soul, blood, not mine. . .But don't get me wrong. . .you make me feel pretty inside. . .*, in addition to this totally transparent stab at replacing his own unwanted pig iron with someone else's steel and pledging himself towards some apprenticeship-like process, really and truly working towards this goal until he felt it part of his new chemistry, in addition to it being pretty late in the game for him to be thinking overhaul personality-wise (because once the deconstruct begins doesn't a whole re-engineering have to occur, if not a full on lot-wipe?) isn't it just nakedly false to deny what he, Sid, is all about? Not just the knuckle-headed hodgepodge of his recent past with its, well, pretty ample list of minor idiocies, over-careful living and comparatively few glories, but the whole incommensurate sum inside calling

itself 'Sid' or 'Sid's past? Yes, foisting incompatible improve-
ments onto your building site is demonstrative of someone
lacking the vision and integrity to make something coherent
and decent of himself. And even if what he creates on his own
is nowhere nearly as pleasing as an admittedly superior model
then at least he will have done so not because he is prideful or
stubborn but because he is afraid to deconstruct the tenuous
structure jerry-rigged on an already spooked building site.
Such an earth-rending overhaul would run the risk of giving
the noxious weed which so riddled his old man an opportunity
to leach up through the new foundation and slowly slink its
way to Sid's upper floors. And since his blueprint for living is
to be nothing like his old man such a project not only feels
foolhardy but terrifying.

—Then X starts crying and things speed up. I want to
keep this woman, right? So I'm in. 'That's good,' she said
'because I already have one.'

In sum, Sid didn't want to take the superstructural hit
implied by such a disavowal of his personal accumulations,
even if he disliked or distrusted most of them. They have at
least gotten him this far and he has avoided being like his
father in any obvious way. No, he would continue his resi-
dency in this slouching but persistent tower. He knows it is a
scared choice but if he started acting 'better' or taking 'good
advice' he'd feel divorced from the queer ghost bumping
around in his upper floors, that unknowable dude he guessed
he would die not really knowing but whose pursuit still
constituted an overarching narrative.

—So BAM the job is already done and suddenly
we're halfway there. My life begins to feel more meaningful.
'I will live for X and my child and that's it.' Period. Full
steam ahead. No second thoughts.

Likewise, Sid will discard any strategy resembling
what he thinks anyone in the population at large might em-
ploy, thus ensuring, by his hermetically faulty logic, that his
plan will spring solely from the original source material he
now plumbs by staring into the dark glass tower above and
waiting for a manifestation of his core force, some gift from
the inner-ether on a par with stealing Woody.

—I'm not as angry a person. I'm pretty damn happy,
in fact. Life starts to make more sense.

One trouble though. Whenever Sid crosschecks his imminent course of action for personal authenticity, engages in this vague q. & a., emerges from his little symposium with a framework of rationales which he thinks will stand up, tests and re-tests them, finds they actually hold water and emerges unscathed somehow, once The Grand Gesture is in his forebrain looking. . .well. . .gee. . .pretty spectacular on mental-paper if he must say so himself, so spectacular he becomes like pretty overwhelmed with how uncommonly his mind works sometimes and allows the Notion to hold systemic sway and to the exclusion of far more viable countermeasures, this tyranny of thought, this hypnotic narrow-mindedness, captured in the twinkling of his un-blinking eyes as the transiting sun reflects off the opaque towers above and brands the Idea onto his consciousness, forces him to conclude that this is the only possible way to accomplish his goal—keeping Ronette happy. Thus, a man achieves a semblance of confidence, however misplaced.

Virgil knows Sid is elsewhere. He could station him in front of Ronette and feed him lines like Cyrano and he would start yodeling Esperanto. His best friend would fuck this up his way and royally. Chastising him will only catalyze more extreme variations of the grand gesture he knows Sid is now pulling from the sky between the looming towers above—a.k.a. his ass. If only his best friend toted around cheaply won verities like the rest of the Co-op circle did then maybe he would at least have some foundational swagger in that thick skull of his when he did his tilting at windmills shit. But no amount of blunt clarity, blunt force, or bitingly sharp commentary ever seems to break through all the noise up in that noodle of his. Sid's pure fool stubbornness is lovable but tragic. Shit, man, there is serious living going on out here. Every single one of our lives is on the line. Dude at least needs reminding that as long as he keeps indulging his insecurities he will remain apart from the world, neither fully open to serious joy nor brave enough to expose himself to the inexorable waves of world-killing pain we must all face at one time or another. Yes, Sid needs to understand that gestures, no matter how ingenious or well-intentioned, are poor stand-ins for what is actually necessary. So even if dude is constitutionally incapable of being decisive he needs to start practicing having convictions. After much failure and suffering he might reach a point where he can start living life straight down the middle instead of sidestepping it all the time.

—But then we lose her and before I get angry I get spooked. Like maybe I cursed the whole thing from the start. Maybe our little girl picked up on my doubts from *inside* of Exene? Maybe she decided she only wanted to be where she was truly wanted. Maybe she *made* X miss that stop sign. All these bullshit questions instead of the hard one. . .

Sid is not so far away he can't hear Virgil start to tear himself apart again.

—. . .Why in the fuck was my wife on a rig delivering at five months pregnant?

—C'mon, bro, don't, okay? It was bad luck, nothing else.

—We were so cool with our 'no scared choices' bullshit. Said our baby was bred for boldness. . .*Your Moms was hauling rig when your ass was more than halfway home, baby. . .*What horseshit.

—*Good* shit, Virge. Valid shit.

—Good for us but not for her. We put our lives in front of a defenseless baby.

—C'mon, man.

—With serious fucking repercussions. Do you dig what I'm saying here, Sid?

—You didn't do anything wrong. Neither did X. No way. Period.

—Man, tell me something. Can you imagine what it feels like to miss someone who never existed?

Sid clears hair away from his face so he can meet Virgil's eyes.

—I can't, man.

—I *can*. You take her to the zoo, teach her how to ride a bicycle, scare away her boyfriends. You know it's impossible but you feel it so strongly that you forget she's dead. But then the feeling wears off and you lose her all over again.

— . . .

—Yet here I am always telling X how to act, pretending like I've got things under control, like I'm not constantly thinking about our dead daughter. Hell, I'm still trying to come up with a good name for her.

—You gotta cut yourself some slack, Virge.

—I'm always seeing her. At five months. . .graduating high school. . .when she's 50. . .on my death bed.

—You gotta stop thinking in hypotheticals.

—Wasn't nothing hypothetical about what they pulled out of Exene's stomach, man. Nothing.

— . . .dude.

—Well? It's time you woke the fuck up, bro. Seriously.

—Me?

—Don't you see what I'm driving at? You're too hung up on your own trip. Life is what's outside that head of yours, man. You're going to die some day. . .hypothetical and alone.

—. . .

—You hearing what I'm fucking laying down here, Sidder?

—. . .

—Ronnie's going to disappear on your ass some day.

—. . .

—And then what you got that matters?

—. . .

—I'll tell you what. *Nothing*. Nothing but you and your precious good intentions and stupid grand gestures.

Sid uses both hands to pull his hair behind his ears.

—I'm hearing you, bro. I've got this. I'm going straight down the middle on this one.

—Then tell me what you're going to do.

—I don't think I should tell you yet.

—. . .

—. . .

—I'll do my best with the eulogy, bro.

o   o   o   o   o   o   o   o   o

Staticcy bursts of Muzak score the hypnotic movements of a middle-aged man stocking grape jelly in a non-Co-op-affiliated supermarket. He pivots to his loaded cart, grabs two jars, pivots back to the shelf, slams the jars down and straightens them. He does this over and over and nearly in time with the Muzak, his rank of purple soldiers methodically marching towards the edge. Though his hands are knobby and swollen and his entire aspect seems bent, his movements are quick and sure.

There is nothing romantic or noble about earning a living with a body failing by degrees, Sid thinks. He has knee and hip tendonitis and often finds himself wondering how many years he has left in the saddle. Kicking upstairs, so unfathomable now, may wind up being his only alternative. And given the direction his life may take after tonight's Grand Gesture, he is thankful to have this option. Leaving behind those wonderfully mindless days in the saddle would be a small sacrifice if doing so helps guarantee his and Ronette's future together.

Yes, this all squared. The momentum of this Grand Gesture continues to be undeniable. Riding to the supermarket his thoughts had had this same fluidity, his mental rig coasting down a seamless grade, the conclusions ticked off with the blocks as he drafted in the slipstream of his newfound organizing principal. So, to shopping.

He counts six different weight grades of flour ranging from the long torsos laying atop one another on the bottom shelf up to these pouch-like plastic re-sealable jobbies on the top. The former are covered with thick font and outsized graphics while the latter are decorated with small pastoral scenes in pressure-inked pastels whose flourishy fonts boast of impenetrability and pure bloodlines. One version, a 10-pound bag of organic white, features a transparent window shaped like a Vaudeville stage with the dense meal pressed up against the plastic. Sid finds this revealing style of packaging grotesque, even a bit profane, and so moves on. He studies the esoterica on the non-windowed labels (heartland vales, millstones, Masonic iconography, regional maps, swaying stalks, stout farm-houses, jowlsy farmland couples) hoping to get an impression off to the side of whatever impression the manufacturers want to give of the mundanely utilitarian contents within. Alright, he needs to prioritize. He needs a sack small enough to fit in his riding bag. Something neither expensive nor cheap. And the flour should be unbleached. This would symbolically acknowledge his recent failures but, more importantly, imply that flaws are more natural than any supposed purity. Ipso facto we should not mourn our imperfections but celebrate how we chose to adapt to them. Ergo this Grand Gesture. Ergo their more perfect union. Yes, the final product will not only be an acknowledgement of Ronette's needs but an expression of his desire to take their relationship to the next level.

Then he sees the sacks with a bull logo. Perfect. He's like the minotaur. . .no. . .a bull who *graduated* from being a minotaur. He grabs the baby blue five-pound sack of generic deluxe all-purpose wheat flour, tells the stocker to 'have a good one,' and hums his way through checkout to the strains of a Top 40 song he didn't realize he knew the words to, thought he hated, but now hears in an entirely different way.

o o o o o o o o o

Ronette takes Evers. Work has done her good; a day of weaving between the tanks on the narrow, streaming downtown avenues, staring into the false reflections inside the warping skyscraper glass, blending into the blur of competing speeds around her, these in-between states sucking her in, obscuring her cares, dissolving her into the beautiful diffusion of lives piling high into the sky, providing that false sense of omniscience which can feel like community, counting the stairs on the walk-ups or dripping next to some suit on the elevator who tries to bridge the class gap by asking the woman in the tight yellow riding kit about the rig over her shoulder or commenting about the state of the city's crumbling roads, they're hard enough to drive on, he can only guess what it's like for a bike messenger in their rainy climate, both finally smiling goodbye at her floor, Ronette used to the eyes on her back, prone to neither scruple nor pride when it comes to honors, not resenting the opposite sex for their general tendencies, just wanting to live and let live, man. Keep it simple. Do no harm, dig?

Then she would talk with the receptionists, pose them serious questions, provide blunt advice, briefly enter their exotic lives, fascinated as she is by others' cares, ever the failed anthro student, anxiously drawing conclusions with a mental rigor she never applied to her own inner-life, happily bored to bits by her holdings, content to merely exist, knowing, though, that she needs to maintain these minor relationships if she wants to avoid estranging herself from the world again, so memorizing and reciting the names of their children and pets, inquiring into their love lives, recalling their lists of joys and grudges, retraining her memory for mundane facts, knowing people enjoy confiding in this sweaty, smelly woman who likes to linger with a cup of water while they treat her visit like a diary entry or confessional. . .*Someday we need to just sit down with a bottle of wine and really hash things out, Ronette.* . .but stubbornly keeping their association transient; slowly filling her days like this until she switches off her radio, takes 500-525 pedal strokes to cross the bridge, gets inside her ride, man, meditates, divests herself of as much of herself and others as she can until she can kick it in the bungalow with books or music until Sid gets home and they eat and maybe she tells him a little about it and they sleep or whatever until they have to wake up and put their helmets on again in the morning for another day of deliveries.

But why the hell did she take Evers? She only takes Evers when Sid wants to take Evers. And for that matter hadn't she told herself before crossing the bridge to strictly avoid even looking at Evers? Because. . .well. . .yeah. . .she is a bit superstitious. . .okay a *lot* superstitious. . .her little quirk. See, in order to maintain the hard-won peace in her life she sees no reason to deviate from the tendencies which have finally landed her there. Food. Bathing. Teeth brushing. Bike routes. Pedal strokes. Training. Just about everything, according to Sid. All measurable and replicable. As long as she stays close to mien nothing very unexpected or terrible should occur. And isn't this just another way of saying she is experienced? Isn't superstition just another regimen? Isn't cultivating habits, however tyrannically, the easiest path to a stable and predictable life? Yes, this is what she has been telling herself and it has worked out just fine. Yet here she is apparently so wigged out on girl-fire that she has skipped the port route, not executed the usual 1,700–1,825 pedal strokes necessary to skirt the poisonous air trapped between the interstate and the train yards and is ticking off these low, horizontal blocks with the lonely little bungalows marooned in their treeless and puddling lots as the sweet-tart chemical mist streams down her face and forces her to consider, not inquire into, but deeply consider what sort of habits, what tweaking in routine would be necessary for her to live effectively trapped inside all this poison and implied motion. However similar these bungalows are to hers, she thinks the residents inside must have radically different customs. Though only a ten minute ride away, this neighborhood feels ominously private, profusely foreign. It is as though each individual structure is a security gate and Ronette has forgotten her credential and must race past before someone plunges out the front door and starts chasing after her yelling 'What are you doing here?! Come back!' Shit, if she had counted pedal strokes on this fucker last night, prepared for just this kind of mishap, she could be making this a race and improving her time. She stands in the saddle to sprint but instead of firing forward she feels like she is cycling in place. Maybe if she turned around and rode back she could reverse the spell somehow. . .*But, no, that's not how this works, dummy. . .You're full of little lies lately, aren't you?. . .*No, it's too late to turn around so she had better sprint her ass off through this fucking whirlpool of a road before it sucks her down a sewer grate and lands her in the lonely life she not-so-secretly wants and in the company of all her supposedly quiet habits.

—Lies! Lies, you bitch!

Since Ronette is yelling at the road she does not notice the four-way stop sign or the beginning of her long tumble through the intersection.

Sid sits in the easy chair with his fingers laced over a fraying black pinstripe suit many sizes too small for him. Beneath the coat is a yellow smiley face t-shirt, yellow cummerbund, and yellow bowtie. When he crosses his legs the cuffs on the slacks ride halfway to his knee and his arms do the same vis-à-vis his elbow. Black tube socks too thick for the black penny loafers they are squeezed into are held up by black garters pinching his mid-calves so tightly blood has collected beneath his skin on either side of the bands and made it look as though his legs are recovering from the shackles. Each item but the shirt, bowtie, and tube socks were his father's. This is the sixth time he has worn The Ensemble. First to a tap recital in ninth grade when the suit actually fit, then to the junior prom when he received pretty relentless ribbing on its disproportionality from his usual tormentors and eventually his date, then to his father's funeral when it was already absurdly small. He had invested in the shirt and bowtie for the third occasion. It had been Sid's inaugural Grand Gesture. By wearing The Ensemble he planned on being hated in small but indelible ways by distant family members who knew him little and mat-tered less. Their outrage, he reasoned, would reveal themselves to themselves. And hadn't even his old man occasionally been capable of seeing the lighter side of things, even fancied himself a bit of a connoisseur of the absurd and sometimes found himself willing, given the right admixture of alcohol and success at work, to expound to the fourth chair on the nihilistic qualities of that unshakable enemy of his known as 'The Modern?' Might not his old man, 19-year old Sid then reasoned, be laughing his ass off at The Ensemble from on high or wherever the hell he was right now? Wouldn't these party poopers do well to realize this and get in on the fun while the getting was still good? Didn't their next family funeral prac-tically demand such and a.s.a.p? Yes, The Ensemble was an homage, he explained, trying to convey the almost artistic seriousness of his decision to his mother, deigning to tell her what the man whom she had submitted to sleeping with for 26 years would want in his hypothetical afterlife, what with its opportunities for reprioritization, temperament realignment, and an almost certainly emergent brand of gallows humor. And, what's more, Mom, he had done his due diligence here. He had asked a close friend (Woody) if he had a right to his own manner of mourning if doing so also compromised others' ability to freely pursue theirs. And Woody had told him that the moment he donned the smiley-face t-shirt he would be convinced of the objective rightness of his choice since. . .*The old guy suffered longer than anyone deserves and we all went through it with him and deserve a laugh or two by now, Mom.* . .Then, in closing, touching her arm, initiating physical contact for the first time since he was a preadolescent, he reassured her that some-where down the line the relatives who scowled acid at him all day long would eventually be able to look back and laugh if not in solidarity with Sid then at least at what a harmless buffoon he was compared to what a moody, mean-spirited, self-indulgent old crank his old man was. Luckily, his mother had drank enough to not object much. And since they were both in a celebrating mood why ruin their celebration with scruples?

So Sid wore The Ensemble to the funeral, burial, and reception, and shook hands with his arm pinned to his body (so Woody wouldn't fall out) while his noodle and insides did the far more complicated work of not quite articulating to these strangers the far more precise reason he had worn this outlandish outfit, namely that he was *overjoyed* that his father

56

had been thoroughly eradicated from this plane and all others and would no longer have any say in what his. . .*moron long-hair son.* . .got up to anymore. What's more, his old man would be completely oblivious to his son's parlay of 'grief' into a furlough from studying Latin and Classics at the community college and would not be there to make his sarcastic donkey hee-haw when his. . .*deadbeat son.* . .stretched the furlough into a sabbatical from the higher education his father had insisted on. . .*wasting his life.* . .to save for. Then, finally, when he told his mother that he was taking. . .*an extended leave of absence from all forms of pedagogy.* . .but was not dropping out, you understand, just reassessing, what with his, well, not being too crazy about the telephone job which barely afforded him the shit apartment in a dangerous part of town, and, well, given the circumstances. . .*what with Dad's passing.* . .he had been forced to consider if it wouldn't be. . .*better for all concerned, me and you, Mom, if I just moved back in for a while, what with Dad gone, and to keep you company.* . . And after she nodded and reflexively fled to the kitchen to drink her feelings away Sid thought about how the old man could not only not go all ad hominem on him for the jackpot of a turn of events which his death had brought about, but could never again say boo about a single thing Sid said or did. No, his old man was thoroughly and finally gone and, just as he had predicted to the fourth chair, everyone was better off without him. Yes, his mother had used the life insurance money to go on a world booze cruise and Sid had the house all to himself to do whatever he wanted, which included filling out the paperwork to have his last name legally changed to 'Doe' and the second half of his first name removed.

The other three times Sid had donned The Ensemble had involved Ronette. The first had been during their fourth date. A longtime delivery customer had gifted him symphony tickets and Ronette had told him she liked classical. On a whim he bought a black bowler at Goodwill midway on the ride to her apartment. She opened the door wearing a black dress and laughed at Sid pouring sweat in. . .*that hilarious costume.* . .His Ensemble was suddenly the doofus' retrograde look to her Greek Goddess. The stylistic imbalance made him nervous. Maybe he didn't know Ronette as well as he thought. Maybe this would be the night she dumped him.

They rode out with Sid preparing himself for the inevitable. Ronette pedaled free and easy in her fluttering dress while Sid slugged and chugged to keep up. He was a sweaty mess when they approached the inner-belt of downtown. Coasting down the ramp to the bridge, an updraft took the bowler and magically lifted it onto the highway exchange 50 feet above. For Sid this was a maddening fit of cosmic whim which he doubted he would be able to recover from. While his vertigo had improved since childhood he still got dizzy if forced to linger at heights. . .*Forget the hat. . .Let's go. . .*But before he could say anything Ronette had thrown herself into the adventure of retrieving it. They slung their rigs over their shoulders, walked back up the shoulder of the narrow ramp, hopped a median, and were climbing a steep stairway when Sid finally shouted his affliction up to her over the roar of traffic. Ronette hurried down, laughed apologetically, slid her red wristbands off, showed him the scars on her wrists, then the not-quite-fully-healed ones in her arm where she used to shoot up and shouted. . .*I guess we know everything about each other now!. . .*She held his hand while they carefully made their way down to the bridge then kissed for the first time while waiting for a garbage barge to pass beneath the upraised center section of the lift bridge.

The second time he had worn The Ensemble for her was when they signed on the bungalow. She asked him to wear the same crummy clothes he wore to the open house. He said her superstitions were 'cute' but that ever since his father's funeral he had only worn The Ensemble during the most important moments of his life. Ronette remembered him appearing in her door for that fourth date, remembered their first hesitant kiss under the descending bridge section, smiled, and said that was enough of an explanation for her. Sid, emboldened, wanting to be explorative with his emotions like a compelling mate should, further hazarded that wearing The Ensemble was also a way of commemorating the death of the bad old days and the advent of a happier life. He had then shyly slid the wooden salad spoon out to show Ronette he also intended to wear him to the signing. And somehow Ronette had dug this, too. A remarkable woman, he had thought. If he believed in marriage he would have proposed then and there.

So when Ronette comes in the door, her knees mushy and running red, her delivery yellows torn at the hip, a dented helmet dangling from her hand, gravel smeared over a purpled cheek, a lens missing from her glasses, her eyes haunted, not so much seeing Sid sitting up straight and smiling expectantly, but looking above and beyond him, pausing to look down from the beckoning firmament of stucco to, if not acknowledge his presence, then at least demonstrate she remembers who he is and that, yes, he more or less belongs here and that it is not so strange to see him leap to his feet, send Woody flying from his sleeve and lunge and trip toward her.

—Ronette! Oh Jesus.

Emotionally condensed minutes pass. He kisses the wounds on her face and asks questions in diminishing volume until she starts telling him what happened and he gradually calms down with the accumulation of facts. She hasn't broken anything. She is not in any great pain. Her rig will be fine. The things he thinks she most cares about are vouchsafed. Then the possibility that things could have been far worse is almost ecstatically detailed in Sid's interpretation of the event. He is breathless and smiling while Ronette looks confused and shy. She accepts his attention without protest, enjoys having him manipulate her limbs, wipe and buss her cheeks, loosen her braids and burrow into her scalp to test for sensitivities, then stroke it all back into place again. Reduced to necessities, life suddenly seems extraordinarily straightforward.

Ronette has had enough concussions to know that this isn't one or at least not a very serious one. But when she tries to focus on any single object in the room without her glasses she feels herself spun and bashed and reversed like a buoy. No, she must look only at Sid whose flitting and stroking is not unlike the physics of the tumble on Evers, just far more deliberate and gentle, perhaps even a kind of template for reentry. She concentrates on the familiar ovular zone framed by his hair. Lips-Nose-Eyes. Lips-Nose-Eyes. His gentle aquilinity. She hears herself asking him to do little things for her (take her socks off, comb her hair out, remove her shirt) just so he will continue moving and perhaps slowly wean her off the tumble by example.

She showers with her eyes closed and the curtain open. He holds her by the hip and periodically asks if she is okay. She hums back affirmatives and lets the water spread her hair out. He tries a joke about reduced cognition. She looks over to smile into his eyes. She has never felt more thankful for him. His soft, warm sounds slowly inhabit her while she washes all the tumbling down the drain. A pleasant feeling close to emptiness or fatigue overtakes her. She thinks she would like him to take her to bed now.

When she turns the water off the toilet belches in sympathy and they laugh at this familiar sound. He helps her dress then leads her back to the sitting room to install her on the sofa. He then resumes his place in the easy chair and is once again smiling broadly. She feels shy but relaxed. Both listen to the quality of stillness in the room. The after-images of her standing there stunned and bleeding quickly become abstract as the euphoria of overcoming a small disaster together transforms its fading horror into light comedy. He makes a few more soft jokes and she smiles again and both of them feel good. The pauses lengthen as they listen back into the quiet now practically ringing with clarity, their feelings and perceptions uniquely acute as they consider each other and then the objects in the room, everything reduced down to form and function, their experience of these silent moments honest, eloquent and beautiful, made more precious by the last strands of rush hour murmuring safely from the other side of the noise barrier. Yes, both of them would like to stay like this for a very long time, maybe forever.

But Ronette notices there is no music playing. Maybe Sid turned it off after she appeared there bloodied and dazed. She can't remember. Then she notices he is wearing The Ensemble and understands that he had been waiting to surprise her with something big. She sees him watching her put this all together.

—Put some music on, will ya, Sid?

—No, we need quiet now, Ron.

—You—

—Listen, I'm going to need you to just sit there, okay? Here. . .

Sid removes Ronette's lucky red wristbands from an inside pocket of the suit.

—Give me the wrists. Tonight calls for formal attire.

Ronette holds out her wrists and Sid removes the black Co-op wristbands. Before sliding the red ones on he gives the scars on each wrist a kiss. She tries to relent a little inside but feels greedy for the silence they are abandoning. Watching him walk to the kitchen, The Ensemble riding ridiculously high up his arms and legs, she wonders if maybe Sid requires more seriousness in his life—from himself and from her. Maybe if she cared more about her inner-life she could share it with him and help him feel less alone or lost inside his sometimes. Maybe what she considers their major faults—his insecurity, her remoteness—would wash away quicker if she reached out to him more. She twists the tips of both braids. Yes, and if only she could annihilate every last preconception she had or at least the ones which prevented her from being more present sometimes then maybe he wouldn't wind up feeling like these grand gestures were necessary.

—Sid, wait.

He turns around to see Ronette dandling at the elastic on her underwear.

—Are you sure you don't want some fucky-fuck first?

The smile on Sid's face is unchanged. He pushes into the kitchen.

She remembers that they had fought or done something like it last night. Sid will have taken it harder than her and prepared a grand gesture which will unintentionally enshrine an argument the crash had helped her forget. There are blundery noises then crashes in the kitchen which are followed by Sid's muffled shouts of reassurance. Ronette takes a breath and gives it back, takes a breath and gives it back, then tries to slow her heart rate. Maybe she can regain some of that silence, the—

—Okay, here we come. Close those eyes.

Sid keeps colliding with things and knocking them over. It sounds as though he is pushing something towards her. Each new crash makes her eyes and head ache.

—Oops.

What's left of that sweet silence is quickly rampaged over. She tells herself not to be angry. Then there is another crash closer by and Sid goes 'oof.'

—*Sid?!*

—I'm alright, I'm alright.

After a few final thuds she hears a faint squeaking sound. It's how her rear wheel sounded as it spun just above her head when she came to in the intersection. Strangely, laying there on the wet asphalt, hearing the first hesitant voices of the motorists surrounding her, she had only then realized that the wheel had been squeaking all day. Yes, just before her brain had shut down to prepare her body for impact that one last suspicion had snuck in. . .*Did Sid tech my rig this morning?*. . .She had crashed enough—and far more violently—to know that an intensely watchful silence is supposed to take possession of you in the moments before impact. But instead she had flown through the air feeling slightly annoyed. Yes, she remembers now. It had been that tech-needy wheel which had awoken her and now here it was again drilling down through her and returning her to the tumble and what she had been thinking just before she crashed which, in turn, flashes forward to place her back in the doorway when she got home, feeling elsewhere or nowhere, refusing to *see* that Sid was wearing The Ensemble but *knowing* he was and the *reason* behind what was about to happen, the explanation for her breakdown at the dinner party, her shit rides home, the argument with Sid and her stupid crash-out, all this flailing and tumbling occurring not *in* but *around* her, this whirling vortex deactivating her failsafe, shoving the truth to her forebrain, making her admit what she had been so desperate to ignore the clues of for so long—i.e. the tensile qualities of Sid's hand on her thigh, the fucky cadence of her pedaling, Woody's angle in the bowl of macaroni—God, come to think of it, even while she was enjoying a day delivering she hadn't been able to shake the feeling that once she was over the bridge she was going to have to outrun something. Yes, that vague opponent had probably been running the show for months, years maybe. And Sid, judging by the happy-dumb tone of his voice, had succumb to its influence and was well stoned on the damn thing by now. Yes, this world-rending squeak just a few feet away now is unquestionably the demon laughter of their opponent lording their victory over them.

—Alright, here we go.

Between them is a tattered black baby carriage which they sal-vaged a few months ago and have been using to dry dishes in since. Sid pulls back the dome.

—Have a look.

A baby blue sack of flour lies on the torn lining. Its top tapers together and is bound by stitching. The two-line product title—Generic Deluxe All-Purpose Wheat Flour—frames a wild-eyed bull leaping and contorting away from an unseen antagonist. Motion lines on either side of his tiny red tongue indicate he is bellowing. A silver ring pierces his septum. He seems terrified.

—She's five pounds even. Let's call her Flora.

6.

—Yo, Sister Ronette, where's The Sidder?

A runty messenger dude holds the door to The Percolator open as Ronette noses her bike into urgent-sounding guitar music and the smell of coffee.

—I thought you guys always came together.

The kid yucks and snorts and works up the courage to give Ronette an up and down. His is the jittery swag of the new school messenger who thinks city delivery is like running with the bulls. Ronette did this cocky phase in her early druggy days and so doesn't begrudge how puffed up he feels. A certain amount of bravado is required to tamp down the fear of navigating mechanical beasts even more dangerous than spooked bulls.

—I saw you at Velodrome last week. Killer stuff, Sister Ronette. Kill-*urrr*.

Sid mentors many of these newbies. They quickly learn that the tall and quiet hair-veiled dude can tech a rig cleaner and faster than anyone else. Also, since it is well known that he has not crashed once in six years of delivering it wouldn't hurt to get a contact hit of luck off of him now and then. But, most importantly, he is coach and partner to that championship Cooper Ronette Okampo. So they not only gravitate to Sid but are somewhat in awe of him, often pulling him into one of their cock-and-bulls to mediate a disagreement or pronounce some ineluctable truth about life in the saddle. When this occurs Ronette—stationed across the room and hiding behind a book—listens to Sid's usually so quiet and hesitant bungalow voice confidently rise above the noisy room to become just what the newbies would expect from someone in his illustrious position. She must then remind herself that we are all many people and not very well-acquainted with most of them. Therefore, she should not feel somewhat frightened by this pedantic, almost cocksure person she strains to recognize. Anyway, she can love this version of him, too, and doubts he even recognizes himself. Besides, it's probably not so different from how she feels when she is racing—so intensely engaged that she forgets she exists. Yes, temporarily reducing one's self so—Sid the Tech Expert, Ronette the Racing Champion—can come in handy when you want to disappear in public view.

—Thanks. Now step aside, little bro.

Ronette noses her rig past the newbie and rolls up to a long bar of old jewelry display cases filled with pastries. She waves to the two calisthenic barista/dispatchers wearing small earpieces who bend and stretch and dodge each other while fielding drink orders, ratcheting espresso machines, shouting business addresses, registering payments, and updating the delivery logbook. Above them, hanging from the fir beams climbing into the exposed ductwork of an ancient ventilation system hang classic bicycles, obsolete race rigs, bent wheels, disfigured frames, a maze of innertube intestines, and the pretzeled handlebars of the rig Warren Renshaw once flew over in the Basque Pyrenees. Further back are the three wide entrances opening to three stairwells whose steps creak and crack as Co-op employees jog up and down between the endlessly intertwining enterprises filling The Hive, the ten-story Co-op nexus housing a music venue, recording studio and booking agency on the second floor, a restaurant, caterer, and gallery on the third, a yoga studio, naturopathic pharmacy, and day spa on the fourth, traditional and alternative medical/dental practices on the fifth, micro-lofts for in-residence artists and sleepover studios for visiting artists on the sixth, community outreach and a charitable foundation on the seventh, sales on the eighth, and admin on the ninth and tenth. Shouts fly up one stairwell, laughter down another. Doorless entrances thrust you into the center of open floor plans surrounded by the massive paneless windows a 19th century gem king installed so his jewelers' eyes would not fail quite as scandalously as they did for his eastern concern and, more dramatically, so the citizens of the foundling city could crane their necks into the then still starry evening sky to see the tiers of alchemists hunched amid kerosene lanterns conjuring faceted dreams deep into the night, encouraging the optimists on the streets below to limn a promise from the display. . .*One day soon any of you might have the means to walk into our glorious showroom.*

But where the gem concern only dangled abstract futures to the citizens below The Co-op now *models* the transformations available if they will only step inside. You can watch them in the windows striding from suite to suite, bent in yoga poses, cross-legged in meditation, supine with a counselor, on their back being worked over by a masseuse, congregated, lounging, dancing, magnetically attracted to the curtainless windows, often staring down to the streets below, catching someone's eye, actually waving, smiling invitingly, gesturing 'come on up.' Yes, the former World Gem Center still contains transformative matter, only now *you* are the only thing stopping yourself from getting in on it. And, heck, you've walked by a million times, right? Seen their imprint all over town? Why not go on in? There's time before work. That is if you have work these days. You've heard they promise entry-level jobs for going through the training, right? It doesn't mean you have to sign in blood or anything. Or maybe you've power-walked down the hill this morning and want to try something *recherché*. Word is this booming little cult is doing gangbusters business. Your friend ____ is a member so how weird can it be. So come on, go on in. Have a complimentary espresso drink. See the jobs counselor on Seven. Check out the free art exhibits on Three. Get a facial on Four. Because once you enter The Hive you are suffused with the sheer bright bustlingness of real and implied motion. Cheerful strangers make direct eye contact with you. An air of extravagant youth and sturdy health carries you through the crowded tables full of earnest conversation, vigorous pantomime, and context-heavy shine. None of this feels common to the uninitiated and the more frequently you partake the more necessary it feels. Lo, inside of ten visits (The Co-op goal is five) everyone knows your story or your business or your hang-ups and soon you are swiveling your chin from the place setting of your hands, recognizing the songs blitzing from the speakers, learning the names of the barista/dispatchers, artists, messengers, chefs, agents, producers, and work-a-dayers just like you and finding yourself not wanting to let go of this. So you take The Knowledge. The modules are free. They only require that you volunteer ten hours of your time each week. The discounts are heavy and the benefits estimable. Don't worry, there are only unwritten rules and new-comers quickly learn that disparaging talk and cynical behavior are the only things which do not fly here. And since spending any amount of time in an atmosphere of intense positivism renders outliers absurd if not somewhat monstrous there is nothing to worry about—Their kind don't last long or have much of a chance to ruin it for everyone else. This is not to say, however, that those who take The Knowledge and become members are brainwashed into becoming some smiling sycophantic drone. No, independent thought is institutionalized as a core value here, my brother. Moreover, how applicants or members conduct themselves outside the ever-widening reach of The Co-op eye is strictly their own affair. They may cling to as many heretical notions as they please (doing so is strongly discouraged of course) just so long as they refrain from voicing them while conducting Co-op business, using Co-op facilities, or occupying Co-op premises. So, yes, you're a Co-op member sporting the ∞ pendant now. This is your new lifestyle. These are your new friends. What's not to like about any of this? Nothing, nothing at all, my sister, so please stay the duration. Though we have only just met, understand that we are all your long estranged family. We will never abandon you. Your organic funeral will be extremely well-attended.

As Ronette pushes her rig toward the back third of The Percolator a low-slung multi-color skyline of plastic jungle gyms comes into view. Small children yelp, waddle, teeter, collapse, crawl, think, stew, laugh, cackle, and cry as pods of adults look on from the tables positioned just the other side of the multi-color plastic picket fence. There are open shirts, breast pumps, diapers, strollers, overflowing bags, and an overwhelming odor of powder. This is The Brood, an ongoing experiment in creative childcare where Hive employees supervise Hive children and talk in what sounds to Ronette (who has always avoided this area) like a bizarrely coded language.

—Yeah, Alex likes to chew on'em then suck'em dry.

—Ha! Saves some nipple time I bet.

—Ha! No. Actually? She's just wild about sucking. Pillows. Blankies. Bibs. Nipples. The cat's tail once. Just acknowledging her inner-animal, I suppose.

—Heh, nipples. Fond memories, pleasurable ones even. But now—

—I just don't know what to do about her, bro.

—The chafes? The oozes?

—No, the fixating. The me-me-me-ness of it all.

—Well, babies can't help how self-seeking they are.

—Yeah, I mean what are you gonna do, muzzle her?

—Chastity! Don't!

—Careful now, Brother Jim. That's not far from being some pretty serious negative-think there.

—Presley is a manic hand washer. You turn your back and you hear water running somewhere.

—Sister Momma taught her well.

—Isn't there a tincture of some kind on Four?

—I hide her steppy stool so she can't reach the sink? She uses a pile of boardbooks. I tell her boardbooks aren't doctrine in the potty? I find her teetering on the seat of her tricycle!

—Resourceful little Little Cooper isn't she?

—Should we really be saying 'manic' though?

—Earnest! Don't put that in your mouth, hon, okay?

—Just get some from the pharmacy across the street. Our tincture prices are a bit. . . erm. . .self-seeking just now.

—Works for teething, too.

—I tell her she can only wash before eating or after getting messy. . .*Your motives are sound, honey. . .your dedication laudable. . .but you need to ask Mommy's permission to go wishy-washy from now on. . .*Then she starts getting her hands dirty on purpose, comes in with mud smeared all over her clothes. Or she keeps herself awake hours after beddy-bye so she can sneak into the bathroom while she thinks we're sleeping.

—Has Teddy started training wheels? I thought I saw him racing Trudy.

—She locks herself in, turns the water on, and sings her wishy-washy song over and over like some lunatic!

—Oh how nice of you, Bubba. What do you say, Phoebe?

—It's just that the term 'manic' has such negative connotations. You need to be careful not to language-model, Sister Jen.

—Ooo, I'll have to try that.

—And 'lunatic' too.

—Fine. How about. . .'intensely devoted.'

—Okay sure.

—So anyway I put a combination lock on the bathroom door and she starts compulsively. . .devotedly ramming the bathroom door with her trike. I tell her wishy-washy is now confined to the kitchen sink and turn off the water line on the chance she finds a way up there.

—No, that must have been Justice. Junior Velodrome is his new sweet spot.

—Now what do you *say*, dear? *Hmm?*

—An hour later I find her jumping up and down with like no shot of reaching the kitchen sink. But she keeps trying and trying and I stand there watching her get more and more frustrated but don't step in, don't want to be too harsh, don't want to be too doctrinaire, criticize her initiative, crush her dreams—No, I just stand there watching her jump up and down, sniffling and crying, and hope there might be some kind of lesson in this for her.

—When does Thor start Co-op school?

—Finally she gives up, is sweating and exhausted, wipes her tears, and starts angrily shouting 'Wishy-washy! Wishy-washy! Wishy-washeeeeee!' at the sink.

—'Discipline. . .um. . .' how does it go again? It's one of Brother Warren's favorites.

—But I just let it all happen and sneak away. A few days pass. She has been doing perfectly polite little wishy-washy's with me in the kitchen sink. Her clothes stay clean. So I take the lock off the bathroom door because she's been such a good little Little Cooper. And she only washes after wee-wee or poo-poo like I taught her. No midnight excursions. No signs anywhere of unnecessary washing. A week passes. Nothing. Then one morning I need something from the basement. I go down and find a massive puddle in the middle of the carpet. There's wood rot on the wall where the pipes are. Mold everywhere. I go outside and find a small lake around the hose spout.

—Ha! Whoops. Sorry, Sister Jen, that's not funny.

—You're right it's not funny. It's freaking terrifying is what it is.

—'Discipline is the goal, not the goal at the end of the discipline' or something like that.

—But I thought he had passed his pre-K modules.

—Can you stand up tall like a big girl for Mommy. . . Hmm? *Can* you?

—I've learned I need to be more respectful of Satchmo when I ideate for Satchmo. . .Maybe Prez should do her own ideating here is what I'm saying, Jen.

—I mean she's gonna have a full on fucking. . . shoot. . .a full on freaking complex!

—Where is he today, Brother Dylan?

—Satch is with Sister Nona. Warren thought it'd be good for morale on Three. The distillery ramp up? *Muy* stressy. You know what a little charmer Satch is.

—Like, sometimes, Sister Mommy Jen? I don't realize we're doing something I prefer until it's over and he's had a miserable time and cried or got cranky and spoiled the fun I thought I was going to have in the first place because I lied to myself about how much I thought he would like it.

—Like I'm wondering if I'd be enabling her by saying, fine, here, upsy daisy, wishy-washy to your heart's content. 'You go, girl,' basically.

—Ha, naw. No.

—Maybe? Who knows.

—Some things there are no modules for.

—Yeah. . .erm. . .yes. Sometimes it's like totally boring seeking your own ideal is what I'm saying, bros and sisses. Pleasures, too.

—Oh, I've back-seated my pleasures for the time being and I'm fine with that.

—I'd ideate myself up to the freaking day spa.

—Can you guys watch Fitzroy for a second? I have to run up to Five. Don't let him act out.

—Maybe we need to start them in on modules sooner. Like Year 2.5 maybe.

—Are you're sure that isn't a little self-seeking on your part?

—Well, I mean is there some sort of law that says we can't.

—Run it up to Nine.

—Aw, in a year you won't remember any of this.

—Yeah, you'll wonder how you could have been so petty and childish. Nostalgia's a form of non-life, brothers and sisters.

—He was standing up for Maximilian's honor. Someone tackled him from behind and well let's just say we haven't gotten to the 'two wrongs' thing yet.

—Winsome! Put that down! *Now!*

—What a little gentleman.

—Maybe Prez and him'll get married some day.

—Yeah, and then they can honeymoon at the Co-op laundromat.

—Sister Jen!

—Well?

—Listen, my little miss over there isn't getting in the way of what I want for myself. Nuh unh. We are separate entities.

—Like I'm supposed to say '*Upsy-daisy let's go wishy-washies. Let's go wishy-washies yay yay yay.*' Like suddenly wishy-washy is the most wonderful thing in the world when it might be the beginning of the end for her and here I am singing the wishy-washy song like there is absolutely nothing wrong with this picture.

—Don't sweat it, Sister Jen. Next month she'll have a totally new hang up.

—Like I forget that by putting him first chances are I'm going to have a better time than if we had done what I felt like doing. Yet the more I follow my own advice on this the more I feel myself losing track of my sweet spot, you know.

—Kurt went from dollies to *U.N. Peacekeepers* in two weeks. He demanded it!

—Are you going to the show tomorrow?

—On Two? Oh heck yes.

—I mean, personally? She can be as filthy as she wants for all I care. She's a kid for cris— for golly. But *Jennifer* doesn't agree. You know her. She's all like unga-bunga, 'set-standards,' unga-bunga, 'win-the-day,' unga-bunga-wunga.

—How is Sister Jennifer, anyway, Sister Jen?

—Have you tried the black Dalai Lama doll?

—Oh, she's fine. Cross-river at Orb. Facilitating *Compromise and Death*, I think.

—Did we get that by Legal already?

—I mean here I am this supposedly educated woman, not some nerd or some. . .some. . .*suburban queen* or something but a woman who going into this thought she knew better about a ton of stuff, you know, someone who was righteous enough to really nail this thing. Motherhood. You know: 'Roar-of-the-crowd-here's-your-medal?' and all that? But actually? 9 times out of 10? I think well, yeah, I guess I nailed it but what if I had done X? Or said Y? Wouldn't that have been better? Wouldn't that one little tweak in my style stop Horace from being something more than. . .well. . .pretty non-doctrinaire for his age sometimes?

—Does Horace still do that thing with his you know?

—Like can you trademark infringe a living deity?

—No, that was just a phase.

—My goal is to like entirely forget what I want sometimes and just listen to the poor kid. My sweet spot can take care of itself.

—Crap, the worst part is when you sound like your parents.

—Or one of your brothers or sisters.

—Like I'm done with the baby thing and ready to get on with the *child* thing.

—Is there such a thing as a nipple transplant? Can our aestheticians do a fact-find?

—Go ask Five.

—Try Nine.

—A module for my nodule?! Ha!

—Oh yeah, that? It's like suddenly your 9 out of 10 isn't even *your* 9 out of 10 because your like *reciting* this cra— this doctrine you've learned without even thinking about it.

—I never do that.

—Yeah, that sounds bad, Brother Manuel.

—No, listen, respect my self-story for once guys, mmkay?

—Sorry, BroMo.

—Thank you. See, it's not like you're plagiarizing someone else's parenting style. It's more like you're tired, okay, just really darn tired. You're holding down a job, doing your +10, trying to be the best darn daddy you can be, but in a weak moment the little stinker challenges you on something—

—Language Brother Manuel?

—. . .the little dude really challenges you and it's like a pretty legitimate challenge and you just don't have the energy to like deeply listen to what your little Little Cooper is saying and you wind up hearing yourself repeat something that you always tell him, whether its something straight out of the Co-op parenting handbook or your variation of hip parenting or whatever. Either way it sounds cold and predictable, like you are just going through the ideations.

—Well you need to give them some kind of positive modeling.

—What I'm saying is is there aren't many chances to shine but tons to fail.

—And after we do a one-on-one with a counselor she gets completely *weird* about wishy-washy, builds up little rituals around it, sets up menageries of stuffed animals, runs through these weird hand motions and dances I have no idea where she got them from, makes up these complicated songs to go with each new round of paw washing, gets like incredibly serious-looking whenever she is close to a water source.

—Lighten up? Are we allowed to say that? It seems appropriate. . .

—Yes, it's doctrinaire.

—. . .maybe even a little philosophical, too. I'm jotting that down for the rhetoric bros.

—Like put me on the waiting list is all I'm sayin'.

—*Five wishy-washy, six wishy-washy, seven wishy-washy, eiiiiiight? Nine wishy-washy ten wishy-washy LET'S DO IT ALL OVER AGAIIIN! HooRAAAAAY!*' Over and over. Over and fuhREAKING over.

—You'll be fine. It's funnier than you realize. You just need some distance before you close space again.

—I mean here is your child screaming her head off to do what you taught to her to do and now you're turning around and telling her not to do it and the kid has no idea how to please you anymore and winds up thinking Mommy is a total head-case hypocrite psycho and Sister Momma Jennifer is the voice of reason in comparison.

—Then he started not liking mushed peas and so I was like totally sad you know because he was like this early adapter of mushed peas and all.

—Nipples have a very dynamic place in our culture I would say.

—Pfft, in the end I just wanted to give her space.

—I mean my 'hoorays' are less than sincere is what I'm driving at here.

—And I'm looking at this full bowl of peas. . .you know. . .and I'm. . .well. . .actually pretty sad because it feels like this major turning point in our lives, you know?

—And then Momma, *Jennifer*, she's like unga-bunga 'just look at our water bill'. . .unga-bunga. . .unga-bunga-fuh-REAKING-wunga.

Ronette needs to get this over with pronto. After the membership has buckled at the knees and descended upon her she will answer a few questions then beg away on a fictional delivery. She and Sid had decided this was the best way. Word would wildfire up through The Hive while they were on the streets. (Sid having arrived early and fled already.) The onslaught of attention could then be handled piecemeal in the coming days and weeks until they finally became just another pregnant Co-op couple.

But Ronette distrusts how easy this sounds. After all, their private lives were about to end, weren't they? *Everyone* was going to want a piece of them. Their brothers and sisters would break down the door to get their hands on the latest Little Cooper. They would insist on play dates. Enroll Flora in Junior Little Cooper Camp. Schedule toddler socializations with-out the parents' permission. And the new parents would be thrown kicking and screaming back into the world they had kept at bay for so long. This single decision—to create and love another being together—would expose them to an onslaught of socio-familial *oppression*. And even if she knew facing this down was necessary if Flora was to successfully integrate into the vast and complexly cooperative world, Ronette, staring open-mouthed at the bizarrely casual, almost fatalistic faces around her, now realizes that doing so will mean reacquainting herself with many of the old horrors—others' expectations, notions of family life, the general tendencies of the modern world.

She just had to keep telling herself wonderful possibilities lay ahead, that by becoming parents they would distill all their best qualities into this little composite being, their mascot and diplomat. And, who knows, perhaps by exposing themselves to all the popular routines and implicit priorities of parenthood, they would not only feel less isolated from others, but a little less untouchable inside. Yes, the bulk of their (child-centric) concerns would be extremely common and whatever stubbornly personal trouble remained would be suppressed or perhaps even forgotten or discarded once they were swept up by the fast approaching storm of popular modes. And perhaps these new people they become will seem less obscure (to themselves and others) once all the junk surrounding them is left behind.

Yes, she just needed to keep reminding herself of the rightness she and Sid had felt after conceiving symbolically, then laughingly, then in dead earnest on the shag, breathing heavily on their backs afterwards, smiling sideways, barely recognizing their newborn selves but feeling unified, both wondering what it would be like to place their magic seed in the public air to germinate, both certain that their chosen method, however imperfect, however controversial, was the most suitable one for their needs.

Can it be this simple, Sid?

Absolutely it can.

So suddenly we've made this major life decision?

Yup. Presto change-O.

Hmm. Wow. Okay.

You should have seen the look on your face when I pulled back the dome.

Relief. Total relief.

I mean, what did you think I had in there?

I dunno. I guess I was afraid it was empty.

Huh?

And you like wanted to fill it with the appropriate cargo or something.

Ah.

Yeah.

We could some day, Ron. I'm not saying we can't. Or that I won't.

No, this is better. Fleshy babies are too fragile.

Plus, they complain too much.

And they cry all the time.

And when they're not crying they're pouting.

Ha. Okay, okay, enough.

Don't get me wrong, though. That is our daughter your holding there. You understand that, right?

I'm all gushy, aren't I? Just look. I can't let go.

C'mon, gimme a turn.

No, not yet.

Listen, just to be clear, this isn't some metaphorical thing. Flora is our child, our ultimate collaboration.

Yes, I'm with you. It feels like we have an actual family now.

Right. So I refuse to think there is anything unusual about raising her as our daughter. Our family is just as good as any other.

I agree.

Now your pangs probably won't just magically disappear. You're going to want one of those baby eels growing in your gut whether it grosses you out or not. Flora probably won't change that.

Screw the pangs. I'm already having these like pretty intense ma-ma feelings.

Really?

Yeah, like I want to go down and hang out with all the mommies at The Brood. Talk shop. Get hits off each other's hormones.

Ew. Seriously?

All this like totally conventional stuff.

Powerful stuff, though, I'm guessing.

Yeah. And, also?

Hmm?

I want to be pregnant. Weight gain, cravings, waddling around. The whole shebang.

That sounds fun. I'll spoil Mama rotten.

Not too much. This should be like training.

Getting inside *your pregnancy, basically?*

Yeah. Give my body what it's telling me it needs, basically.

You're already feeling sorta. . .um. . .expectant, you mean?

My stomach feels. . .needy. It's like a deep down itch.

You're sure you're not just hungry?

No, it's more like. . .I'm inhabited.

Whoa. Okay. Weird.

Especially after what we just did.

Oh. . .ha . . .yeah. Gotcha.

Yeah.

Well, a prosthesis on your stomach would be good for your abs and quads.

If this is too weird I—

No, Ron, let's just roll with it. There's bound to be lots of surprises ahead. Our general tendencies are pretty much gonna fly out the window, I'm guessing.

What about my job?

I'm sure Warren'll find something for you upstairs until you're ready to get back on the rig. Or I can pick up more hours.

What about training?

I can take the stationary out of the basement.

What I mean is maybe my body won't even be up to training when we get further down the line.

We'll just let whatever's gonna happen happen.

Do we tell people? I have to tell Exene immediately. Like tell her the whole truth. I mean, Jesus, otherwise she'd think I was delivering pregnant like she did.

Totally. I was thinking the same thing about Virge.

Are we supposed to lie to everyone else? I mean people I haven't spoken to in years will be quizzing me about the prosthesis under my shirt. They'll be saving places for me at all the maternity modules.

Relax, Ron, relax.

Oh god, I don't think I can lie to Warren. Not even a little bit. Maybe Flora should be a premie.

Look, there's nothing wrong with keeping our process private here.

Yeah, but we can't expect everyone to play along with this after we go public.

That's fine. Just so long as we are allowed to raise her however we want. If I want to ride with her on my handlebars? I'm going to ride with her on my handlebars. If we want her sitting in the bleachers for your meets? She's sitting in the bleachers. Screw anyone who thinks this is some big joke.

Yeah, but—

It's not like we're looking for special accommodations here.

But holding back this like vital piece of information feels manipulative. . .like something The Bad Old Ronette would do.

Listen, from what you've told me the Bad Old Ronette was incapable of sacrificing her general tendencies in the name of a child.

That sounds sorta vain, though. Like we just want to see our sacrificial selves reflected back in this sack we carry around?

Us? Vain? Get real. This is about transcending ourselves, leaving behind all the stuff we don't need anymore, making a family out of only the good stuff.

But think about the pressure that puts on Flora. Like through no fault of her own she has been born into the responsibility of helping Mom and Dad forget how bored with themselves they are. It sounds like we're using her.

Well, we are, Ron, just like other parents would. The fleshies aren't so sentimental about the human species that they have one just to feed the fire.

Ew, Sid.

Well? Listen, they want a child because it sounds fun or important or like the most intense expression of two people's love possible. Like I said, they're no different from us.

So what if I become bored with her? What if she isn't giving me this like transformative experience? What if she becomes nothing but a sack of wheat flour?

You're worrying yourself silly before we've even chosen a conception date.

Well this is freaking huge, Sid!

Okay, steady now, you're squeezing her too hard.

Oh geez, sorry. Sorry, Flora..

Now listen. You and I as parents and individuals will be changing over time, right?

Sure. Right.

That means Flora's place in our lives will be changing along with us. Right?

Erm, right. I guess.

What she means to us. . .how we think about her. . . what we say to her. . .how we treat her—these things will all evolve over time. They're beyond our control and we should just embrace that.

But she's not alive, technically. She can't even talk.

Is that really what you want to say to your daughter? The one you keep stroking so sweetly? Do you really want to feel that way?

No, I don't.

Me neither. Heck, I won't even grant you that she can't communicate. But let's say she can't. Fine. Why is it so important that I know her thoughts or feelings? Why do I have to know how our sack of wheat flour experiences being a sack *of wheat flour? Isn't it enough to* imagine *what she might be experiencing? Isn't that just as valid a way of loving as asking her a bunch of invasive questions all the time? Being these like totally overbearing parents?*

Yeah, I guess I agree. I'm just—

Flora could never say a single word to me and I would still love her.

Yes, I like how that sounds but what if I want her to love me back?

Isn't it enough to love her because she is our creation?

Yes. Maybe. I dunno. Probably.

Let's just take this one step at a time, Ron.

Okay, but there are questions I could ask about projection and objectification. Totems. Idols. Our pretty severely lapsed social membership.

I like your textbooks as wallpaper, Ron, but all that college talk is a sham. You're not capable of being such a tool.

I just think we need to be brave about discussing our motivations here.

This seriously isn't my Ronette Okampo I'm talking to. I mean I loved her, too, but the new one thinks too much.

Well?

Look, all I know is that I love my daughter and so do you. You hit it off immediately.

She does have a real nice heft to her.

Give me a turn.

No, not yet.

But that was all in the abstract. The *reality* of parenthood, though, would come crashing down on Ronette a few days later.

They had forgotten to lay the sack on its side before bed. When Ronette found it in the morning slumped over face first she gasped, quickly snatched the sack up, gave it a few gentle shakes to redistribute the flour, watched the folds flatten, put her ear to its stomach, listened to the soft rushing sounds of gratitude and started to cry fat tears of care, worry, and guilt.

—I'm so sorry baby had a rough night. Can Mama cheer Flora up with a little wheee?

Ronette nervously wiping her face so Flora wouldn't see she was crying.

—Huh? Baby wanna go *big* wheee?!

Giving the sack a daffy, fake-evil look and tossing it in the air, watching the slow half-revolution before it fell back into her waiting hands with a nice dry thwump.

—Again? You want to go again? Mama make it better? Okay, here we go. . .*Wheeeeee!*

Bending low to the floor so Flora would have more hangtime, heaving the sack in the air to complete a revolution before thwumping back into Ronette's hands.

—Wheeeeee! Isn't that fun? Higher, you say?

Laying on the shag, clutching Flora to her chest, torquing the sack and throwing.

—*Wheeeeee!*

Flora whipping around once and then once more before bashing into the ceiling, deflecting away, and thudding down in the easy chair as the stucco rained down around her.

—Flora!!! Oh God!

Frantically examining the sack for rupture, smoothing out the folds until the insides distributed more evenly.

—I'm so sorry, Flora.

Cradling the sack, tearfully pleading with the bull logo.

—Forgive me? I don't blame you for being mad. You're right. Mama totally sucks.

Kneeling there, holding Flora over her head, sniffling with re-morse, it took no effort at all to believe she had just caused Flora actual pain. Yes, the gap between imagination and belief had shut tight with a queasy thud and there was no longer any meaningful difference between what Flora might be and what Flora was. The truth in all cases could be reduced to. . .*She is my daughter.*

Disgusted by her carelessness, realizing that the smallest misstep might doom Flora, Ronette cradled Flora in her arms like any other fragile child and made soft shushing sounds to soothe her. And it had felt good holding her close like that, molding that tiny little body to her stomach, making the site they shared warm and secure. A child isn't a play thing, she told herself. Without her mother's protection she is completely defenseless. How awful for Flora to have been wounded by the only person she can trust.

—Yeah. Totally.

Thinking back on that morning now, staring dumbly into the chaos in the playpen, sinking into the babble of the parents surrounding her, Ronette must yell at herself to avoid the creep of the failsafe. . .*Cut yourself some slack. . .Remember, they're all just as flawed and crazy as you are. . .We all make mistakes and we all suffer for them because whether we like it or not we all live through our children to a certain extent. . .It's how we choose to adapt to our inevitable failures that defines what kind of parent we are.* . .So, no, there is nothing so strange then about hoisting Flora to the stucco sky every morning and promising. . .*I'll never let you go, baby.* . . then joyfully whooshing her around the towers and mountains and installations, re-exploring those territories through her daughter's eyes, investigating all the messy borderlands between, kicking up clouds of clothes and junk, allowing Flora to make her claim on the bungalow as her mother pleads with herself not to trip or fall. . .*This is a guitar. . .GI-tarrr. . . thwoing-ng-ng. . .This? This is a pillow. . .zee-zee-zee-zee. . . zee-zee-zee-zee. . .This? This is a mannequin leg.* . .Nor is it abnormal to worry over every single maternal decision she makes. Whether to leave Flora in the alcove window or the street-facing window. Which swaddling blanket to wrap her in. The right color. The right texture. The best location in the window relative to the weather and the gap in the curtain. The right piece of classical music. Medieval or baroque? Romantic or minimalist? The right audio book. ABC's or Durkheim? Seuss or Dickinson? The right kind of secret note to leave tucked under her bottom. A promise or an endearment? A piece of wisdom or a confession? Recalibrating her decisions in cascades of tweaking. Constantly projecting herself across the river to see what Flora is up to while she is at work. Was she studying the mysterious stillness of the world outside the window, perplexed by the subtle changes in the light falling on the neighboring bungalows, nervously trying to come to grips with the infinite assembly of objects, insects and sky, wailing in fear at the stunning appearance of a stray dog jogging down the street or, more terrifyingly, a slickered postman in a pith hat charging up the stairs with a sack full of riddles and threats? Accessing her motherly ride in this divided way, trying to reassure her daughter, transmitting images of the fantastical architectures of downtown, trying to convince her that if she concentrates hard enough she might smell the same chemical sweet exhaust that Mama does, look into the same pale sky, feel the same cold rain streaming down her face. . . *There. . .that-a-girl. . .here's Mama. . .just a little more to the northwest.*

And even Ronette knew enough about pregnancy to know that it was not unusual to have painful mood swings, suffer from some pre-postpartum thing, mourn in advance the separation to come, sometimes project her motherhood way too far forward, confuse a shift on the rig away from Flora with the day when there might be more than a river separating them. Kindergarten or college? Play dates and socializations? Marriage or death? She had talked about this with Exene, told her best friend who couldn't conceive how she had or was going to, or at least was supposed to be in the process of doing so and was feeling both exhilarated and frightened about it but wanted Exene to know she was not so over the moon as to not be super mindful of how it might impact her and that this mindfulness was not a preemptive attempt to guide how the friends would go forward with their secret knowledge but a declaration of her wish that Exene participate however much she wished and, again, no pressure, would like her to be whatever kind of aunt she wished just so long as she understood, again, not to be melodramatic or anything, that she considered Exene far more of a real sister than either her forgotten foster or Co-op sisters and her saying so wasn't like some stratagem to lock her into a yet-to-be-determined role with implicit responsibilities or cushion the unspoken but inescapable blow (barrenness faced with productivity) but to speak a truth she had been derelict in expressing until now. . .*I mean, I love you, Exene. You're my sister in the only ways that matter. The best ways. . .*And when she started babbling about her premature fear of losing her daughter and had finally dissolved into the arms of her sister whose actual, living baby had died inside her body, Exene had stroked Ronette's hair and said she understood. . .*My miscarriage is similar, I think. . .It has never really ended. . .I lose her and get her back all day long. . .Sometimes I can almost make her face out. . .even feel her close by. . .But the harder I try to get her to stay the more vivid my memory of the accident is and then I have to start all over again. . .I know this sounds horrible or crazy but this way I at least get to feel like I'm still* *her mother. . .*Yes, we all live with the ghost of the process which lands us in the moment. . .*It gets less tragic, I think. . . or maybe the tragedy becomes the baby. . .The thing you will always carry inside. . .*And instead of mourning absence we create a composite, dead-alive being. . .*We set a plate for her . . .take her to movies. . .We even took her to your last meet. . . I know this sounds nuts but it makes us happier than just going 'she's dead, she's dead, she's dead,' ya know. . .I mean she is. . .I know that. . .but not in every way. . .not in a lot of really important ways. . .*Loss is not necessarily definitive when rebirths are available. . .*I mean either being alive is a little overrated or not being alive is kind of underrated. . . What I'm saying here, Ron, is there are options for those of us who are trying not to care too much about the distinction. . . Flora will always be your daughter. When she goes to college. When you die. When she dies. Period. . .*Life and death, presence or absence, animate or inanimate—these are all false parameters, echoes not dualities, transparent glass. . .*Having a sack of flour. . .having Flora is what the brainiacs might call 'an elegant solution'. . .She can never run out on you. . .*Exene then pulled the stray hairs from Ronette's forehead and Ronette, usually so retreating with her body, not only loved this touch but felt desperately hungry for it even as she balled and balled more apologies to Exene who then rubbed Ronette's knuckles with her thumb to extract a whole new series of disorienting tears, love, and doubt which Ronette is struggling not to flood back into right now to comfort herself.

—So speaking of kids and all. . .me and Sid. . .uh. . .

Co-op famous but out of place in The Brood, Ronette easily gets her brothers' and sisters' attention.

—Well yeah. . .we're five months in now.

There is something that occurs in crowds where some small event causes uncertainty or pause to blossom around the site of that event, and though the volume and bustle of the crowd at large continues as before the discreet change which evolves locally—whether it be as subtle as a shift in body language or something as obvious as a shout—causes a blossoming of *moment* to cascade outward into the crowd then rebound back to gather and focus attention around the still unfolding event. Everyone needs to know what has caused this shift in the psychological topography of their space because some threat or advantage may result from participating or not.

But usually something relatively mundane has occurred which is only very meaningful or useful to those participating in the event proper and the redoundingness of the moment winds up fizzling.

Occasionally, though, what has occurred is so un-expected, so galvanizing as to completely rearrange the kinetics of the shared space. Heads turn and eyes bulge. Waves of unfiltered emotions crash down on the participants almost in premonition of what is about to transpire. A certain instability enters the thoughts. Some become frightened. Then there is a clap or rumble and everyone either runs to get a piece of whatever is going on or decides they had better make way.

—Holy freak. . .holy freak. . .

—Ron-*eeeeeeeette*?!

—OhmiGod-ohmiGod-ohmiGod.

—Somebody go find Brother Warren!

Belladonna Mabuse sinks into the collapsible leather chair she special-ordered from a catalogue for the disabled. She has just returned from her quarterly budget meeting with Warren to watch her Co-op hatchlings strut and preen. (Those annoyingly wistful sessions with the one man she ever allowed herself to care for instead of just fuck always ending with her solemnly sliding a check across the desk, Warren objecting to the amount, and Belladonna sighing in departure.) Encamped just east of the playpen but close enough to the stereo speakers so she doesn't have to hear quite so much screaming and crying, she notices Ronette slogging through the thick gaggle of parents and looking lost. After she speaks there are gasps, though. Then it is as like everyone is goosing one another. Cheek hugs, high fives, and little jigs spread. Stunned, exhilarated talk follows. It's telltale. Ronette Okampo is freaking preggers. Just look at all these spontaneously kind and gener-ous people fluttering about, smiling knowingly, looking relieved—She finds the whole display. . .if she understands herself right. . .well. . .unambiguously *nice*. Oui, she does.

You see, her hiatus from The Co-op had been pre-dictably awful. It had begun with an especially intense booze jag and ended with her dabbling in sadomasochism. At first both blended into the other and had her believing that taking the whip to the needy's flesh or shoving rubber balls in among their tusks and nethers or choking them half-dead while they squealed with gratitude were among the few laudable pursuits available to a hopelessly abusive soul like hers. These people would understand her, she had reasoned. Relationships would be more straightforward, even pre-ordained. Yes, this might be her long lost family.

The initial sessions had been empowering. She would lock the submissive into grand muh-Ma's bedroom so they could yank on their leathers in private. Then she would enter having made no alteration to herself at all, cherry pick from the toys and gear they had splayed over the nattered wool bedspread, and discipline them in a manner and to a degree they had decided upon on the telephone beforehand. Invariably, her quarry would kneel on the floor in some ridiculously vulnerable position or attitude and she would play her role straight down the line. She struck and flayed them howsoever much they wanted, called them all sorts of denigrating names and playacted to the hilt in their absurd little scenarios. Once it was all over she would tiptoe downstairs while they dressed feeling as though she had done something useful, if not rather kind.

As discussed, and in order to stay in role, they would wordlessly show themselves out. This was the only part Belladonna struggled with. She wanted to touch them, share a small little smile, say 'goodnight' or 'thank you,' let them know she really wasn't as mean as she pretended, suggest they grab a drink some time, maybe get to know one another better. But they always went straight for the door and climbed the twisting staircase to the street without once looking back. This made Belladonna feel increasingly detached. The affection was too indirect and the cruelty was simulated. And when she deviated from the pre-discussed parameters (i.e. became violently furious at how unlovable they were) to instigate something a bit less choreographed her pathetic little captive only moaned and groaned all the more obsequiously and called the next morning to bashfully compliment her passion and timidly ask for another appointment a.s.a.p.

The whole thing finally collapsed in on her the night she identified with a powdery little waif who tearfully berated herself while Belladonna savagely whipped her. This was too much. Belladonna had no idea who she was anymore. She yanked the woman to her feet and began covering her cheeks with hot, apologetic kisses. . .*Please. . .hit me instead. . .I*

*deserve it. . .*And while she had at least succeeded in humiliating herself, her submissive was deeply offended. . . *Let go of
me. . .I would never do such a thing. . .*Watching her stumble
up into the rain-splattered night, Belladonna, now almost
laughably alone, feeling the oak floor plummet away from
her, wondering if she finally had cause to drink herself
irrevocably into The Remove, decided that the only alternative was to return to The Co-op where she at least knew
where she stood with people.

The two weeks of preparatory heavy drinking which
followed had taken its toll. Her legs atrophied so badly from
sitting and sleeping at the dining room table she had had to
order the specialty chair. Trying to dry out at The Percolator,
whole mornings were now lost in hazes of groggy spectation
as the children's ridiculous behavior and the adults' breezily
bizarre conversations snaked in and out of her bedimmed
consciousness and blended into a tidal wash. But to her
surprise she found that these sessions had a noticeably tonic
effect on her. The children were amusing and harmless and
there was something refreshingly low-content or maybe just
encouragingly indecipherable about their parents' mutually
supportive discussions. Yes, it felt good to not have any stakes
in anything happening around her and just allow all the
frivolous positivity to wash over her in dull, warm waves. And
even as she slowly regained her strength and many of the
boring old awful thoughts popped up, so also did a new fragile
hopefulness, a beaten down neediness. Yes, she just didn't
have the energy to be so mean-spirited anymore. Even as her
mind continued to present her with ungenerous reactions to
what she observed—mumbled largely under her breath—she
found herself believing less and less of it and identifying with
those she had been attacking for so long. Don't misunder-
stand, though, she wasn't turning into some kind of softie or
something. Just. . .well. . .maybe something had been beaten
out of her in the last month.

So she wants to go say something unmistakably nice
to Ronette. Only how does one go about this sort of thing?
Talking sweetly without snorting at herself would require a
conviction in the purity of her motives she just doesn't have
yet. And so any chance of transcending her parameters, of
accessing all the lightness which has built up inside over the
past month, goes straight to hell once she wonders if she is

capable of sounding genuine. Who was she kidding? No way was she built for getting in on this little mommy jamboree. The Co-op's mothers continually pleading 'the kids' 'C.P.T.A.' 'childcare' 'career' 'the +10' 'bills' whenever she shyly invited them out for drinks only demonstrated how comprehensive her isolation has become. Children cannot go to shows. They cannot booze themselves silly. No, the innocent little stinkers needed to be sheltered from the pain and ugliness seeping out of a Belladonna Mabuse. But just too-too perfectly the Little Coopers not only tolerate her when she sneaks over to get a closer listen to their adorable nonsense but seem to *gravitate* to her. Probably there is something about her caricature of an oversized goony bird that makes the darling little poo piles come teetering so they can tug on her leathers and confirm that incredibly bizarre creatures like her are included in this already pretty tripped out, fantastico realm they had lucked into. God, she can only imagine how ridiculous she must look when she goes all googoo gahgah while the nonjudgmental little squawk boxes drool on and fawn over her. No, the best she would ever be able to do was get Mom alone for cocktails and maneuver her into dishing about all the terrible things involved in ministering to her adorable little tyrants. Yes, then she could regale these burden-bound momsters with tales from their former realm—the parties that somehow still went on without them, the dating game, the latest humiliation she had endured at the hands of some fictional barbarian, the stakesless living for *numero uno*. O god she missed being that mouthy scapegrace she has been trying to phase out. The native acre still beckoned so. And The Remove, sufficiently provoked, would clamber up the ravine, mount the west hills and come crashing through downtown for her throat if she let it like this. So by the time she has risen from her chair, recombined it into a walker, teetered over to the melee near the baby fence, recombined the walker into a chair and sat down, she has already pleaded inside for Ronette to hear what she truly feels . . .*I am happy for you, Ronette. . .I just can't help myself. . .Please save me* . . .and lost her battle with the vocal cords long prepped with malice.

     —And of course you did remember to get blood tests? *Didn't you Sister Ronette?*

Two women sprint for the stairwells leading up into The Hive. Ronette spins around and sees all these smiling brothers and sisters closing in on her and wanting to touch. She is disoriented but happy. Their cuppings, nudges and hugs, the smiling alertness in their eyes, the troubled surveys of a far from convex stomach, the promises of hand-me-down gear and future socializations, the comments about the regular little community they have grown from their stomachs and how wonderful it was for Ronette to join them, the jokes about how. . .*knowing our Sister Ronette*. . .she will probably give birth in her rig; this outpouring making her swoon with embarrassment and forcing her to begin to extricate before she started crying. . .*again!*

—We don't want you to give birth to some kind of *monster*.

Ronette turns on Belladonna. Just look at this fat, sputtering bitch. Ronette wants to sink her claws deep into her flesh and dandle the kill in front of Flora so she can practice her claw strikes. Yes, this was a terrifying but delicious urge . . .but wait. . .whoa. . .whoa. . .wasn't she feeling incredibly non-exemplary here? Wasn't someone five months along supposed to be commensurately advanced in prioritizing her energies by extracting only the best and necessary from those who either by choice or unavoidable circumstance were going to participate in her Process? Hmm. She and Sid had talked about this that night and agreed that since there would likely be a sharpening of certain unambiguously positive personality traits within the parents during the pregnancy it stood to reason that those around them would have to evolve similarly or compatibly or at minimum tolerably—put up or shut up, basically. So accessing the more ruthless wing of their evolving selves would occasionally be necessary if they were to efficiently transform the unifying principle of their life from a bike into a trike, from a tumble into a long-haul Tour. So, yes, this checks out. Shaking Bella's half-dead carcass from a height before letting it plummet to the earth was not only justifiable but necessary. The bitch needed to know her place.

So just listen now as she starts gleaming with clichés about appetites and puking and fatness, telling her brothers and sisters to put their ears to her gut and see if they can hear anything yet, watch as she inflates herself to give them something to rub (Ronette feeling a tickle of hysteria in her throat for the reservation made, even if in absentia, on that stomach) while also fixing Belladonna in her crosshairs with her third eye . . . *My terms, bitch. Get with the program or fuck off.* . .Yes, she is a little high on the extreme economy of thought she is experiencing, the sensation that everything she does and says is unequivocally right and necessary for the well-being of the haughty little Eel Princess who will be Flora's physical surrogate, that particular thickness and twist in her guts demanding sustenance, the nauseating but right-eous little tugs, the total organizational supremacy she now knows she has no choice but to answer to, this bio-psychic mandate telling her that all the fine words she had spoken to Sid, not to mention all these cooed congratulations from the broads greedily copping feels and scoring contact highs, the whole lot of it could, when the time came, collectively go screw.

—You know I should probably try to catch some deliveries, guys.

And so she finds herself carefully pushing away, her freshly minted two-headed being feeling more like three or four as she starts to float over the smiling heads in the room so her body can close on its prey.

—But thanks for everything, guys. . .brothers and sisters.

But just as she is about to seize Belladonna by the leathers she hears the unmistakable sound of cycling shoes bashing downstairs and the booming voice which accom-panies them.

—Where is she?! Where's our girl?! Come here, Ronette Okampo! Come here right now!

And so there is a whole new gauntlet of strokes and kisses to pass through before going behind the barista-dispatch bar to disappear into the outstretched arms of the Co-op's COO.

Warren Renshaw, three heads taller than Ronette, is bent over her and sobbing. He still remembers visiting her in the hospital after yet another concussion. She lay there mumbling, her eyes wildly scanning the ceiling, her right hand manically rubbing the needle hole in her left arm. This was all his fault. He had failed to see the warning signs and Ronette, barely a woman, his little lost sister, could easily have died. He leaned down, captured her frantically searching fingers in his and whispered. . .*We won't let this happen to us again.* . .He then paid her hospital bill, silently drove them through the country for three hours, dropped her off at a rehab facility, and watched her flail and claw at the attendants who dragged her away.

He had been a domestique in the grueling slog of professional cycling and cobbled together a career in Europe on a third-class American reputation for nine vagabond years before crashing out in the Pyrenees and coming to in a hospital with a doctor trying to explain to him in Basque that he had a collapsed lung and that his brothers in the rig—that womb-like *peloton* of cyclists swarming along narrow roads together for six hours a day, 200 days a year—were wending away without him and for good. He returned stateside to open the bike shop that eventually became the messenger service that miraculously became The Co-op. He remains happily stunned at how easily this new life came to him, especially given how fresh the feeling is of waking up disoriented in that hospital and being told his umbilical connection to his cycling brothers had been cut. And while this towering, barrel-chested man beloved inside the *peloton* for his practical jokes and foolhardy breakaways had developed an acute sensitivity to others' wellness while acting as workhorse, nurse maid, and scout for his teams, he would never have guessed that sexually ministering to Belladonna Mabuse for the few weeks before she cut things off. . .*Your heart just isn't in this, Warren.* . .*Go make someone else your cause, darling.* . .would lead to her cutting him the massive quarterly endowment checks which even his rudimentary business skills couldn't help but parlay into a burgeoning Co-operative empire.

One of his first projects had been to renovate a ramshackle cycling velodrome on the southern outskirts of downtown. Area professionals suddenly had a world class track to train on. Club teams sprouted up all over town. He hired a few of his old friends from the Euro circuit to develop young riders from The Co-op and their team became regionally renowned. So when he learned that his once so lost little sister who had been keeping herself straight by doubling her delivery hours and living as far away from downtown as possible was not only training at Velodrome but, according to reports, had all the makings of a natural, he rode fifteen miles through the rain to tell her he was sponsoring her whether she liked it or not.

And here he is now with his mane of somehow still sun-bleached hair twirling around Ronette's head while he whispers and sniffles.

—Of course you understand Herr Cooper will provide for you during this important time. All of the advanced parenting modules will be free.

And Ronette cannot help but glow back and pat the shoulder of this man whom she has never had the moral energy to resent on behalf of Exene and Virgil. He has always treated her and all of his employees like family; gently inquiring into their lives, cheerfully dispensing blunt but well-meaning advice, invoking hierarchy only if he had no other choice, preferring to be a brother instead of a boss, crying freely over their disappointments, cheering their smallest achievements, giving others as much of himself as he could.

—Maybe we can get you off the streets now, Sister Ronnie.

She looks into the chest of this man who took control of her life when she no longer could and tries to imagine what her life will look like in the coming months. She wants to see something so she can tell him about it but finds nothing but a buzzing black void.

—Sid, too? Kick upstairs? Enjoy some free daycare? That would make Señor Cooper so happy.

She looks down. Both are wearing the same brand of black cycling shoes with the yellow ∞ on the sides. She remembers when he showed her how to lace them, a technique which maintains the structure of the shoe during even the most violent of sprints. Kneeling down, gently manipulating her foot in his catcher's mitt hands, a tear fell from his face onto the shoe and he told her he was proud of her.

—Also, I wonder if you would consider not riding your next meet.

Both remember that moment now as Warren kneels down, pinches up some fabric from the stomach of her jersey and sticks a ∞ pendant through. She had said nothing in reply then because she was embarrassed. But now, thinking out into that vague darkness of the future, she realizes that she still wants him to be proud of her and how much of a responsibility that is for both of them.

—I'm going to do just this last one, Warren. Don't worry, I'll ride straightforward races.

And before he can list all the reasons why she should reconsider and before she can start crying apologies for all the lies she will be telling him in the coming months, she gives his chest a final pat, turns her rig around wanting desperately to hurry away and sort out all the guilt and tenderness she is feeling, notices the sunken form of poor Belladonna Mabuse having her dress tugged on by a toddler desperately reaching through the fence, pities this miserable woman, leans down, pats the child on the head, and gives Belladonna's forehead a quick and soft kiss.

7.

Chain link scrapes against concrete as voices come echoing down the concourse. Riders and techs lean into the curving cinderblock wall floodlit dark orange. Competitors are reduced to signature visual traits. The woman built like a linebacker. The Amazon who qualified for the Olympics. The woman with the braids.

Sid's hair hangs down around him as he adjusts the derailleur on Ronette's rig. Her braids arc and loop while she counts off shoulder rolls. Both wear distinguished black racing kits with a small yellow ∞ on the front and back. A meditative bubble surrounds them. Competitors roll by wondering what kind of magic allows these damn Coopers to keep winning trophies. They raise their voices hoping to break their concentration only to wind up feeling guilty about it. Man, those two couldn't hurt a fly.

They had delivered for The Co-op for three years without knowing the other's name. Though both were solitaries yet disliked returning to their intentionally ugly apartments where, in theory, they would be better off if there was someone there to keep them company. So after work they aimlessly cycled around town or, if they felt like trying to spend more time around their brothers and sisters like everyone told them they should, inside at Velodrome. Eventually they recognized themselves in each another and Sid forced himself to approach Ronette. She saw a rare harmlessness in this stutteringly sweet person trying to ask her out. Soon they would begin the delicate work of becoming indispensable to one another and would no longer need the formality of 'dates.'

They were racing each other for fun one night when a Co-op trainer approached Ronette and told her she should train for competition. Sid said he would coach her, Ronette figured 'why not', and soon Warren was practically breaking her door down to sponsor her. They threw themselves into it, talking deep into the night about tactics, mechanics, and training; how a front derailleur should distribute tension but never mitigate it, how a calf muscle has an optimum slackness relative to the flexion of the knee joint, how the interconnection of parts—in Ronette and her rig and altogether—should coextensively inhabit a remove of pure instinct and function. During this seamlessness the rider no longer hears the crowd, forgets who or what or where she is, is stimulated only by the other rider, and remains possessed until she suddenly finds herself nosing the line. This process repeats two or three more times during the evening before she wheels the rig back down the concourse with a medal around her neck and her boyfriend jogging towards her so he can pull what's left of the seamlessness close and share it for as long as it lasts. And on the increasingly infrequent occasions when the seamlessness does not occur and she does not win any medals they hurry down the concourse overjoyed to have lost so they can breathlessly break down what went wrong and puzzle out how to fix it.

This is their last meet until after the birth. Ronette will have to ratchet down training to nil over the next four months in order to. . .*get inside her pregnancy*. . .As much as they will miss the training, the layoff will give them an opportunity to start from scratch again—that is if they have the time. . .or the inclination. . .what with the new responsibilities. . .the altered relationship to time. . .the many other seamlessnesses blossoming up around them and inundating the bungalow with joy.

—Heat 1! Riders to the central staging area!

Ronette holds her wrists out so Sid can remove her black wrist-bands, kiss her scars, and slide the lucky red ones on. They then lean forward, touch foreheads, close their eyes, and hold hands. They have always made perfect sense to one another here, felt seamless. But tonight both are distracted by the riding bag leaning against the concrete wall. They open their eyes sooner than usual.

—Ready?

—Ready.

He removes her glasses and puts them in his pocket, snaps her into her black racing helmet, moves behind her to tuck her braids into the back of her jersey, pulls her yellow competition bib with the black double zero and ∞ on it over her head, pauses, then breaks ritual by reaching around to hold her around the stomach. Ronette squirms free, wishes she hadn't, and puts her hand on the back of his neck.

—Don't worry, Siddy. We'll be fine.

She wheels her rig away and doesn't look back.

Scattered shouts greet Sid as he walks up the ramp then crescendo when he reaches the top. Everyone is standing. Velodrome is shaking. Co-op blacks dominate the crowd. He squints through the blaring stage lights at the woman halfway up the wooden slope with her arms raised. A name and number are announced and the crowd stomps their approval on the squeaking bleachers as she thrusts her black helmet back in gratitude. Once everyone is seated again Sid removes a pair of binoculars from the riding pack and trains it on the dented and scuffed track. A few pine slats are set unevenly in their seams and there is a wet spot near Turn 1 but nothing poses much of a hazard. Satisfied, he scans over to the top of the bleachers on the opposite straightaway and raises both his fists over his head until two fists shoot up in reply. Exene remains seated but Virgil stands to shout over the rhythmic clapping which anticipates the start of every match.

—Here we go, Pops! We're gonna *kill* this!

Sid pumps a fist in reply then walks to the narrow end of the stadium over Turn 1. The long straightaways slope at an angle of 40°. The two banking turns slope at the same angle then abruptly straighten until they are perpendicular to the bottom of the track. A rider moving at high speed uses centrifugal force to whip into the banking turn and briefly travel parallel to the earth. Sid always sits in the front aisle of the Turn 1 bleachers so he can be as close as possible when Ronette defies gravity.

o   o   o   o   o   o   o   o   o

Since X was happy about it Virgil was happy about it. And after thinking about it for a few days he decided that their best friends raising a sack of flour made him feel less lonely inside his and X's loss. Not that he thought it was sad or pathetic to call a sack of flour your daughter. No, it was more that they now had company in not having an actual baby. . .*We have our pretend baby ghost sitting next to us on the bleacher and they have their sack of flour in that riding bag*. . .Bottom line they were both doing something to make themselves feel better. So even if they've chosen an alternative which sounds pretty fucking frivolous if not borderline insensitive to their loss he can't blame them for not knowing exactly how fragile X is right now and what kind of impact their decision might have on her.

One week after that fucking soiree he had had to lock a frantic and pleading Exene out of their spare room so he could tear down the baby wallpaper, take down the mobiles, and disassemble the crib. And a week after that he had told her they both needed to stop pretending their daughter went everywhere they went. In protest, she had refused to go to physical therapy for the back injury which the x-rays said were long healed and had only given in when he agreed to put a baby seat in the back of the car. . .*I just need the idea sometimes. . .I promise not to talk to her too much*. . .Navigating the killing streets which had taken their child was traumatic enough so why not help her if he could. . .*But we need to get back to living in a realistic way soon, X. . .leave a few of the crutches behind. . .This is what our daughter would want.*

But hypocrite that he is he still asks his daughter for advice while he's in his rig, tells her he has no idea how to help her mother anymore, cries and rages into the pouring rain while delivering downtown. Then he comes home to see the woman he loves bracing herself against the wall to walk, humming tunes to keep her mind occupied, breaking her back to be philosophical, broaching the idea that they would heal more quickly if they returned to The Co-op. . .*What's the point of being isolated anymore. . .Our daughter will forgive us. . .That's what family is for, right?. . .They have no choice but to accept each other's weaknesses. . .that is if they want to keep on being families. . .I think that's something The Co-op kinda gets right, you know?. . .They tap into everyone's need to fit into something meaningful while still holding its members to a high standard.* . . .And sometimes he hides in the bathroom to pound his fist into his palm until he thinks he has calmed down but later finds himself snapping over nothing, yelling incoherently about how. . .*this all has to end soon or else.* . .and winds up sinking into X's arms to make her care for him in lieu of the actual baby she needs.

But seriously it's all good. Deep down somewhere he's happy for Sid and Ron. And honestly? He's glad they aren't having a real one. No way he wouldn't be jealous. It was small and selfish but what are you gonna do. Wasn't it his right to be a bit of an asshole about this a while longer, at least until the rages and tears eased off and the sympathy pains in his gut died down? Yes, soon he'll get himself straight enough to feel only tenderness for this thing his best friends feel such tenderness for.

Ronette is *not* ready. The stretches were fine and Sid's tech was fine but crammed in the stable, rattling wheels with the other girls, nervously snapping her breaks on and off, already sweating inside her kit, she knows the entire pre-race ritual had been off because she had been worried about Flora being trapped inside that dark and stinking riding bag. Bringing her was important, though. She should witness what will be her mother's last meet for a while or maybe forever. But, wait, she resents how melodramatic that sounds. Every little decision she makes doesn't have to have major ramifications for Flora. She is still her own woman, remains in control of her own fate. A child doesn't change that, right?. . .*Wait. . . wait. . . whoa. . .Okay. . .Sing the prayer. . .The meditations have been helping. . .Om mani padme hum. . .Om mani padme hum. . .Be fair to yourself. . .Be realistic. . .Slow down your mind. . .Om mani padme hum.* . . .Anyway once she was out on the track she would revert to form and everything would fall back into place. Her opponent would be all nervous and reactive while the seamlessness transformed her back into the track-slaying bitch everyone tells her she is.

Maybe she's squeezing Virgil too hard. Not that she has to fake it but. . . well. . .yeah. . .she probably *does* since once she starts *acting* as anxious as she *feels* he will start saying. . .*We should go-We should go-We should go.* . .and asking. . .*Is it your back?-Is it the nausea?-Is it the noise?.* . .all while she smiles and says everything is fine and his eyes call bullshit. Then she would have to make some little proof of her stability—a jokey hrumph, a flirty pshaw—anything to allow them to at least feel light-hearted about the lies she is dealing. But, jeez, wasn't it about time she stopped behaving so *tragically*? Shouldn't she stop wearing maternity clothes hoping to simulate or even magically renew her pregnancy? Shouldn't she stop wearing the back brace which she mostly wears because its bulk makes wearing maternity clothes more justifiable? Shouldn't she be able to walk down a flight of stairs without holding Virgil's hand? Shouldn't she not freak out whenever someone sits down next to her without pausing to wonder if they might be crushing her imaginary daughter? Shouldn't she not be trying so hard to get a better look at her dead daughter? Shouldn't she not be searching the crowd for a glimpse of her eyes, her nose, her hair? How she might be hiding under the bleachers? Or in the infield under one of the pylons? Or on the catwalks just below the dome? Shouldn't she not panic at the slightest suggestion of gravity? Wonder how the next fall might scare her daughter away for good? How she should be able to look at a bicycle without becoming nauseous? How if she is serious about rejoining The Co-op shouldn't she be seated in their cheering section? I mean a lot of the time she was perfectly happy or at least temporarily forgot all the pain (whatever the distinction, damned if she saw one anymore) so why not just try to will herself into behaving other than she felt? Take Virgil. He had shouted over at Sid and had at least found a supportive way of channeling his rage. Maybe she could manage a few hoots for Ronette if she didn't stand up too fast, if she stopped fixating on how much she has regressed since the last meet, how trapped she feels inside this cage full of yodeling wahoos covered in face paint, bellowing like animals, reciting chants, doing the fucking wave, and generally acting as though pain and death and abandonment were the furthest things from their fucking minds, how every single noise in this acoustic nightmare was piercing her branules and making her want to jump out of her skin to flee for a more car-centric city.

The trouble is that when she behaves other than she feels Virgil, instead of becoming angry, increasingly pretends to feel only patience for this new coping strategy. So she worries that if she even just partially succeeds in conning herself into believing she is getting better this way, he will continue stumbling all over himself to keep saying the supportive words-making the supportive sounds-doing the supportive things and turn into someone she neither knows nor remembers. God, what a terrifying responsibility it is to hold someone's fate in your hands. Maybe it's better to be your damaged self so you can at least remain in love with the damaged person you continue to torment. But, no, honesty about their feelings hadn't gotten them anywhere. Clearly their quota of suffering, however they chose to endure it, will continue stretching out in front of them, never allowing them to believe life might become manageable again.

And what was the appropriate amount of sadness here, anyway? Just how crazy was she allowed to be almost two years after losing her baby? Was there some cliché out there which might magically bring her solace?. . .*This too shall pass. . .Time heals all wounds. . .*some form of brainwashing to replace her hourly involvement with her loss? God, *fuck* that. Mourning never ends. Besides, her daughter was *plenty* alive. She hadn't shut herself in this nuthouse to *prove* she was adjusting to her 'loss.' No, she was here because it was what a good aunt would do and her daughter needed to learn the importance of loyalty. Yes, attending to a greater good might marshal her through or at least distract her from her pain. So stop squeezing so hard-thinking so much-being so honest or Virgil will notice and say it's time to go. Yes, if she can just gut this one out the next one might be easier.

But wait that was what she said last time when she somehow managed to get through watching woman after woman wheel her rig up the incline, wait for the starter's gun (which always nearly makes her pee with fright), slowly start pedaling, then speed up, then nauseously ride parallel to the ground, then dive down, then swoop up, all at terrifying speeds, always watching the other woman's wheels churning away as they race into a frenzy, thrusting away at the weaving mechanisms they are strapped to, desperate to separate themselves from the other, desperate for the end, the crowd screaming, the formal blacks roaring, all those dancing ∞s making her dizzy, the entire velodrome crashing down around them until the riders nearly superimpose at the line and Exene leans into Virgil's chest to hide her face and throw up in her mouth.

But here she is anyway and there is Ronette in the stable looking burdened and disheveled, sweating already, manically rolling her shoulders, unaware one of her braids is sticking out of her jersey. Christ, was anyone besides Virgil and maybe Sid and Ronette sensing the bad juju here? The overlapping circumstances? Five months pregnant? On a bicycle? Sack or no sack? Was some sort of trespass against fate being committed? Don't all these chanting motherfuckers remember the circumstances? Is the air inside Velodrome poisoned against Ronette? God, it fucking feels that way! It's bad enough that the acci. . .*Let's not use that word anymore, Virgil. . .As they say: 'There are no accidents in life'. . .*that the. . .er. . .*loss* recurred every time she saw a bicycle or a baby but now her best friend and sister was about to step into the saddle of one of those killing machines to chase down. . . to chase down *what* exactly?

—Virgil, someone should stop this. Something's not right here.

—Where's Brother Jim with the O?
—Do they sell beer here?
—No they do not, my brother.
—Yeah, shit, it's warm.
—Shoot. You mean 'shoot,' Sister Rhoda.
—Crowded. Hot. That's all I'm sayin'.
—Sister Ronette looks ready.
—Are we all ready?
—Can you watch Prezzy while I powder my nose?
—Warren prefers a family friendly environment is all.
—God, even here?
—Yeah, this is church for him.
—We sure turned it out for Sister Ronette tonight, didn't we?
—Maybe we should do an r.f.p. anyway.
—A beer garden?
—No, more like members only luxury suites.
—Throw in a conference center. You never have enough conference centers.
—Yes! I'll make a note for Nine.

—No the N sits there. Move now please.

—And pronto, BroMo

—I was *born* ready.

—Whoops, I didn't necessarily mean anything by that Brother Manuel.

—Fitzroy! I do not want to see you do that ever again. Do you understand me?

—Tinted glass, Co-op Brew, Co-op Cater, a portion of the proceeds going to Co-op Charities.

—The Mabuse chick will pony.

—No problemo, *hermana*.

—Just not too *big* a portion.

—Then I want you to promise me you will never do that again.

—Yeah, she'd have a nice private suite to get wasted in.

—Pfft, we can afford this thing without her.

—It's a good thing for us philanthropy's her sweet spot.

—Hey, Warren. Brother Warren!

—Hey, Jim. *Jim*! *Brother* Jim.

—Yeah, that and Jim Beam.

—Momma, I wanna i-scream.

—It'll be a d.o.a. r.f.p., though. South Waterfront has tied up too much dough.

—Does anyone know who Sister Ronette is taking out to the woodshed first?

—Does anyone else think she looks different?

—Yeah, bro, she's pregnant.

—Yeah, you can see it in her hips.

—I dunno, though. Never underestimate Brother Warren's optimism.

—Not that. Her face. She looks pale, less beautiful than usual.

—Momma!!!

—Jim! Over here! No, over *here* you big jerk!

—She gets the Olympian first.

—The lighting is pretty harsh in here, though.

—No, I'm the last E this time. Make way, *por favor*.

—Did you wishy-washy, Momma?

—The old lady, you mean?

—She's not old, just grey.

—Her name is Farrah Tyler. We recruited her but she said she prefers to ride unsponsored.

—I'm just going to ask. Sue me if this isn't doctrinaire. . .

—Does anyone besides me think it would be a good idea to child-proof these bleachers? A Little Cooper could fall through.

—I don't see any extra weight. Pfft. *Classic* Sister Ronette.

—. . .or sexist. . .or ignorant. . .or self-seeking. . .

—I think that's just what they call 'in the zone,' Jen.

—Fuhreaking move, please, Brother!

—Yeah, god, it *is* hot in here. . .and sticky.

—I see, Sister Jennifer, thank you.

—Is that what they call it, Brother Warren?

—Psst, hey, *bro.* You should watch the language around the big man, man.

—. . . but isn't it weird to be competing when you're so. . .*pregnant?*

—Presley, for the last time. . .No!

—Like even the simulated bad language is a no go, mmkay?

—What do you think, Brother Warren?

—Sister Ronnie knows what's best, brothers and sisters. Athletes understand their bodies in ways others don't.

—Come here now! I want you to hold my hand. Nooooo. . .*hold* it. Like *this.* There.

—No. *No!* There. Next to the T. And try smiling more this time, sis.

—Yeah and according to my pre-natal counselor? Well, she says vigorousness is totally fine.

—We should all support what she chooses to do with that body.

—Yeah, Sister Ronette will be doing *laps* around us when that li'l Little Cooper is ready to fall out.

—What did she say again? Oh yeah, it was something like 'overextending yourself is the only way to learn your limits.'

—I know it almost sounds like bad doctrine to point this out but, well, that's just not good doctrine, bro.

—Do you realize what she could mean to us. . .like *financially*. . .if we marketed her a certain way?

—Now if she were further along I would have insisted.

—Now don't tell the big man I put it that way. . .

—I mean we're going to have to *drag* her off that bike.

—But not letting her ride tonight would have been selfish.

—. . .and I know that sounds self-seeking but. . .well . . .there *are* bills to be paid. Expansions to secure loans for. And etcetera.

—But I'm sure Sister Ronnie knows her limits.

—All I'm trying to tell Brother Warren is that one wrong step and one of our Little Coopers would fall down there and break something or worse and we would have no idea how to get them out of there. . .

—Brother Chris, I want to tell you something. There was a time on the Euro circuit when you could enter some small town—French, Italian, Dutch, Spanish, anywhere—and the fans would be sitting at tables at an outdoor cafe waiting for the riders to come through and you would stop and they would surround you, practically pull you over to their table, beg you, and force you to drink, say, their *patxaran*. They'd be smiling and laughing, wiping sweat off you with their napkins, introducing their wives and children, shoving more *patxarans* at you. God, it was so beautiful.

—. . .not to mention be liable.

—Here we go, Ronette, HERE-WE-GO! (clap, CLAP-CLAP)

—I'm just saying that maybe it might be a good idea to take better than just *good* care of this woman after her pregnancy. Something beyond free modules and childcare. I mean there's talk about *The Nationals.*

—Hey, psst, hey. Brother Warren's telling the newbie The Origin Story.

—I'm just afraid all these shortcuts are going to catch up to us some day.

—I mean for starters? Regional expansion? Television money? Advertising space?

—A couple of miles outside of town you'd pull over to pee in their fields and think about how those kind people had organized their day around giving you their *patxaran.*

—Nah, it's no biggie. I was still on my bike at eight months.

—Yes, but aren't we overextended as it is?

—Yeah, but this is blood sport, Jennifer.

—I mean she could be *huge* for us if she would, well, allow us to, er, allow her to, um, capitalize on her talents. . .

—Hey, isn't that Exene Gibson over there?

—It's just that no matter how optimistic we are about projections or even if we choose to be as optimistic about projections as Warren *tells* us to be. . .

—What I'm saying, Brother Chris, is that cycling taught me the importance of belonging. Whether in the *peloton* or on the team bus or in some small Basque village in the Pyrenees. We all need to feel like we belong. And the trick to belonging—and this is almost shockingly simple, Brother Chris—is realizing we already do. . .belong I mean. Wherever we go, whoever we meet. We are all brothers and sisters. The only thing separating me from a Basque villager in the Pyrenees is circumstance. Now circumstance may mean that villager's horse just isn't up to a 40 kilometer ride around the mountain and back anymore or maybe his wife is ill or maybe the race has been rerouted that year—However you slice it it would *appear* that we are separated. But there it is, Brother Chris! We *aren't* separated. You know why? Because I choose not to be that's why. You see, I may never see that old guy yanking his horse by a rope and shoving a glass of *patxaran* into my hand again but that doesn't mean he isn't still my brother. Just think about that. To call everyone—near and far, alive and dead—*family*. To disintegrate every barrier that exists and melt into brother and sisterhood. Imagine how liberating that is for a moment.

—. . .possibly. . .er. . .suggest. . .she. . .erm. . .*soften* her image.

—Brother Warren!

—. . .I'm just saying that at a certain point organizational growth ceases to be sustainable.

—I'm glad you could make it tonight, Brother Chris. Congratulations on completing the introductory modules.

Sid looks at the riding bag. It's silly but he wants to unzip it to let some air in. Even if Flora doesn't have a respiratory system in the traditional sense she still needs to breathe. This was good care, what a good father would do, what Ronette would want him to do, not a make or break type thing, but one of the many small efforts a parent was supposed to make in service of their child's comfort and short-term welfare. Yes, this feels right. But then what about how loud it is in here? Even if Flora can't hear in the traditional sense might not her sack register in vibrations how nuts Velodrome is tonight? Let's hope all the noise doesn't distract Mama from the race. See, Dada loves you, Flora, but he's wondering if they shouldn't have brought you. Mama and Dada could probably have used one last night to celebrate the seamlessness together, to say goodbye for now to their most beautiful creation. . .besides you of course.

And Mama really doesn't look right, Flo. She's sweating too hard. One of her braids is sticking out. Even from here Dada can see she is stretching her calf like she's cramping. Did she get overheated in the prep stretch? Or was it the proper stretch? Has she read the note he stashed in her helmet? She knows he always puts one in there. It's part of their little ritual. Anyway, blah-blah-blah, Flo. Mama's a pro. A total freaking pro. Let's just get her through to the next round and take it from there. And honestly? It's totally cool if all of our seamlessnesses will be three-way dealies from now on. Here, you can sit in my lap for the first race.

Just stick to the back wheel. Let her set the pace. You're not overheated. It's just sweat. But is that a cramp? The calf feels off. The lower back feels off. The rig feels off. Will you fire the gun already? Just stick to her back wheel. You are incapable of seeing anything but that tread-those spokes-that hub. Fire the gun, bitch! Fire the fucking fun!

    —God, she's beautiful.
    —This is it, this is it. Start clapping everybody.
    —Shhh.
    —I mean I can say that, right? *Shhh?*
    —I mean consider how far she has come since rehab.
    —Psst. Hey, Brother Warren.
    —Mawwwm-i-i-i-iii!
    —Shhh!
    —Then imagine how far she might go.

—Brother Chris, I want you to remember this moment. . .the pause. . .the waiting. . .

—Shhhh-sh-shhhh.

—. . .At this moment everyone in Velodrome is the same person.

—It's our duty, as her brothers and sisters, to help her explore her full potential.

—Wah-hah-hah-hah-haaaa. Waaaaaaaah!!!

—Just think about that.

Ready?!
(powff!)

Go bitch, go. Oh god.

—Go Ronette?! Go!

—Why are they going so slow?

—Yeah, what's going on?!

—Brother Warren, they're just standing there!

—Tyler wants a tactics race.

—How long like this?

—Sister Ronette?! Go already!

—One little bob or weave, one wheel too far out of line and the other rider takes off while their opponent is off-balance.

—Brother Warren?!

—Yeah, why doesn't Sister Ronette just dust her.

—Yeah, that old lady can't keep up.

—Maybe Sister Ronnie wants to see if she can win this way, too.

—Mawm-i-i-i, why aren't they *go*-ing?

—Maybe she wants to suffer a little first.

Fine, bitch, fine, we'll do the standoff. Give me the pain. Fire in the calf-fire in the knee. Is this early arthritis? Well fine, give me more. Burn me to the ground. Let's stand in our machines all night. I can watch that little grey bun bobbing up and down forever. Whatever you put us through will be just. Slower, you sadistic bitch! Slower!

—Why are they on the infield now?

—You can *go* down there?

—Tyler taking them down there could mean she wants a pure tactics match and wants to rest in the flats. Or she is tempting Sister Ronette to make a move. And in order to make that move Sister Ronette will have to climb the slope and that requires an incredible amount of energy after the track stand they just did. If Tyler expended less energy than Sister Ronette during the track stand her initial move will be far more powerful. She might get far enough ahead that Sister Ronette won't be able to draft off her.

—I don't get it.

—Come on, Sister Ronette!

—But the first attack in a tactics race is often a fake attack, a way to feel out how much was taken out of their opponent by the track stand. Tyler's strategy is to repeatedly burn Sister Ronette to the ground and pick up the pieces at the end. She's betting she has more endurance than Sister Ronnie.

—There they go!

—No. See? They're slowing down again.

—We believe in you, Sister Ronette!

—I thought these were always speed races.

—Go already!

Go baby, go! Go baby, go! Go baby, go!

—Most of the attacks are fake, in fact. The winner of the final sprint in a tactics race is usually the one who suffered less earlier.

—Holy crap they've stopped again!

—How do you know Sister Ronette isn't trying to burn *Tyler* to the ground?

—It's one of those things where you can just tell.

Go baby, go! Go baby, go! Go baby, go!

. . .No. . .No. Don't stop. Don't take us up there. If we stop that means we'll have to go soon. And for good. No, you bitch. No. Don't make me listen to the shouts. I want to pretend we're alone. I want to forget my life-my daughter-my man. I want to dig a little hole out of this pain and volume and hide inside forever. There are responsibilities at the finish line. A whole series of things to do-feel-enjoy. Let the Eel Princess keep howling in her calf-her back-her stomach. I would rather

be flayed with fire like this than be responsible for someone else. What arrogance! To demand care! Don't tip the wheel, bitch. Don't go. I want to watch your grey bun trace ∞s in the air forever.

Both women are red and streaming but Ronette is the first to have to whip her front wheel from side-to-side to remain in place. When she does this her opponent departs, slowly at first, but gradually gaining speed.

No!

   Go baby, go! Go baby, go! Go baby, go!

After a quarter lap of increasing speed Ronette's opponent once again slows down hoping to goad an obviously far more fatigued Ronette into a desperate attack. She could then draft off of Ronette before starting her actual attack. But since Ronette stays back her opponent slows to a crawl and brings them to a halt for another track stand. Ronette is breathing far more heavily—a major tell. She tells herself to think then remembers she usually doesn't have to. Then all the pain in her body starts to articulate itself—a horrible ache behind her eyes, a spasming lower back, a cramping calf, the need to vomit.

   Go baby, go! Go baby, go! Go baby, go!

She tells herself to bottom down through the pain to complete one pedal stroke and then one more. Yes, the only thing necessary now is the will to repeat. Some distant mechanism will accomplish this for her while she tags along. Suffering will occur off to the side while she slowly gains control over her conscious mind. Yes, this is a lesser form of seamlessness and not so very different from the failsafe. Maybe a friendly little minotaur is nearby to give her rig a shove.

   Go baby, go! Go baby, go! Go baby, go!

Only she has forgotten to watch her opponent who has launched out straight and hard.

No!

Ronette sees the grey bun flying away and fires off a pedal stroke to launch down the slope into the middle of the straightaway so she can start gathering speed to take the banking turn and whip round after her opponent. But when she enters Turn 1 her rig briefly goes parallel then starts to tip over.

Go baby, go! Go baby—

Sid bolts upright and nearly sends the riding bag flying. Exene screams. Virgil yanks Exene by the wrist and barrels down through the crowd. On the opposite straightaway Warren jumps down to the track and runs. At the bottom of the incline Ronette is curled up holding her stomach and her back wheel is spinning over her head. Sid repeatedly shouts Ronette's name down from the ledge but she doesn't respond. He wants to jump but it's a 20-foot drop and his vertigo swirls and plummets him inward. As he trips and gallops and falls across the bleachers his hair plasters over his eyes and his dizziness worsens. The riding bag swings wildly, hits people in the face. Melees break out around him and bar his way. He cannot see Ronette or how he is supposed to get down to her. Warren reaches her first. He cradles her neck and palms her stomach. Seeing her helmet is dented near the crown he tells her. . .*Lie still Ronnie. . .Lie still. . .We've got you. . .We've got you. . .* while removing her helmet. A note written over the fortune's secret numbers falls out. . .*To Ronette, We're with you all the way. . .*which no one will ever read. Virgil has pushed through the chaos of Co-op blacks, jumped down onto the straight-away, and reached up to grab Exene who is staring in horror at Ronette splayed on the track. She whimpers and looks over her shoulder at the bleachers above. . .*I'm sorry. . .We have to go. . .*Virgil pleads with her. . .*I've got you, X, come on!. . .* Exene forces herself to sidle closer to the ledge on her knees. Others realize what she is trying to do and grab hold of her to help her down but this only terrifies her into preemptively throwing herself out into the leverageless air. She swims once then collapses with a moan into Virgil's arms. He is kissing her cheek over and over. . .*I've got you. . . I've got you . . .You did it. . .*He holds her for a long moment while the world tilts around them. . .*That was some scary shit and you did it anyway*. . .And as they jog to the spot where Ronette is curled on the track Exene smiles wildly at the joy of those words while trying to ignore the sensation that her intestines are about to come flooding out of her vagina. And Virgil squeezes and yanks the hand of the trembling body behind him so the soul inside won't flutter away before he can get her to Ronette and show her she is alright. . .that they are both alright. . .that everything can be alright. Sid reaches the ledge of the straight-away but since he can't propel himself downward and break his fall without risking damage to the riding bag he hangs it around his neck and shoves it inside his shirt. Warren has put his free hand around Exene's shoulder. Exene is gently stroking Ronette's arm. Virgil squeezes his free hand into a fist to control his anger. Warren is sniffling. Tears plink onto Ronette's helmet. Virgil notices and gently places his fist on Warren's shoulder. Then Virgil also begins to cry. Seeing this, Exene cries too but then smiles because Ronette has opened her eyes. . .*Ronette? Ronette, honey?*. . .There is no blood. She seems alert, even keenly focused, almost freakishly normal. Exene is relieved her sister has not died. . .*Can you say something for us, Ronette?*. . .Without any safe option on how to jump down and strands of hair still plastered over his eyes Sid finally just throws himself over. Ronette's lips flutter. . . *Flora?. . .Where's Flora?*. . .Sid's foot catches on the ledge and his trajectory veers sharply downward to send him falling face first. . .*Is she alright?*. . .Inside all this chaos Sid hears a pocket of silence turn into a collective gasp. Before or perhaps just after he lands he will have the sensation of having forgotten something but not be able to remember what it was because of the pain from the blow to his stomach and the glass thrust into his thigh.

8.

Summer sun slants into the ninth floor of an otherwise shuttered former shirt factory where 21 women with yellow ∞ pendants on their enlarged stomachs bend and lift and step to throbbing music while a slim woman in a black leotard shouts encouragement at them. They huff and gasp, barely disturbing the curtains of dust hanging from the ductwork above, squinting into the silhouette of their gyrating trainer and trying not to lose track of the bobbing yellow ∞ on her stomach while she pleads with them to give her more.

—Come *on*, ladies! You're letting your Future Little Coopers down! And two! And three! And *one*!

Then there are the screams of the children crawling and flailing and romping around, dancing and jumping and crashing on the mat, yelping and pleading to get the attention of the sweat-strewn giants above who don't have enough breath to reprimand them.

—Your *children* are working harder than *you* are, Sisters! Now come *on*! And two! And three! And *two!*

Ronette sees double and triple in her beater glasses. She wants to keep up with the other women but keeps losing her balance trying to dodge the little monsters at her feet who the others hardly seem to notice. One doughy little thing in particular, dressed only in a diaper, has been slapping at her ankles for minutes now. When Ronette moves away it only crawls after her to renew its saucer-eyed pursuit. What exactly—it's hard-blinking blue eyes ask—is Ronette trying to accomplish here? When no answer is provided the toddler straightens itself on the wobbly canes of its sausagey arms to state something between a belch and a wail.

—Blaaayp!

Ronette motions for it to shoo but the toddler waves back, almost falls over, rights itself, quaveringly looks up, and indicates that this reply is shockingly unsatisfactory.

—Baayp-wehhh!

—No, *shoo.*

Ronette points at the other women and whispers.

—Go back to Mommy.

Ronette only recognizes a few of the other prospective mothers but thinks they must be Co-op members. The cost for a class like High Impact Aerobics for Mothers, Module II would be prohibitive for most non-members since the Co-op only accepts its own insurance and sets its module rates far above the market standard in order to imply an advanced level of quality and innovation. Even with Co-op coverage the class is costly, but Warren had told Sid to tell Ronette. . .*Uncle Cooper's got this so just go and enjoy or else. . .It's high time she started taking better care of herself . . .Remember, Brother Sid, that's our niece or nephew she's carrying around in there. . .And for goodness sakes keep her* *off that rig. . .*So here is Ronette doing what Uncle Warren and Papa Sid had persuaded her to think was such a good idea. Yes, everyone has been teaming up on her since the accident. Warren with his twice-weekly deliveries of groceries, gifts, and get-well cards as a pretext for lecturing her. . .*Uncle Warren has been reading about the importance of pre-natal exercise in early cognition. . .low-impact pre-natal exercise that is. . .And since we need you off the rig for the next, oh, 6-8 months I've taken the liberty of signing you up for a few advanced mother modules. . .What I'm saying, Sister Ronnie, is that you need to start getting more serious about your child's future. . .*X and Virge stopping by to say all the right things but telling her with their haunted faces that she had better not put them through anything like that crash ever again. Sid micro-managing her. . .*You need to get out more, Ron. . .Breathe some fresh air. . .Recuperate. . .Let yourself heal. . .Read less . . .Eat more. . .Spend more time with Flora . . .Practice getting around in the foam rubber. . .Remember how badly you wanted to be pregnant. . .*giving her all these searching looks since she confessed that this was probably her sixth concussion and letting Warren wheel her rig away one afternoon, reminding her she needed to be more cautious now, asking her if she was okay-did her head hurt-did she need to take something more heavy duty than what they gave her at the hospital. . .*And, no, I won't let you get addicted. . .*But most of all it was the Eel Princess. That self-righteous little tyrant was constantly making demands, questioning her motives, whining and complaining. . .*Take us for a walk, Mama, we can't breathe. . .It's so hot in here, Mama. . .Can't we just take the foam rubber off this time?. . .We're suffocating, Mama. . .Why won't you listen to us?. . .We're dying in here, Mama. . .We're hungry. . .We want to eeeeeat. . .Just because you're not hungry doesn't mean we're not. . .Ew, that was gross. . .We're going to make you throw up now, Mama. . . Yes, Mama deserves punishment after that crash-crash. . . Quiet! We're sleeping. . .Wake up!. . .Mama! Make our owies go away!. . .Don't you care, Mama?. . .Don't you love us?. . . We hate you! We hate you-We hate you-We hate you!*

—One! and two and One! and two and One! Good! *Good!*

Ronette thinks she remembers having once shot up with the woman leading the class. What was her name? Alex?

Devon? She was about thirty pounds skinnier then but seriously *heavy*. Now she is the sort of hyper-kinetic Co-op goddess who makes the abandoned warehouses, shuttered machine shops, and infrastructural malaise sprawled behind her seem exotic instead of depressing. So it matters little that Ronette can only count two lazily turning fans boxed into the buckling particle board walls or that some of the women in the class seem on the brink of cheerfully hyperventilating or that there are too many obvious code violations to count. No, the Alex-Devon's of the world remind us that doing things against our better judgment is sometimes the only way we can make any progress.

—One! and two and One! and two and *One!*

Yes, Alex-Devon is absolutely *energizing*. She knows this module will be one of her many successes and that however long the final renovation of the building is delayed by The Co-op's liquidity issues she will never once regret having spent her own money to install the studio mirrors which multiply her inspiring image for her students and the future students in their stomachs. Ronette replays the one-sided conversation they had when she arrived.

—Oh my goodness, *there* she is.

Alex-Devon advancing on Ronette's stomach with hungry hands, wanting to tap the pendant. Ronette intercepting them with an awkward little shake.

—Well, I should say 'There you *both* are.'

Alex-Devon knifing her hands into her hips, surveying Ronette's body proudly.

—Well just look at us now, Ronette. Can you believe it? Her eyes twinkling, fixing Ronette with a conspiratorial look.

—After all we've been through.

Refurbishing their pasts with one sweeping sigh.

—Oh, but that's all over now, isn't it.

Smiling to finish the spell.

—Anyway, I was thrilled to squeeze you into the class. Warren only had to ask once, you know.

Alex-Devon then introduced Ronette to some of the other women and they quizzed her about the accident. She lied that she was fine-the baby was fine-everything was fine while The Eel Princess yanked the leash tight. . .*Yes, Mama needs to seem like a good mama even if she is really a selfish, careless,* *crazy Mama. . .Her Little Flora will want playmates some day, after all. . .And who wants their child to play with the daughter of a sick, mean, nasty old Mama?. . .*Yes, The Eel Princess has cracked down since the morning Warren showed up with that pre-natal health counselor who Ronette, to her own surprise, wound up being uncharacteristically honest about her symptoms with. . .*Migraines. . .Nausea. . .I'm peeing all the time. . .My skin is itchy. . .I feel a little crazy. . . Sleeping terrible. . .Horrible dreams. . .Terrifying premonitions. . .*only to learn that this was all perfectly normal. Then she had confessed that she had no idea what she was going to do once the baby got there, felt completely unprepared, panicky and angry, doubtful she was a fit mother. But the counselor said that these were perfectly normal thoughts and that while it was a little late in her second trimester to be feeling quite so anxious she would soon be too happily distracted by her baby's imminent arrival to dwell on her insecurities. . .*Things have a way of just working themselves out from here on out. . .You'll see. . .*Her gentle Co-op sister had then given her hand a squeeze and left before Ronette could further confess that she was already a bad mother, that she sometimes forgot to leave the curtain cracked so Flora could see out, often neglected to say good morning, had allowed Sid to relocate Flora from the baby carriage to a cardboard box on top of the mannequin arms dresser, spent entire days reading about infant psychology, linguistics, birth rituals, transcendental meditation and raw foods diets while lonely Flora whimpered in frustration as the many hands so tantalizingly close refused to reach out and touch her. Yes, with the departure of that kind stranger Ronette had lost her last chance to admit how nuts she feels when she finds herself snapping at the Eel Princess. . .*Can you possibly understand how difficult it is for me to be off my rig. . .how terrifying it is to walk to the store worrying about your shirt popping out of your pants and spilling the foam rubber all over the sidewalk . . .to have to constantly worry about the shape of your stomach and how faithful it is to yesterday's state of pregnancy. . .to constantly be distracted by your whining, to juggle all these lies, to make sure not to get high on these pills, to prove to Sid she was still sane. . .to sometimes feel grateful for how stressed she is because that at least distracts her from the* *guilt over the Velodrome accident which had ruptured Flora and wounded Sid?*

—Two and three and *two!* Good, Sister Ronette! *Good!* Just a little higher on the recoil, mmkay?! Two and three and *two!*

Okay-okay-okay. She should run through one of the meditations. Her body can follow Alex-Devon's instructions while her mind counts off to the side. . .*one*. . .*two*. . .*one*. . . *two*. . .She can slowly *become* her breathing. . .*one*. . . . . .*two* . . . . . .*one*. . . . . .*two*. . . . . .as the numbers slowly lose their lexicality. . .*one*. . . . . . . .and become her respiration. . .*one*. . . *no*— . . .*two*. . .*um*. . .But then she thinks that if she's having such a hard time balancing her needs with The Eel Princess's won't it be even more difficult when it's time for her motherhood to go *public*? If she can't handle what is *inside* now how will she handle what's *outside* then? And if she somehow does manage to quiet all the doubts in her head what will be left to raise her child? Yes, now that her general tendencies are long gone, stampeded over by motherhood and pulverized to dust, wasn't she in fact in the process of giving birth to *two* babies here? Not only a daughter, but a new mother, a woman who would have to start from scratch again? And if that's the case then who will be the bigger baby? And who will be in charge?

—And *one*!!!

Christ, why can't she make pregnancy seem easy and light-hearted like Sid? Why can't she ask him to help her get inside her pregnancy instead harping on him all the time? Had he paid the guy who knew the guy who could get them a social security number? Had he applied for food stamps yet? Had he priced diapers? Had he put together a believable budget? Had he told Warren that they would be flying east for the birth, seeing a specialist out there, taking all the appropriate steps and, no, the anomaly the tests had shown after the crash was probably nothing and if all went well they would be back a week or so after the birth so please don't come by with any more goodies. But since Sid isn't hormone sick or worry-bloated he keeps on cheerfully accomplishing these tasks, self-righteously positioning himself to recalibrate her emotions in these like totally cliché ways which are starting to drive her nuts. . .*How's the Mama doing today?*. . .*Me and Flora are so proud of you, Ron*. . .*We know how hard this* *must be for you. . .Just tell me how I can help. . .*I mean does he hear himself sometimes? Laying down this like totally boilerplate shit? Shouldn't the father of her child try to understand, like *deeply* understand that a woman sometimes requires a little more oomph from a mate and that no matter how much she loves the dumb sap he should be hustling his ass off to make damn sure he brings a little more imagination to the table vìs-a-vis Parenthood and de facto Marriage lest loving him becomes nothing more than a habit, a valuable habit no question, one just as powerful as any other superstition, but not so droningly predictable as to imply she was one-dimensional, a Mother before a Wife, a Wife before a Mother, either/or instead of freaking *and*, a composite being crazy enough to sweat her ass off with twenty pounds of foam rubber on her stomach but smart enough to know she really doesn't have to?!

  —Two and one and *two*!!!

  At least he understood that she needed to see the light at the end of the tunnel and had suggested they do the birth at their secret spot on the river. They would make a week of it down there. She would plan a ceremony and end her pregnancy on her own terms. X and Virge would witness. Yes, she was thankful someone knew what she needed when she probably never would. What a hag she's been. Sid had been like a total saint since taking that gainer over the wall. Imminent Fatherhood was totally reorganizing him, taking all the commas out of his sentences, turning him into this like declarative *stud*. Do this Ronette. Do *that* Ronette. Here are our options, Ronette. Yes, efficiencies were flooding out of that once-so-hesitant mouth and he was totally kicking ass on his end; logging ridiculous hours in the rig, rounding into ridiculous shape, training for the short track while Mama napped, making the flying ponytail his signature, experiencing all of this personal momentum around the advent of their daughter, proudly demonstrating the laudable traits of discipline and drive for Flora the way Mama used to. God, he was almost unrecognizable, what with his suddenly double-corded limbs habitually posed in attitudes of frank intelligence or cheerful forbearance, his new go-to posture being chest out and hands on hips like Superman or Alex-Devon. Yes, he had joined Ronette's old tribe and she was desperate to clutch the membership back.

—And one! And two. And *lift!* And two. And step!

So every time this new Sid puts his hand on her stomach these days she blushes like some dumb weak woman and allows this visceral thing to occur between them which has her frequently needing to fuck his brains out. But what he happily mistakes for love and seamlessness Ronette knows is nothing more than her body's jealous desire to cling to what she has lost and perform the act that feels increasingly necessary, however symbolic.

—Bayp? *Bayp!* Oh-wuh. Waaanh! Waaaaaaaaanh!!!

And the sun radiates deeper into the room while the city behind sprawls away.

9.

It is a starry morning before dawn. The moon glows through the fir boughs and glistens in the packing tape wrapped around the sack's midsection. Ronette squats down next to Flora, removes her new glasses, reaches into the riding pack for the Buddhist prayer wheel, finds a note wrapped around the handle. . .*To Mama, Om mani padme hum, MamaRon*. . .smiles, shakes her head, composes herself, removes the acorn she has kept in her vagina overnight and begins chanting. . .*ob lo ko say coo, fo lo ko say*. . .*ob lo ko say coo, ob lo ko say*. . .A breeze makes the surrounding limbs clatter and clack. . .*ob lo no say coo, ob no no may*. . .as she empties her mind of these last syllables of doubt. . .*Twa fo no ko say jo bo, ob lo ko say* . . .In their place faith floods in. Her daughter is real. Her daughter is alive. I will be a good mother. Yes, do the reps. Breathe in nothingness like the one book says. . .*djo mo lo bo fo ho ko, ob lo ko say*. . .and the mind will become more fertile as she releases and relents, releases and relents. . .*fo fo ko no say lo, om, fo fo no say*. . .Speak away the barriers which are words. . . *rab ko no, nab bo lo toe*. . .Empty the soul of sounds so belief can flood in.

All week she has been stealing away from the others, plumbing deeper into the woods and doing the reps. And as the sessions lengthened and she freed herself of more syllables, both sides of the argument (alive or not alive) were reduced to wordlessness until nothing but instinct and will remained. . .*to jo bo no, fi ni ko day*. . .Her daughter is as alive as her mother wishes. . .*ha ha to no, ho no ha fo day*.

All contrary notions are rendered tolerably absurd. As another books says. . .*The mind of perfect equanimity is an infinite plane without architecture.* . . .So when The Eel Princess starts snickering at Mama's funny little exercises and tells her to focus on the physical end of birth and not all this spiritual mumbo jumbo, Ronette only smiles at what a. . . *needy-baby-big-mouth*. . .her Flora has for a spokeswoman and becomes increasingly uninterested in the distinction between real and surrogate voices, her ballooning bosoms and her flat stomach, her now living daughter and a sack of wheat flour. And even if more than one of the books say she must not construct hypothetical realities like 'past' and 'future' she cannot help but hope. . .*goe toe fa ni, pa toe sue ko*. . .that motherhood washes away her contradictory thoughts and renders her mind a Nothingness which is also Oneness.

For now, though, she must simply do the reps. In time, the labyrinth will turn to dust and the minotaur will be set free. . .O but if only she could leap onto his back and ride way with Flora. If only she didn't have to return to the judgmental city. If only this stubborn little Eel Princess didn't keep telling her to go back to camp where there are men who might actually impregnate her and a wombless woman as warning. . .O if only she could do the reps in such a way that she and Flora might completely disappear together without hurting those two men and one woman. If only she could keep this acorn inside her for another night and not have to bury it now and join the others.

Exene snaps on her back brace, pulls on three oversized sweaters and shines the flashlight into the corners of the tent. After Velodrome her daughter started appearing in a more vivid form. She is three, maybe four years old and wears a pink dress. Her eyes are brown and she has pigtails. Sometimes she plays hopscotch or jumps rope. Mostly, she watches and listens. And though she hasn't appeared in the woods yet Exene thinks she is just waiting for the right moment.

When she told Virgil he said. . .*Let me know the next time she comes round*. . .then lowered his eyes . . .*I'll try not to scare her away*. . .Since then he has become quiet and gentle, smiles more easily, and touches her more. And while he has obviously given up on her or him or both of them ever getting 'better,' he at least seems relieved to have done so. Peaceful, relatively happy weeks have followed and camping with Sid and Ronette has helped consolidate their gains. They remain fragile but suffer more honestly now. This, coupled with the maturation of her daughter, has helped Exene feel less alone, more capable of hope.

During the night she had listened to Virgil softly snoring, told herself not to think about how each breath was so precarious, tried not to worry she would commit some fatal error at the birth ceremony this morning, and eventually convinced herself to think about only good things—How all the sun and air and laughter has helped her relent inside, how helping prepare for the birth has felt healing not bittersweet, how once or twice she had felt more like her old self or at least the new version of her old self, the one who might finally be recovering from the miscarriage, the one who felt no shame over secretly wishing she were irretrievably insane and therefore not to be judged for overturning the tent to make sure her daughter wasn't hiding underneath.

She stumbles along the crooked lip of the bank above the boulder-strewn river while training the bouncing beam on the narrow path. She must steady her step, walk closer to the precipice, and not look down. Today will not necessarily include pain. She can improve. . .*Come on, improve. Improve-improve-IMPROVE!.* . .Yes, however badly she wants to return to the tent and hide there until her daughter appears, she suspects that if she doesn't keep going she will become one of those people who look back for the rest of their lives. So even if body and soul say there is absolutely nothing wrong with totally disappearing back inside her loss she. . .*unfortunately . . .freaking unfortunately, Sister.* . .is not so far gone as to be unaware that the vast body of evidence suggests that in the long run. . .*in the besainted long run.* . .doing the opposite of what she wants right now might give her an outside shot at getting better some day.

Yes, she refuses to ruin the most important day of her sister's life. So find some perspective. Just look at all this. . . this. . .*um.* . .multitudinousness. . .the forest-the animals-the one planet among billions. . .*the like total freaking productivity of it all.* . .Remind yourself that one woman's singular loss is overwhelmingly common in the grand scheme. Play the philosopher but don't overdo it. Remember to laugh at yourself. Enough of this stricken woman business. . .*Yes.* . . *Freaking yes, okay?.* . .And when Ronette officially brings Flora into the world and she probably breaks down, tell. . . *freaking beg.* . .everyone not to worry. . .*It's nothing.* . .*really* . . .and find an upbeat way of explaining that *sharing* her pain is the same thing as *inflicting* it. And, shucks, guys, she just isn't up to feeling guilty on top of everything else, you know. So truly. . .her cracking voice? These welling tears? Ignore them. They have nothing to do with how happy she is for Ronette. . .for all of them. . .*This is a day of birth and rebirth, after all.*

     Exene enters a broad clearing bounded by towering old growths and the curtains of darkness they hang. Low-slung stars impart a thin phosphorescence above the tree-line while a naked harvest moon looms above. Glowing river stones arranged in a circular path lead to a small roiling fire where a dark form breaks sticks and throws them into the flames. There is a small explosion, dying sparks. Exene turns off the flashlight and enters.

     She sits down on the rock next to Ronette and takes her sister's hand. Their nervous, smiling eyes meet before both look down at the riding bag in her lap. Shadows accentuate how bony Ronette's face has become. All the lightness and confidence of the last week has drained away. If only the sun would wait, Exene thinks. She wants to sit warming Ronette's hands while smelling the gathering dampness of the earth with her, remain *partial* mothers just a little longer, delay those first rays spilling over the wall of hills cross-river and heralding the ceremony which will make everything final. But when she hears one of the men laughing down by the river, then the sound of plunging water, she knows that the judgmental dawn will soon break over them and they will all have to begin stoking the fire.

     Too soon.

     Too soon.

Dawn brings dimension to the surrounding forest as the four faces in the innermost circle of stones are gradually, flickeringly illuminated. Ronette sits at true north wearing a black peasant dress which would slide off if not for her swollen breasts. Exene is at south in her many layers. Virgil is shirtless at west and Sid is dripping wet in The Ensemble at east.

Ronette silently counts to herself and breaths rapidly while the others stoke the fire. As the flames climb, piles of objects are illuminated. Ronette points at Sid. He will be the first to throw something in. Still shivering from the baptism he gave himself in the river, he teeters when she stands.

[He had stayed under for a ten count in the icy, rushing water to wash away what remained of his bad old self. Even if this didn't work it would constitute another small moment of joy in what has been the happiest period of his young life. It turns out fatherhood (or, more technically, 'imminent fatherhood') was what he had needed all along. The imperative of caring for his wife and daughter had put all his ducks in a proverbial row. And since everything else seemed so petty in comparison there was far less to worry about. He could now devote himself to a universally laudable pursuit. And however cliché, parenthood made him feel more connected to others and gave his life newfound purpose. There was nothing hypothetical about these gains, man. So kneeling in an icy river at dawn, about to witness the birth of his daughter, Sid could not contain his excitement and so started laughing and sucking up water and gagging. Virgil, who had already dunked himself and was in the process of skeptically assessing his shivering body, had heard Sid's coughs and waded over. Sid had given him a thumbs up, caught his breath, and re-submerged. The water was so cold it seemed to pass *through* him, so he counted past ten to twenty thinking that if he stayed under long enough he might turn *into* the river which was traveling to the ocean to combine with all the others to encompass and unify the world. And when Virgil abruptly yanked him from this reverie. . .*What are you thinking, man? You want to freeze to death?*. . .and tore the hair away from his face to search out any further foolishness, Sid slapped him on the shoulder, smiled, and reassured him he was not trying to escape. . .*Just immersing, bro.*]

Sid tosses his favorite album in the fire. He is about to speak but remembers he is not supposed to and so sits down. Ronette points at Exene who reaches for her pile without looking and feels the hard, cold plastic in her hand. She tosses the baby rattle into the fire. Virgil doesn't have a pile so Ronette passes him over then stands and tosses one of her pairs of beater glasses into the fire. Then her summons come more quickly. They stand up and sit down more quickly.

Ronette has tossed in her black wristbands, Sid his favorite book. Exene gains confidence with each toss, her mouth screwing into a smirk. Virgil notices, smiles at her. The fire hungrily eats paper and fiber and synthetics. The flames flash green or blue or pink. They are all sweating and glistening. Ronette has singed the tips of her unbraided hair. Virgil's chest is streaked with ash. Sid removes Woody from his sleeve and throws him into the fire. Exene tosses a tiny shirt into the fire and then breaks order to also throw in a small pair of pants and then a tiny dress. She then suddenly starts tearing out of her layers, teetering around ridiculously, laughing and struggling until Virgil comes over to untangle her. In reply, Sid rips out of his soaking Ensemble and throws it into the fire. Then Virgil and Exene throw the last of the maternity clothes and blankets into the fire. Ronette waves her hands like a conductor who has lost control of her orchestra. The pre-planned ritual is falling apart. Even if her baby has already been successfully birthed back in the woods, a poorly exe-cuted ritual might have unforeseen consequences. She jumps up and down to get Virgil and Exene's attention but they are too busy unlacing the back brace. Sid walks over to Ronette to calm her down, takes her hands, removes the red wristbands, kisses her wrists, and throws the wristbands into the fire. She hadn't wanted this but allows it to happen. Sid then goes over to Virgil who, like Exene, is only wearing underwear and watching the back brace burn. He points at Virgil and then the fire. Understanding, Virgil takes one step forward, makes fists, crouches into a boxer's stance, torques his body at the hips and throws his chest and arms forward to yell into the fire as loud and as long as he can. Exene stops herself from going to him. His neck muscles bulge and his brown irises bob in the bared whites of his wild eyes. As the sound elongates and rises in pitch he appears to be in both pain and ecstasy. When this long guttural cry is over his hands open and his shoulders fall. He turns to Exene smiling and she leaps into his arms. He whispers. . .*There's no right way to be, X. . .Talk to her all you want. . .I will, too. . .We'll never lose her again. . .*Sid points to Ronette. This confuses her. Then he points at the riding bag with Flora inside. Ronette shakes her head 'no' but Sid thinks there is no reason to delay the birth of their daughter any longer. He touches Exene on the shoulder and makes a hand gesture she understands. As he walks over to

Ronette, Exene, still holding Virgil's hand, stands on top of a rock and begins to recite from the last of Sid's classics. . . *Relentless dawn, free the bloom of your making. . .Let none but the eternal winds scatter your seed. . .*Sid tries to open the riding bag Ronette is desperately hugging to her chest. They tussle. Flora peaks out of the bag. Ronette sees the bull and becomes distraught. This will ruin everything. It's too soon. The sun has not mounted the bank. Everyone is out of order. She wants to run back into the woods but Sid won't let go. . . *and grant us the second flower of undiminished days. . .*Then with one great pull he tears the riding bag from her and sends the sack of wheat flour flying. Its midsection glistens with the reflection of the approaching flames as Ronette lunges in after it.

10.

Belladonna has been staking out the bungalow from the tinted safety of a Co-op limo. In five days of ass-bruising surveillance she has seen nothing but Sid's comings and goings and Warren dropping off satchels full of gifts. And she has had enough of this Co-op Livery driver. He is middle-aged, classy, and utterly professional. There is no challenge in being sweet and solicitous to someone who gives her no reason to be otherwise. So tonight she will call the Co-op livery service and tell them to send someone still taking the introductory modules.

—I need a newbie, someone I can mentor.

When the phone rings the next morning Belladonna hammers her heals across the parquet of the bridal suite. She has been living in the top floor of a downtown luxury hotel for two months now. A reborn woman deserves altered circumstances, after all. And even if she has a view of the west hills, La Petite Manse feels a million miles away.

—Yes?

—My apologies for being so late. . .um. . .Sisterrrr. . . Mabbacy?

This one sounds snotty. Or maybe just adenoidal.

—Alternative side of the street parking is in effect.

—To whom might I be speaking?

—Oh. . .um. . .my name is Thad. . .um. . .*Brother* Thad. I'm your driver for the day Miss. . .Sister Mabbacy.

—It's Mabuse, Thad. Ma-Boo-*Zuh*.

—Oh, I'm sorry, ma'am. . .Sister. . .Sister Mabuse.

—But today you will call me Josephine.

—Ma'am? Er, Sister? Errr. . .

—Josephine. Say it, will you please, Brother Thad.

—Sister Josephine.

—Not 'Sister,' Thad. *Josephine*. Can you please say it?

—Josephine.

—Very good, Brother Thad. I will be down in a moment.

—Yes Ma'am. Oh. Sis—

Belladonna gently places the receiver in the cradle. Her spirits are high. Yes, this will be the day. She must remain methodical, though. Tolerating Thad will be a good first step.

She studies herself in a bathroom mirror framed by golden bulbs and shining aluminum. Much of the strain and rue has drained from her mouth and left this perfectly sweet little smile in its place. Vanished layers of make-up reveal facial typographies which might even be considered hand-some in certain cultures. A 'Thad' might even want to *notch* this. Hmm, yes, just so long as they aren't lovingly tearing each other apart when Ronette opens that door.

But boy was she was wrong about Thad. Just look at him. Another Adonis. Maybe even an artistic *sensitive*. Some 6th floor type picking up some working class cash. A painfully polite man-child who'd be forgiving of her slipups then write something obliquely moving about it. God and now with this smile? This Thad is freaking *winning*. He wouldn't notch *this* in a million years! No, however much sensitivity and open-mindedness has entered her life lately, she cannot trust a *Thad*—which is to say he was just the kind of challenge she needed to stay on top of her game.

—Miss Mabuse?

—Yes, Brother Thad. It is I, Josephine.

—Good morning. It is good to meet you. Oh, oh yeah. . .*Josephine*.

—Well, I am glad to hear you think so, Brother Thad.

When she puts her hands on her hips to appraise him her purse swings out wide, slugs him in the gut, and causes him to quietly say 'oof.'

—Yes, Miss— Yes, Josephine, truly. I look forward to driving you today.

—Well, off we go then, Brother Thad, oui?

—Yes. . .er. . .oui.

No one has seen the baby yet. Not even Warren can get inside. He had only learned from Sid (talking through a crack in the door) that it was a girl, her name was Flora, and that she has some kind of immunological disorder which requires a quarantine for the time being. Warren has spread the word and said that if you want to send gifts or casseroles you should bring them to Nine and he will drop them off. . .*They need their space now, people.*

Belladonna knows zilch about immunological disorders but sees no reason why the mother also needs to remain quarantined. Besides, how bad could things be when that once-so-hangdog little puppy Sid was prancing around The Hive giving breathless updates on the little bugger to anyone who'd listen? No, this was not the father of some catastrophe. This was an emboldened man backslapping and glad handing around like a new member of some prestigious fraternity. But just in case things were worse than he let on Belladonna was prepared to be there for Ronette in her time of need.

You see, the night after Belladonna had made that crude remark about the blood test and received that forgiving, almost benedictional kiss from Ronette, she had dumped her drawerful of self-help brochures onto the dining room table, desperately rifled through them looking for some last ditch regimen to save her from herself, and chosen a barebones mimeo issued by something called *The Radical Love Network*. During the next few days she had recited her many deficits to their operators and listened to their terse, sometimes angry voices tell her how common her complaints were. The solutions, they said, were radically obvious. . .*We are all hopeless devils. . .Love others' for their bad behavior but despise your own. . .Fail frequently, succeed occasionally, try unconditionally. . .Embrace neutral outcomes. . .Remember, there is not a single thing you necessarily deserve. . .The only love that matters is the kind that you give away. . .So just get over* *yourself. . .Once you accept this you will be ready to begin practicing Radical Love. . .*Being told she was suffering from a shockingly conventional disorder. . .*rampaging solipsism. . .* was just the sort of jarringly humiliating revelation she had been looking for. Suddenly she was just as pathetic as everyone else. She was hooked. She called their hotline ten, fifteen times a day. Then, deciding to up the ante, and calling in as a certain Josephine Larochefoucald, she confessed to things which she may as well be guilty of. . .*I was a lady of ill repute down south. . .killed one of my madams. . .put a newborn baby in a basket and left her in front of the nearest Catholic church* . . .Yes, she came clean in code like this half-hoping her new friends would tell her she was truly hopeless. But they only had more good advice for her. . .*Get over yourself, Josephine* . . .*You're boring us. . .Aren't you bored with you . . .Grant acceptance to others, Josephine, don't ask for it for yourself* . . .*Think about out how flawed and vulnerable everyone else is for a change. . .Remember, very little separates your evil from others' silence. . .And isn't this really Belladonna?. . .* And, finally, after candidly unburdening herself as Belladonna of the most revolting flashes of her untamable mind she thought she might actually cry when the Radical Love counselor told her. . .*You have finally freed yourself of your past, Belladonna. . .Congratulations. . .It is time for you to write The List. . .These are all the things you want for yourself which also benefit others. . .Don't call us back until you have begun living by The List. . .Then maybe we can talk about your future and your place in The Radical Love Network. . .* She immediately called a taxi, shoved her leather dresses in a suitcase, bashed down the stairs so hard the candelabra was swaying when she charged across the dining room, and blundered up the rain-strewn stairs to the street without once thinking she needed to use her walker. Once installed in the bridal suite, she ordered seven vases of red roses (each with it's own inspirational Radical Love message written on the card) and retired to a heart-shaped bathtub with a bottle of champagne and a Gideon bible for a notebook.

The next morning she put La Petite Manse on the market. An estate sale would empty it of everything but grand muh-Ma's 4-poster and muh-Ma's vanity. Yes, she was finally putting her ducks in a row for a Big Push of some kind. Her new hotline family would help her turn The List into a Manual of Living. Deep into the night she scribbled in *Psalms* and soaked. Far down The List, between *32. Burn that fucking house down* and *34. Adopt a parakeet* she had written *33. Find a true friend*. Then a few nights later, copying from a 12-step pamphlet some sarcastic bellboy must have slid under the door, she had written *64. Make amends*. She then thought of Ronette and how she might check off all the entries relating to loneliness, friendship, radical love, and who knows how many the hell else more.

But this morning's optimism is waning. The late autumn rains are battering the roof of the limo and her head aches from the bottomless mimosa. She lowers her window and listens to the rush of interstate traffic thinking it may as well be a cresting river—so relentless these rains, so flimsy the pebbly barrier. And the port air which should have been cleansed by these downpours has a sooty-sour stench. And just look at these sad little homes, the treeless lots, the crumbling sidewalks. How much radical love would it take to rehabilitate such wretchedness? She lowers the tinted divider to pose these questions to Thad, loses her courage, visually dandles his depressingly tanned neck and curly titan's locks and becomes melancholic. Did she have the stamina for much more of this? Why respect Ronette's boundaries if it meant delaying sisterly love? O god she missed the sweet lassitude which stole over her when she practiced being humane with her brothers and sisters at The Brood. A week away and she was already hungry for that sweet stuff, i.e. putting others' cares first, asking after their children, and loving everyone unconditionally. And The Membership were no longer so skeptical in their after-aspects. Yes, she was really beginning to blend in. But with each passing moment spent trapped inside this limo with her mounting melancholia and alcoholic chemistry she gradually slides into the kind of moral boredom which encourages hypothetical thinking and all that pointless philosophy which obscures our more straightforward selves. Why had she chosen Ronette for friendship? Was it because she understands how much effort Ronette puts into not being just as awful a person as Belladonna? Yes, she is probably just as plagued by her Outer Rightness as Belladonna is her Inner Wrongness. O god the poor woman needed to *get over herself*! Everyone remembers how the Old Ronette ran roughshod over this town—tromped on feelings, lied, abandoned, disappointed. That record doesn't just *disappear*. But suddenly here we are not five years later and she's supposed to add motherhood to the act?! O god she feels so sorry for her. Just think of the effort required to maintain such a twofold lie. Yes, the sooner Belladonna positions her radically imperfect self in front of Ronette's radically im-perfect self the sooner they can start forgiving themselves by loving each other unreservedly.

      —Thad? Oh Brother Thad?

      —Yes, Josephine?

      —I need you to do something for me.

      —Alright.

      —Park further down the block.

Thad Wallendorf has no scruples about having few scruples and is a good fit Co-op-wise for driving their diesel limo. He is cheerful, polite, and looks pretty damn sharp in his for-mal blacks and that is more than enough to give the impress-ion of scruples or whatever lesser discipline is required to not peer through the divider or leave his com open or score over many bottles of *gratis* champy. Plus, the tips these suckers give are righteous, man! If the city's well-intentioned elite want to get blitzo and irresponsibly partyish on his watch it's no skin off his college-debt enslaved ass.

      But when this nasty ole dog asked him to spy into the bungalow. . .*Unfortunately, Brother Thad, I am not over-fond of getting wet. . .My complexion, you see. . .*he wondered if he was discovering a new scruple. I mean spying? Objectively wrong, man. But. . .um . . .hmm. . .if you spy well. . .that is if you don't get caught. . .the human trespass element could be confined to his retinal linkups. . .and if he liked the people he spied on he would tell this devious broad less than she needed to know or just plain lie. . .anything to indirectly defend the interests of the victims he was already developing a soft spot for. Besides, are you really harming someone if they don't know they are being harmed? Yeah, man, this was kosher. He'd be furtive. Freaking *slick*. He was even dressed for the part. So yeah, totally, over the low wall of that diminishing scruple Thad was espying some gen-u-ine on-the-job excite-ment here. And the woofer had promised a serious bonus, too.

      —If they see you just make a run for it. The woman is ill and the man is probably pacifistic.

Well, Thad Wallendorf had been a bit of an athlete himself not too long ago so a hundred yard dash back to the limo? Pfft, he liked his chances. But there wouldn't be trouble. The woofer had done her groundwork. Or more likely she had had another driver do the groundwork for her. She said the place only had five windows. Thad started in back. The first room was cake because it was papered over. Next an empty bathroom. Whoops, he missed the kitchen. Hard to see through the opening. A tidal wave of dishes and bottles and produce and toys and books. The walls and the window papered over with pages from books. Artsy cats, Thadder's thinking. That's cool. Next a sort of alcove. A tall dude on the floor doing sit-ups and yeah there's some cord in the arms and legs but little in the way of muscular *bulk*. Not like the Thadder. Naw, he could take that dude easy. Anyway, nothing much was going on in there so don't sweat this, Thadder, keep hustling. So you'll be wet all afternoon, maybe catch cold. Big deal. You've got Co-op health and get homeopathic discounts with this gig. Concentrate on the bonus you're scoring here. I mean the howler was a ben-E-*factress*. So let's go. Around the side at the last window he does a quick glance-and-hide like how the cops do around corners on television but his retinal linkups are confused by what they are transmitting. It was like a rhino had rampaged through a storage unit in there, man. Piles. Mounds. Towers. Junk. Art? The window was dingy and birdshat so Thad had better look again. Yeah, man, just some strangely organized mess going on. Bike parts. Clothing. Baby gear. Tarps. Mannequin limbs everywhere. And oh shit a woman lying on a sofa made of phonebooks (?! Whoa.) Yeah, that is one artsy garbage dump in there, man. And it looks like maybe the place is *getting* to the chick. She is fetal and red-faced and clutching a sack of flour. And there's some intense classical music making the window vibrate a little. Some serious cats in there, Thad is thinking. Oh, here comes the dudeski. Careful now, Thadder. Lessee here. Hmm. Dude looks nervous. . .no. . .concerned. . .yeah. . .dude looks *muy* concerned. . .glances at the chick like someone's died. . .a pathetic looking couple on hard times seems he's thinking. Shit, Thad'd like to light a candle for them or something. And here that bitch in the limo had him spying on them? Shit, Thadder's outta here.

—So. . .Brother Thad. . .my goodness. . .so brave. . . so. . .*effective*. Bold, Brother Thad, *très-très* bold. Just too-too.

Jesus, the bitch is such a bitch you can't tell how far in the bag she is.

—And potent. *Oui,* just teeming with potency.

—Thank you, Josephine.

—So here is what I need to know, Thad. Are you ready?

—Yes, ma'am. Oh—

—I'm going to make this very simple.

—Yes. Thank you, Josephine.

—Now, based on what you saw and in your undoubtedly quite worldly opinion. . .

—Yes ma'am?

—The man. . .in one word. . .how would you describe his mood?

—Happy, Josephine.

—Hmm. Well, he's a simple person after all.

—He was humming to classical music.

—Are you fibbing to me, Brother Thad?

—No ma'am. It was an orchestra. I'm sure.

—Alright. Anyway. . .now. . .the woman.

—Happy, ma'am.

—Really?

—Very happy. She was baking cookies. Oatmeal raisin, I think.

—Of course. The Wundermartyr. Pathetic. . .tragic. How she must be suffering.

—Ma'am?

—Well, alright, how did the baby look? My little niece. Was she hooked up to something?

—Baby ma'am?

—Yes, Brother Thad, baby. Wasn't there a crib or something?

Thad has no idea which way to go here. He had wanted to provide her with the opposite of what he saw, defend the helpless suckers in that crumbling bungalow from a woman who seemed to have it in for them. But since she seemed to care for this niece of hers could he bring himself to say the child looked unwell? That was bad shit, man. Like beyond scruple. Like some serious jinx stuff. What if he wanted one of the little stinkers one day? Imagine if some scrupleless jerk like him laid down the jinx by foisting imaginary bad health on Thad Jr.? No way, man. But shit. . . there was no baby in there. . .no crib. . .no baby hammock or whatever. . .nothing. Thad had looked carefully, dug on their art, and scoped the place thorough-like. Jesus, the lady was probably trying to entrap him and would withhold his bonus out of some bitch scruple. Hell no, man. *Hell* no.

    —No baby, ma'am. No crib. Nothing like that. I'm positive. I saw everything.

    The woofer was suddenly far less in the bag.

    —I. . .oh no. Thad? Oh *no*. The baby isn't there?

    —There is no baby inside, Josephine.

    —O god she's probably been taken away. . .is off in some. . .some *ward* somewhere?

    —I wouldn't be able to say, Ma'am.

    —She might be dying or. . .or incredibly deformed.

    —I'm sorry, ma'am.

    —All this time they've been lying about how bad it is.

    —I wouldn't know, ma'am.

    —And it's all my fault, Thad! I joked about the blood test!

    —Uh, no ma'am. No, uh. . .

    —Yes, Brother Thad, yes! I cursed the child with my monstrousness.

    —I. . .

    —It's all my fault, Brother Thad! All mine!

    —I. . .I'm sorry, ma'am.

    —O god what have I done to those poor people!

11.

Aisle 5 at the _____. Bottom shelf. Generic diapers. Sid stares blankly into the pastels and wrinkling plastic, whips his ponytail to the side, shakes his head, laughs, and feels certain there is nothing transformative about diapers or shit or the ideation of shit and that any product in this aisle which would attempt to persuade him otherwise was full of it. No, the high walls of this narrow, paddy-soft hall washed in sallow halogens is only designed to trap the visitor in layer-upon-layer of its numb-dumb, semi-absorbent sheathing. However jubilant the infants on the packaging, however placidly gay their mothers, the implied activity will only bring them closer together in the most rudimentary physical way.

Ronette would disagree though. She thinks that by streaming goo down Flora's baby clothes to simulate feeding and wrapping Flora in generic juniors to capture the hypothetical result she is caring for their daughter in this like bioelemental way which will somehow tighten the mother-daughter bond. Sid had tried to feel what she felt, took his turns changing her, looked deep down into himself while he made the folds and occasionally felt a pang or two of nurturing but usually wound up feeling bored and ridiculous. He loves his daughter, okay, but lacks the key integer which allows Ronette to be moved by placidly swapping out pristine diaper after pristine diaper. And when he had begged off diaper duty, she had leapt at him, actually *leapt* at him, seemed ready to claw his face, opened her mouth to yell, and then slumped in on herself looking tragic. That had been the beginning of this bizarre snotty phase. Instead of yelling or moping she now met herself somewhere in the middle by nervously asking if he had done this or that, would he make sure of X, do a better job on Y, consider that Z might occur if he didn't attend to X and Y just so. He whips his ponytail to the side again, chokes it in his hand and re-tightens the rubber band. Man, it was like he could hear her chastising him from 40 blocks away, her once rich alto gone all stringy and nasal, haunting him from the supermarket p.a., rising and falling in this hectoring under-chide between the sales alerts. It's as though she's more concerned about what he can *accomplish* for the family than what he can *share*. And even if he knows Ronette better than that, loves her deeply even as she becomes increasingly unfamiliar, he is wondering if his newfound confidence will be equal to whatever the next phase brings. It's so much easier playing father at The Hive where he is actually digging hanging out with the brother and sister parents, practicing being the brave new parent, playing spokesperson, reiterating the family themes and lying more and more comfortably as he glances at Ronette's twisted rear wheel hanging on the wall next to Warren's old handlebars. . .*Oh Ronette is doing great. . .And Flora is fine, just fine. . .We just need to keep our girls away from bad germs a while longer. . . No, the prognosis is excellent. . .Ha! I'm thinking we'll have her on a trike far ahead of schedule, yeah. . .Oh, yeah, we* *brought a stationary up from the basement. . .We're shooting for the Spring Invitational. . .Nah, sleeping great. . .Yeah, her temperament is totally mellow. . .She hardly cries at all. . .Oh no, the doctor said that doesn't necessarily mean anything. . . Got it from her mother probably. . .Oh, no. Thank you, though. . .No, please, we're good. . .Everyone has been so generous already. . .*And in between the lies he carves out space to honestly describe how when he holds Flora sometimes he feels this like whole new version of seamlessness, a kind of *nowness* which has him more connected to the moment, more attuned to the world which his daughter has been born into. And his brothers and sisters will smile knowingly and touch him, provide him with these unprecedented sensations of support and belonging which have him returning whenever he can, even wandering upstairs hoping to bump into someone who hasn't congratulated him yet.

Riding home he would feel optimistic. . .*Okay, tonight's the night we start turning this thing around. . .*Then he would barge into the kitchen, try to hug and kiss Ronette through her winces and dodges or before her anxious eyes could start ticking through the surrounds of invisible text, pecking the air with silent conjectures as they now do, wielding these anthro-ethno-socio-psycho-whatever textbooks Exene was always bringing her from the library, firing out stats and folkways as though this was her new version of loving, rifling through the notebooks she fills with increasingly ominous clinical observations. . .*Child not obviating. . . no affect. . .zero emoting. . .Mother instigates Reflex-Response Scenario 1. Wheee!-Boo! Abbreviated Wheee!- Boo!. . .no response. . .Mother (crying) emotes with rattle in front of child . . .no mirroring affect in child. . .Mother spins round thrice while chanting incantation sequence. . .no mirroring affect in child. . .Mother leaves test site. . .suddenly returns initiating fright scenario. . .peek a Boo! x 3. . .no affect. . .Mother experiencing diminished play-pleasure response. . .Child appetite unchanged. . .*having concluded apparently that their daughter had been born with additional limitations beyond those of a somewhat charred and torn sack of wheat flour. And before he could object she would shove a rattle in his hand and tell him to shake it a certain number of times while she stared deep into the sack and took notes, Sid waiting until the end of another disappointing experiment to tell Ronette she just needed to be patient, allow their relationship to evolve naturally instead of trying to coerce Flora into some preferable behavior, that while, yes, it hurts, really hurts sometimes to not be able to *directly* relate to their daughter they—Sid and Ronette—could at least relate to each other *through* Flora, and this was a pretty nice thing if Ronette stopped to think about it for a sec. Then Ronette would broadly agree in a purely intellectual way, promise to mock up some three-way communication exercises but never follow through because she was too busy mocking up two-ways.

Sid didn't want to think about Flora's limitations. If he started feeling disappointed in her where would it end? She would never be perfect and he accepted that. And if his daughter was never anything more than a five-pound sack of wheat flour then there wasn't anything intrinsically 'good' or 'bad' about that. Desiring more would be tantamount to saying she wasn't good enough. And that would only lead to doubts about his priorities. So vehemently does he feel this way that sometimes when he is bonding with his brother and sister parents at The Hive he finds himself ranting about the fictional doctor Flora was seeing. . .*with his gauges and ranges and standards*. . .and saying how frustrating it was to go by. . .*someone else's ideas of 'normal'*. . .There had also been the confusing afternoon when Virgil had visited the bungalow for the first time since The Birth. Sid had gone on a tirade about how. . .*society felt threatened by the 'it' in Flora because she existed on separate terms*. . .*mysterious terms, man*. . .and would have continued if Virgil hadn't shown how irrelevant all that was by gently hefting Flora over his shoulder and smiling like a proud uncle. God, Sid was so grateful he hadn't had the slightest bit of wiseacre going, sounded incredibly serious in fact as he tip-toed across the room to put Flora back into her nighty-night box. . .*Next time, your Aunt X and I will bring your cousin Alma*. . .*She can't wait to meet you*. . .then thrown an arm over Sid's shoulder and smiled. . .*I'm real proud of you, dude*. . .*I think she's beautiful*. . .*Who'd a thunk it, huh? Here we are. Uncles and Fathers*. . .In reply Sid had hunched over like he had been punched in the gut, grasped Virgil by the shirt, glanced at the kitchen, started to cry, then whispered between gasps that sometimes all the beautiful ruthlessness of parenthood he had preached to Ronette about? How transformed everyone was telling him he looked? This supposed New Confidence he was demonstrating? Well, shit, Virge, it all felt like anger in disguise sometimes. Like just because he was all corded out and cathartically slaying dudes at Velodrome practice sessions didn't mean he wasn't also strung out from irregular sleep what with having to set an alarm to go off every two hours so they can take turns soothing Flora who even if she might not be crying would still require the same reassurances any other being with an underdeveloped intellect and a near-total ignorance of context and milieu would when waking up in an unfathomable world—The very thought of their daughter. . . *and I'm dead serious about this, Virge. . .*staring at the ceiling waiting for someone to come pick her up totally tearing his heart out. The upshot being he is not particularly enjoying the *practice* of fatherhood but loves talking about it in the abstract, describing the nowness he feels to the other parents even if he seldom feels it when he is actually *with* his daughter. . .*And it kills me to say this, Virge. . .like completely murders me. . .*but sometimes he *does* find his daughter's limitations wretched, to the extent that he had once dug his fingers deep into her midsection hoping to get a peep out of her. . . *What kind of monster does something like that, man?. . .*then tried to bribe her into forgiving him by tickling her hips and blowing in her face even while he got the strong impression that she was just perceptive enough to know that her father was a bit of a freaking cad, unable as he often was to hustle up little more than resentment for this child who had robbed him of his *de facto* wife, the Ronette who would massage her championship hamstrings on the floor while he played music for her, the still very distinct loss of that woman and their life together sometimes making him want to acquire an actual human child, a being who would *react* to him for once, even if just to spit up on or non-hypothetically shit in his lap, *anything*, a single clue they were something more than a *de jure* daughter and *de jure* father. And when he was finished Virgil had smiled and said. . .*It's all totally normal, dude. . .Having a baby is confusing stuff. . .You'll never be perfect. . .You'll wonder if you're cut out for it or not. . .But you'll do the best you can with whatever you've got.*

Sid swings into the kitchen and slams into a wall of humidity. Baby bottles click and tumble in a double boiler. Ronette, bent over a deep green bowl, repeatedly pushing her glasses back up her nose, sweating through a pink t-shirt with a black ∞ on the stomach, awkwardly stirs an orange-pink sludge with her right hand while trying to squeeze a rubber ducky in her left armpit. Her left arm is wrapped in bandages from elbow to wrist and she wears a cycling glove to protect the hand.

Suspended above the counter in a matching shirt, bobbing and swaying and twisting in a pair of denim overalls hanging from the knob on the cabinet door, squeaking loudly in her oversized diapers, Flora bounces off her mother's shoulder and soars away. She has a fresh white bandage to cover the burn on her side but the packing tape around her midsection has begun to yellow. Dancing around and away from Ronette, she resembles a ragtag speed bag dodging an unorthodox boxer.

—Wheee! Is that fun, bay-bay?

Ronette follows the swaying Flora with a silver spoonful of goo and offers it to the bellowing bull.

—Eat-eat, bay-bay.

When nothing happens Ronette frowningly appraises Flora. Then, as though shocked by current, she whips to the counter, rips open a textbook, tears through the pages, scans feverishly, marks the book with the spoonful of goo, whips back to Flora, squeezes the rubber ducky in her armpit three times while re-extending the spoon, lets the ducky fall honk-ingly to the floor, picks up a Buddhist prayer wheel, spins it between her hip and her bad arm, winces, silently chants something, lets the prayer wheel clatter to the floor, takes the spoon out of the book, and once again offers it to the part of the bull not covered by the bandage.

Nothing.

Frowning more severely now, kneading one of her ballooned breasts, she bends to join the visual plane occupied by the spoon and makes a few soft sounds of encouragement.

—Please, Flora? Like I taught you, okay? One-two-three: *eat*.

The muscles shift in her pale neck as she changes the angle of the spoon. Her body is torqued and shaking slightly. Slats of sweat-wet hair stick to her forehead and neck. There is a damp spot on her shirt over either nipple. Long gone are her tanned muscles, the way her swaying braids framed the stray wisps of spun gold on her nape, the equipoise she brought to bare on the most physically awkward of tasks. Sid's old sweet-heart has been replaced by this cross-purposed woman fluttering over their daughter, desperately trying to anticipate her mysterious needs, frantically spinning this disheveled web of care over their impassive child.

—Please, bay-bay? Num-num-num?

Sid wants to gently massage away this stranger to isolate the Core Ronette, save her from the cloud of drudgery and whacko regimentation she is lost inside or addicted to and thinks this should not be so difficult, a matter of imagination really, a more flexible outlook, a confident phrase or two to rouse her from this bizarro maternal scene and bring even a little of her back to him, save them both from the sickeningly hot seep of the kitchen's atmosphere, the taunts of the peeling textbook wallpaper, all this junk and muck which has absolutely no subtext of old freedoms anymore, the sum dreary power of this enclosure making him sleepily nostalgic until Ronette startles him by singing a few lines from of an old song of theirs to Flora while dangling the goo-smeared spoon at the bull and kneading her breast.

> *All I'm saying, pretty bay-bay,*
> *La-la-luv ya, don't mean may-bay*

It's a good lyric for teaching phonemes but her alto cracks and the notes all run together. Sid wonders how so much could have gotten away from them so quickly.

> *All I'm saying, pretty Flo-Flo,*
> *La-la-luv ya, don't mean may-bay*

When Ronette dabs the bull's lips with the spoon two strings of goo distend from the ∞ to her diapers.

—You say you want the *wooden* spoon, bay-bay?

Sid shoves four wet plastic grocery bags through the clutter on the counter.

—Oh!

Ronette lunges to contain the mysterious order Sid has disturbed. But since her bandaged left arm is little better than a club, she fails to stop a baster from poking Flora in the rear.

—Oh god!

Ronette smacks the baster clear and it goes clattering to the floor. No damage has been done.

—She's fine, Ron.

Ronette abstracts into the floes on the counter and is probably thinking this latest little calamity is due to her lack of foresight. As with Velodrome and then The Birth and all the little accidents which have occurred since, she is probably blaming herself for failing to create some methodology by which she might have anticipated her carelessness. An old pathetic part of Sid would prefer if she blamed him instead. That way he could go back to relentlessly doubting himself and they would have it common. But watching her stand there sadly letting the goo drip to the floor he decides this whole shebang is ridiculously melodramatic. This latest small incident doesn't have to *mean* a goddamn thing. Yes, he is like so done with all the *sturm und drang* shit. He must remain strong for her.

—Okay, Ron, what can I do for you here?

He takes the spoon from her while she scans the counter looking defeated.

—The salad spoon. . .in that book. . .the one under *Forgotten Societies*.

—Yeah. Sure. Here you go.

Ronette scoops a huge pile of goo out of the bowl and apathetically offers her daughter a portion an adult would have a hard time getting their mouth around. Flora, no longer swaying so wildly, calmly does nothing. Ronette sighs, puts the spoon back in the bowl, and scribbles something in the notebook.

—Not hungry today, huh?

Sid squeezes his ponytail out into the sink, makes a daffy face at the bull, gives the sack a tickle, puts his elbows on the counter, rests his head in his hands, and waits for Ronette to answer him.

—No, not really. Still won't breastfeed either.

Sid glances at the 'Time' and 'Amount' columns in the notebook then tries not to stare at the wet, burdened breasts on Ronette's otherwise shrinking body.

—You should pump again, Ron.

He shoves around the objects on the counter, notices a fortune cookie, cracks it open, starts chewing, silently reads the fortune. . .*A grown woman should never jump rope. . .*

finds a purple sippy cup, sniffs it, takes four gulpy pulls, swallows hard, and belches as loud as he can. Maybe she would consider laughing at him.

—No. I mean yes. Maybe later. Before nighty-night.

He takes the wooden spoon out of the bowl, offers it to the bull who, in his inveterate bellowing, could appear enthusiastic or even desperate for its payload.

—Good. Sounds good.

After an acceptable interval, one Sid imagines to be adequate to feed a sack of flour if a sack of flour were inclined to eat (even if doing so seems counterintuitive, if not pretty disgusting, even cannibalistic) he tells himself there is nothing so hard about doing just as Ronette wishes and continuing to offer their daughter this spoonful of goo. This was standard father fare and he got a nice little pang out of providing his daughter with an option, even one as straight-forward as eating or not eating. A nice family moment might be constructed around such a beginning.

—Where are the diapers?

But then Sid sighs and thinks he cannot remember the last frivolous thing Ronette has said. What could be more burdensome to someone trying to maintain forward momentum in his life than the constant tug-pull of responsibilities. . . constant freaking responsibilities. . .*I mean is that what I signed up for?. . .Is this the best that can be done?. . .*And what is more destructive to someone trying to maintain perspective than a freaking rhetorical question?

—They didn't have the ones you wanted, Ron, okay?

He turns his back and begins to unload the produce and powders which will be turned into intricate forms of nutritious gruel.

—So which did you get? I don't see any.

—I didn't get any, Ron.

It shouldn't be so hard to not yell at the mother of his child but maybe that's why he wants to yell so badly.

—It's a waste of the food stamps. There was barely enough for the rest of the stuff.

Ronette looks worryingly into her notebook.

—She's been off-schedule for two days. We need to get her fresh diapers.

—A sack of flour doesn't need fresh diapers, Ron.

She closes her eyes and starts doing one of her whacked out chants instead of balling him out like he wishes she would.

—Om fa ko lo ko lo fa, do so ni do. . .

—Ron. . .

—Si no to lo, fo no ko sah so. . .

Sid stares at the wooden spoon. It is part of a set they received as a gift from the baby shower neither of them had attended. He hadn't named it Woody II because of the old regime connotations. Still, in weak moments, he wonders if this spoon, through some inexplicable sympathy, might understand him as well as Woody I did.

—Can't we just pretend Flora doesn't like diapers?

—Pretend?!

Ronette flares then quickly remembers herself. Only a bad mother would shout in front of her child.

—There is no *pretending* in parenthood.

—Isn't there, though, Ron? I mean for us? At least just a little?

She scowls into his neck. At least he can feel her warm breath.

—I don't want to go over this again.

He sees her mouth caked with goo from all the demos she has given Flora. At least she has eaten something today. She might forget to if he didn't remind her. It's the same with sleep. But helping her care for herself isn't what she is looking for. Likewise, all his newfound clarity is useless when he doesn't know who she is from moment to moment.

—I just don't think she is ever going to have a b.m., Ron.

—Well, then you can think that they keep her butt warm.

And since he has no choice but to talk to her on her little understood and ever-shifting terms he never knows if he is helping or hurting her.

—Ron, it's okay if this is more about you wanting to do it just because it makes you feel good.

Ronette turns her head, kneads a breast, stifles her anger, and speaks in a series of slumping sighs.

—Yes, doing what I think is necessary for our daughter *does* make me feel good. I'm sorry you don't feel the same way yet. Truly sorry.

Even if he were to leave her a sweet note like he used to she would probably pretend not to have found it.

—What I mean, Ron, is that's its totally fine. . .even kinda cute if you want to do the diapers thing. I'm just saying that maybe if we're going to be these. . .these like *uber-*imaginative parents. . .these. . .

When her body sags at his words he tells himself not to lose heart.

—. . .well couldn't we consider going with *cloth* diapers? I'll do all the washing.

She starts shuffling things around on the counter. Something has just ended but Sid is not sure what.

—It's a good idea, Ron. Yes?

—Om lo no ko no, ob fo toe lo—

—Ron?

—Yes. . .a good idea. Yes. Thank you.

Wanting to put this small conflict behind them Sid starts un-loading. But when he opens the cabinets to put away a sack of generic wheat flour Ronette turns on him angrily.

—That's not organic flour!

—Flora's generic. It makes sense to do the repairs with generic.

She returns to the bowl, stirs with her bad hand and buckles in pain. Sid grabs her by the waist but she wrenches free.

—Just because she was born generic doesn't mean she can't be exposed to better things!

He stares at her helplessly, thinks he hears her after-aspects collide and ricochet around the jungly kitchen as the water in the double boiler begins to bubble over.

—We're a generic household, Ron. And it's half the price.

Thankful for a task to temporarily remove himself from the mounting conflict, he turns the stove off. But Ronette's hot breath pursues him.

—Why can't you put your daughter first for once?

He had once staked her tent to keep her grounded but now she was kiting a million miles above the bungalow with Flora at the spool. He doesn't blame either of them for these arguments. Raising a family is a collective learning process, after all. But if no one is to blame then how will any of them learn what *not* to do in the future?

—When will you start making sacrifices for this family, Sid? Huh?

Merely living under the guidance of one phase after another like this feels like treading water. And an accumulation of days together doesn't compile some laudatory family statistic. No, nothing *useful* is occurring here. Nothing *vital*. He is willing to make sacrifices for his family but not at the cost of seeing Ronette recede further into the stucco clouds.

—Well?

So, following an instinct, he stands next to her and reaches around her waist to start tucking in her shirt. She startles, continues scowling at him, but lets him continue. They both remember when he used to help her in and out of the outfits she wore in the last trimester, tenderly pushing the foam rubber down her shirt or pulling it out, how this ritual seemed like a small re-insemination and often had sexual consequences. Trying to channel that intimacy now, wanting just a shred of sweetheart back, he gently removes Flora from the overalls then pulls out the collar of Ronette's shirt. She is confused at first but then remembers to lean back so he can slide Flora inside to nestle against her mother's belly. In an extra touch, Sid rips a piece of paper out of a notebook, writes. . .*Dada loves Mama.* . ., shows it to her, and tosses the note inside.

—Why don't you two have a nap. I'll finish up in here.

Ronette wants to resist but smiles bashfully, relents, nods, then carefully pushes through the door. As he listens to her kicking a path through The Big Room, Sid feels his confidence come surging back. Yes, this could be the day they really turn this thing around.

An hour later Sid tiptoes through and around the big room's many obstacles, kneels over Ronette lying on the sofa with Flora still inside her shirt, and carefully nuzzles his head into her neck. Catnaps have become Ronette's one form of true rest. Her body simply exhausts, dies, does not dream, then refreshes somewhat. When she wakes up Sid steals kisses and whispers something he thinks she would like to hear.

—Ronette, we're in this together.

She searches for her glasses with her bandaged hand but he holds her head fast and gathers her hair together. For a wonderful moment Ronette's clarifying eyes enter his. She squints to focus and tries to show him that she sees him there. Then, after a self-conscious look towards the window and a brief survey of the stucco, she shakes her head in apology and tries to free herself from his arms to go attend to something in the kitchen. But Sid takes one of her hands, guides it to the lump on her belly, stares deep into her eyes, and tries by force of intellectual and emotional will to help Ronette and Flora understand that Mama and Dada may argue sometimes but this was bound to happen during the sometimes stressful undertaking of raising a child.

—Tell me what you are going through, Ron. Tell me how I can help.

—I'm trying to get through to my daughter but nothing works.

—You're trying too hard. Your expectations are too high. Give things time.

—Nothing pleases her. She isn't making any progress.

—Ron.

—She cries all the time. Sometimes I can quiet her down but the same thing never works twice. She seems miserable.

—Ronette.

—And I keep dropping her. I tell her I'm sorry but she doesn't believe me.

—She's a sack of wheat flour, Ronette.

—*Ob no fo go to so lo kay. No joe toe cay cay dope*—

—You gotta cut yourself some slack here.

—And once you come home she pretends to be this brave little girl for Dada.

—I now Ron. . .

—Do you know what it feels like to have no idea where your child is coming from?! To constantly feel rejected by her?!

—I do, Ron. I feel the same way sometimes. I—

—*Fo ko no lo. Cho bo ko lo mani.* I won't lift the quarantine until I know how to be a proper mother.

—Now wait—

—I'll work from home. We can have a phone installed.

Ronette abstracts past him. The future lays itself out in shadowy stucco code.

—I'll home school her.

—Ron, listen to me! We just need to get you back to some of your general tendencies. Get you back on your rig, maybe. You're putting too much pressure on yourself.

—What good are general tendencies when my daughter isn't interested in her mother's *tits* yet?

—Ron, I—

—*Ob lo ko no so, go so fa toe ki nay. . .joe yo cah si fob. . .toe no lo ob kay. . .*

12.

Propped against the inside wall of the nighty-night box is a note written in a strange hand. The words are scrawled in black crayon on a page of Latin text torn from the bedroom wall. Each thumb-sized letter is spiked with the starts and stops of someone pressing too hard on the paper. Sid can easily imagine the author squeezing the crayon in their fist and screwing their tongue up with concentration.

L E A V E
A L O N E

He laughs. This is so painfully apropos it has to be a joke, right? Maybe the author was shooting for irony. . .*deep dark irony.* . .and hopes to render them all a bunch of drool-mouthed simpletons capable only of primitive speech. Or maybe this is a genius move on their part, a bolt from the labyrinth, a psychic line thrown over the mote by the mino-taur, an admission of spousal neglect and a preliminary offer of apologetic hugs from whoever is offering.

But if this isn't a joke or a gesture there are a million ways to go with this and Sid isn't interested in stomaching any of them right now. These Saturday mornings when Ronette nestles Flora into her riding bag and Exene drives them to the library should be enough of a positive development to waylay the many hurtful interpretations he could drum up. Plus, Ronette was going through a relatively stable phase, a spacey one to be sure, making moony-eyed claims about 'talking' with Flora, but also talking to *him* more. . .*I think Flora responds better to music. . .Singing is best because it turns* *words into notes. . .Halves and wholes are best. . .Eighth and quarters make her giggle. . .But there must be silence in your soul before you sing. . .She won't listen unless you make room for her to join in. . .*Sharing the blah-blah-blah of whatever her ethnomusicology books were telling her was still better by a mile than her previous post-partum versions. . .*There are far worse things than some kooky note, Sidder. . .*Instead, he should concentrate on making the most of another lonely Saturday, busy himself so that the bungalow's reiterating silence doesn't ring in his ears quite as badly as it did last week.

Luckily, there is plenty to do. Today he is under orders to dust and then air the house out to help with Flora's allergies, prep her mash and poultices, swap out her nighty-night box, patch the latest hole in the ceiling, then somehow remove the staples from the shag and curbside it. No, there was no point in trying to make heads or tails of that. . . that. . . that *taunt* of a note. . .*No and hell no, man. . .Forward-thinking bros shouldn't harp on mysteries. . .*But since he is so unused to being alone and his mind has nothing else to occupy itself with, he can't help but think forward to the moment when Exene will drop Ronette and Flora off and he will have to do his level best not to resent them for apparently mocking his attempts to reach out to his daughter by singing in alternating whole and half notes, for meditating for five minutes prior to each of these ludicrous efforts, emptying himself of as much of his new, more preferable self as possible in hopes of communicating with a sack of wheat flour only so she can remain resolutely mum until her mother intercedes and embarks on one of their sing-song and, to Sid's untrained ears, one-sided conversations.

—So I'm not musical.

He pleads to the arms in the dresser.

—That's no reason to exclude me.

He crumbles the note up and throws it on the floor. Enough. There are leaks to attend to.

Before he begins he notices a small tear where the mold has eaten a crooked smile into the stucco. He smiles back. . .*Hello there, my friend. . .*Why should he fix this new ally just because he poses some minor threat to the shag? And why swap out a perfectly good shag which he has pretty strong feelings about? He and Ronette had *conceived* Flora on that shag, after all. If he curbsided it what would be next? His easy chair? The arms in the dresser? Their secret notes? No, Sid will not abandon these old friends, nor even a single object from the pre-baby regime. All this junk constitutes an archeological record of their abandoned general tendencies. He, Ronette, and this bungalow had once achieved a magical order and might do so again if they can just get out from under all this. . .this. . .*babyness* they are drowning in—Flora and her naptime in the mathematical center of the big room. . . *Shhhhh!*. . .Flora and her Wheee! time in the alcove, Flora and her physical therapy ('rolling over' 'sitting up and down' and 'walking'); this total systemic upheaval rendering the present chaotic and the recent past expendable. Maybe, Sid is thinking, if he could do some masterful redecoration job which balanced everyone's needs the magical order might reemerge. A baby bed by the front door. A Wheee! alcove with the bumper pool table he has always wanted. A Mama and Dada crash pad in the sitting room. Their rigs in the mathematical center as a shrine to their particular love story. But Ronette would probably find some flaw in the harmonics and Sid feels foolish and weak for falling for the nostalgia goad. Besides, didn't he used to think objects are as disposable as emotions?

    Leave Alone.

    Christ.

    He kicks through baby clothing, sends toys flying, finds some riding gear, rips it on, grabs his rig, whips the front door open before he can think up some reason not to, fires down the steps, jumps in the saddle, ratchets up his pace to compete with all the implied speed roaring on the other side of the rain-stained noise barrier and tells himself, no, *begs* himself not to linger on a final annoying detail coalescing back there in the bungalow, cranks himself up to a sprinter's pace, starts driving for the phantom finish line at the intersection with Evers where he will nose through the imaginary tape, bring the pace down, and realize that he has not been alone with Flora since the birth, not in the house or even in the same room. Not once.

During the next few days more notes appear in the nighty-night box. Slipped under the sack, laid over the midsection like a sheet, propped against the logo just beneath the bull's bellowing mouth, each strikes an increasingly desperate tone.

MA-MA GO-GO
MA-MA GO-GO

And the handwriting, though still childish, becomes incrementally more accomplished, even begins to resemble an adolescent form of penmanship.

DA-DA WHY-WHY
DA-DA WHY-WHY

But Sid does not dwell on their meaning because with each passing day Ronette returns from the wilderness. She stops being so nervous and distracted. Her staccato chanting is replaced by sweet soothing runs of syllables. . .*la lo la lo-lo toe foe. . .bah la toe moe fo si. . .ya-ya ya-ya yaaa, ya-ya ya-ya yaaaaaa*. . .She starts eating more, regularly uses her breast pump, regains her posture. She spends less time fussing over Flora and more time on the sofa reading. She even smiles over at Sid tinkering with his rig on the shag or hammering another board into the ceiling. And he smiles back hoping the long, silent periods which follow act as a hardening agent, securing their gains while paving the way for more. And when she speaks about her improving relationship with her daughter, it sounds as though a degree of maternal seamlessness has been achieved. . .*We are beginning to come to an understanding. . . It's a matter of keeping things simple on both sides. . .We can tell if the other is fibbing or grouchy or just not in the mood to talk so we agree to empty our minds before meeting in the middle. . .We don't necessarily have to 'say' anything once we're there. . .It's more about having the will to do so. . . Presence is the most eloquent type of speech sometimes. . .The key is not forcing anything on the other person. . .I occasionally find it useful to pretend we are strangers. . .*She could spout all the crypto-Buddhist mumbo jumbo she wanted as long as she did so in that increasingly sweet and earnest way of hers.

HELP DA-DA HELP DA-DA HELP DA-DA

Yes, he nods his head a lot and doesn't ask too many questions. . .*But don't get me wrong, sometimes there's*

145

nothing better than a nice silly song or a good long round of roughhouse. . .And Flora—relocated back to the alcove after a section of the ceiling broke through over the mathematical center—spends more time swinging from her indoor swing set or staring up into the Better Baby Brain Mobile and less time in the crook of Mama's arm. Thus situated, their family quietly devotes themselves to their evolving general tendencies, pausing only so Ronette can broach wonderfully practical matters. . .*You should cut down your delivery hours and spend more time training. . .I'm sure Warren would sponsor you. . .Maybe take Flora with you some time. . .It would be good for her to go back to Velodrome. . .She needs to get over her fear of the place. . . She's been doing great at the library . . .I know she can handle it. . .She's getting to be a big girl now. . .And soon Mama will be back at work and she'll have to become more independent. . .*And on the night when Ronette brings the stationary bicycle up from the basement and starts summoning her glistening sweat back, Sid becomes so uncontrollably happy that he has to hide in the kitchen until his trembling subsides. But he has no doubt that with each of her subsequent workouts he will become more accustomed to this disquieting joy, this unsettling good fortune.

The alarm is turned off. They are sleeping better. Ronette responds to his sexual advances, frequently initiates, sometimes aggressively, almost violently so. And as she becomes more accessible, even sweetly self-deprecating about her strange means of communication with their daughter. . . *We do what we can. . .There are misunderstandings on both ends. . .But good intentions go a long way. . .No one is perfect* . . .Sid feels nothing but gratitude for the seamlessness of the mother-daughter bond, the healing it has brought their family, and whatever mysterious role those notes still appearing in the nighty-night box might play.

MA-MA HURT-HURT
FLO-FLO OW-OW

And since some small variation or hiccup in their evolving rituals might ruin everything he manically maintains his habits, guards against saying or doing the one tiny thing which might ruin everything, and does whatever Ronette tells him to do. He approaches Flora with an open and non-chattery heart, meditates regularly, wades out into the mysterious middle where they might come to some sort of understanding of one another and sometimes fools himself into thinking he hears her talking to him in an adorable little alto.

MA-MA GA-GA
PA-PA STAY-STAY

Desperate to share his excitement, he tells his brothers and sisters at The Hive that mother and daughter would soon be making their first public appearance. . .*The doctor says they are both officially cleared to be around other people. . .We want to wait a bit until their strength is up but I promise it won't be too long now. . .*O but to co-tech his tricyclical life with his girls and only have one general tendency to worry about: Family Life. Man, Sid cannot wait. He just needs to keep getting everything right. Yes, he knows he can do this.

13.

—Wheeeeee!

Exene bends her knees, squeezes the plastic re-sealable bag with Flora inside and leaps towards the ceiling.

—Wheeeeee for Auntie!

It is early evening in late fall. An icy wind rattles the front door and rushes underneath to redistribute the big room's mold-spiked, hovering dust. Drafts snake around and through the remaining towers and tumble-downs, climb the drifts of baby gear, hug the jagged plains of tarps laid against the early snowmelt seeping from the attic, and recombine in the mathematical center to gale down the paths cleared to the kitchen, bathroom, bedroom, front door, sitting room and alcove. Into this howling, clashing respiration, spurred by some coincidence of gustwork in the central zone, scored by the phantasmagorically repetitive electronic organ cycle issuing from the rattling speakers, an abrupt breath ascends the alcove to ruffle the pads on Exene's red snowsuit. Ronette, bundled in blankets, her braided hair unmoved by the draft, sits on a pebble- and dust-covered tarp in the alcove watching Exene swoop Flora high into the spiraling air.

—Am I doing it right? Is she having fun? I'm trying to be gentle.

Ronette reaches up to take Flora.

—Totally, X. Here, I think she's cold, though. I'll do her favorite one then feed her.

Ronette lies on her back then throws Flora toward the ceiling. The sack of flour rotates once inside the plastic bag, hangs suspended for a moment, then drags them both down and into Ronette's waiting hands. On impact, the wet-heavy particulate which now coats the entire bungalow puffs sideways.

—She has always liked the rough stuff.

The anxiety of the first month appears to have ended. Exene sees a woman slowly but surely getting inside her motherhood. Watching the increasingly relaxed way she handles Flora, she is convinced Ronette has accepted both hers and Flora's limitations and decided to make the best of them.

—Wheee!

It was only natural that there had been an adjustment period. Hadn't it taken Exene nearly two years before she became comfortable with Alma? Sure, there was still some fragility there, a softer way of speaking and moving, but the old Ronette confidence was gradually taking hold. Anyway, a good mother should never think she has the whole thing down. Complacency only leads to disaster.

—Here, catch!

Exene startles, takes two quick steps towards the alcove window, blunders inside her snowsuit, gets tangled in the tarp, and lunges to trap the helicoptering bag against the naked mannequin at the last moment.

—Ronette?!

—She's fine, X. That's what the re-sealable is for. Otherwise, she'd squirm right out of your hands and go *ZOOM!*

As Ronette leans over to untangle her, Exene notices that Ronette's breasts do not press against her peasant dress as insistently as they did a few weeks ago. Also, her cheeks are fuller and have more color.

—Yeah, but I'm not a jock like you, Ron. If I had dropped her she might have exploded.

Exene hands the bag back and sits down next to the empty space on the tarp between them.

—Nah, I've reinforced her sack with more tape. That's stuff's like armor.

—Still, you could hurt her.

—Nothing too bad. Pain works differently for her. There's nothing personal about it. Here, we can check her scars during lunch.

Ronette opens the re-sealable bag and lays it against her knees. Nearly half of the sack is covered in packing tape and the bottom is covered by a pink wool hat with a large black ∞. The burn mark is now covered by a patch made from a folded page torn from an ethnomusicology textbook. Most of the ink on the bull's torso has been stripped away and the bottom half of the product title is illegible. Ronette carefully removes the tape from the patch.

—Oh yeah, she looks fine.

Ronette hunkers into her blankets, lowers the neck of her peasant dress, removes her breast, and presses her nipple to the part of the plastic bag covering the wound. Wind whips at the bag. A small wisp of flour escapes.

—And, oh my, bay-bay says she's *hungry*.

As she kneads her breast milk trickles out the nipple and slides down the bag. When she is done she sops it all up with the hem of her dress.

—I know it's crazy, Ron, but it looks like she's gained weight.

Exene looks at the empty space between them and feels a twinge in her nipple. Luckily, her daughter is too old for this. Maybe it would've been different if Alma had ever been an actual baby but breastfeeding grosses her mother out. She is content to simply witness this expression of the mother-daughter bond between her sister and niece. And the twinge actually feels rather pleasant.

—You two have come a long way, Ron. I know it's hard not knowing if your child can understand you or not. I'm definitely still not used to it.

—Meh, I dunno. . .

Ronette puts her breast back in her dress and begins to re-secure the patch over the bull.

—. . .sometimes I feel like I'm wasting my breath.

—Yeah, but a child still wants her mother's guidance. Alma gets nervous if I'm quiet for too long.

—For me, the more I tell her the less she listens. She may still be a baby but I think she's already rebelling.

—I dig. Alma always wants things on her own terms.

—Right. And since we have totally different needs I ask her to meet me in the middle. Usually she ignores me or pouts but sometimes she gives in and we reach a compromise I would never have thought up on my own.

Ronette removes Flora from the plastic bag and places her on the right side of the empty space between the two women. Exene unzips her snowsuit, holds it open, waits a moment, smiles at the left side, and zips herself back up. Both women consider their children for a moment.

—With Alma. . .I dunno. . .sometimes I think she needs to be told what to do. When I overwhelm her with options she sorta shuts down. I don't want to control her but I worry that she'll become lost if I don't.

—I dig, X. Maybe the trick is letting her do what she wants. If she winds up hurting herself then she can draw her own conclusions about how life works and you can be there to cheer her up with a round of Wheee!

—Sounds like a passive aggressive way of throwing her into the deep end to me.

Ronette laughs.

—Yeah, well, tough love is the only thing that seems to be working for us these days.

—Aw, you're doing great, Ron. You, too, Flora.

A sudden burst of wind fires around the room, enters an open gash over the mathematical center, whips around the attic, finds a seam in another un-patched crack above the alcove and widens it just enough to allow a pool of melt water to cascade down from the attic and onto the women and their children.

—Oh man.

When Ronette scoops up Flora she dislodges the patch and flour goes spurting out.

— *Shoot*. Shoot-shoot-shoot.

Ronette grabs at the flour on the tarp and tries to stick it back into Flora but the wound only widens and more flour pours out.

—Wrap her in your dress, Ron! Wrap her in your dress!

Exene lunges over Alma to gather Ronette's dress around Flora. A last plume shoots sideways and rushes for one of the tarp's many crevasses. Exene lunges again and makes a dam with her hands. But then a wide cataract opens above them. All the ungathered flour and particulate are swirled into mercury-like pools which quickly disperse to race down brief canyons before pouring over the sides in cloudy waterfalls. Exene watches in horror as Ronette starts to laugh hysterically.

—Ha-ha-ha! Oh, man. My poor baby. Heh. *Om la fa ca, om la toe no koe*, bay-bay. See X? Mama's a total klutz these days. *Om lo to fo so. Ob lo to no fo.* Ha-*ha!*

Exene laughs in relief, huddles in close with Ronette, and pours the flour she has collected into the swaddling of her skirt. Their faces are red and twisted with joy and tears.

—Looks like we need to do a store run tomorrow morning, Auntie X.

Ronette wipes her face and looks into her skirt with a mixture of chagrin and bemusement.

—Your niece is going to need another transfusion.

—Oh, yeah, definitely.

—Oh and something else.

Ronette leans in close to whisper.

—I think I need to arrange that other thing tomorrow, too.

—Wow. Okay. Sounds like a big day for your girl.

—Yes, definitely.

—Me and Alma will be glad to help in any way we can.

—Thanks, Sis. Oh, is Alma okay? I hope we didn't scare her.

They scan the alcove through their tears and the widening curtain of trickling water. Alma still isn't very good with sudden movement or loud noises but recovers more quickly than she used to. And since she likes playing hide-and-seek she will take the opportunity of this laughable little calamity to delve far into one of the big room's innumerable niches so the women can remain in each other's arms shouting out guesses of where she might be hidden. . .*Is Alma in the. . . . . .dresser?!. . .Is Alma behind the. . . . . .speakers?!. . .Is Alma in. . . . . .Flora's nighty-night box?!. . .*all while Warren stares through the sitting room window at the two women who he thinks have lost their babies, muffling his sobs as the snow silently feathers down around him.

o   o   o   o   o   o   o   o   o

As the Co-op limousine crunches across the snow-caked bridge then slowly banks down the exit ramp Belladonna studies the approaching enclave of snow-pocked bungalows crowded into the long stretch between the interstate and the east side's derelict port. Somewhere deep inside those incongruously sun-blasted flats toothed with regular little boxes and regular little lives is the mundane address of Belladonna Mabuse's final transformation. She hugs a paper bag with a squeeze toy and a bottle of champagne inside and cheerfully takes in a breath of the cold, sooty air. . . *Just be yourself. . . Let them know how sorry you are. . .Tell them you are here to help. . .*Yes, she is going to insist on being installed as Flora's mentor. . .*Flosie-Belle, Auntie-Belle's giving it to you straight here, ma petite. . .Ugly's the new beautiful. . .I'm proof you can see the other side. . .A little bit of radical love goes a long way. . .*She then experiences another one of those totally genuine little surges of empathy she has been having for her new protégée, the intensity of this nascent love having not diminished in the weeks since she had had Brother Thad spy on Sid and Ronette and she had drunkenly and too-too melodramatically taken the blame for the child's affliction. Whether the guilt-ridden penance which had followed was necessary or not, Belladonna had cleared some final hurdle in the process. Her nice-nice tendencies were not only emergent but beginning to hold sway. Yes, she could already see how this would play out. She would be the fawning aunt barging through Sid and Ronette's door shoving a bottle in their hands and advancing on the baby with moony-eyed love. Before long she would be taking her niece on excursions while Sid and Ronette patched up whatever scars this stressful period in their lives must have opened. There would be long afternoons of childish games and radical, though gentle love. Yes, caring for someone as helpless as Flora would be the stuff of an entirely new life scheme for Belladonna, the beginning of her full rehabilitation.

—I know about Flora. . .I mean with her challenges and all. *Oui,* I do.

Belladonna is talking into her compact.

—And while I would not wish them on my worst enemy I am not going to stand here and tell you I am sorry for her. Absolutely *not*.

Her pink-painted lips and lightly rouged cheeks move within an alabaster field of powder. She must rehearse like this so her old face does not resurface and betray her with some sudden paroxysm of snideness. No, she must look and behave how her heart feels—soft, sweet and innocent.

—I wouldn't have her any other way and I bet you wouldn't either.

Honesty has a hypnotically calming effect, she finds.

—I would do *anything* for Flora, for all of you. Please forget how awful I have been to you in the past. That was the old Belladonna. I have started over. Truly.

O god but this feels good. She is becoming a loving woman full of conviction. Yes, she is beginning to understand now why the membership, especially their relentlessly im-pregnating wing, has always treated her so self-righteously: Because it was the same way they treat their children. You see, unless they are 100% behind every little fact and dictum they pass down their children will begin to doubt them. Think of the pressure involved in that!? The effort required to achieve such consistency!? Yes, parenthood demands a radical form of self-righteousness. No wonder Belladonna has been anathema all these years. If she got too close she might infect her brothers and sisters with her own doubt and they might pass it down to those future Little Coopers of theirs. Fortun-ately, she no longer poses such a danger to her niece.

—All that matters to me now is love.

—I'm sorry, Sister Belladonna?

Thad has spoken over the com.

—Nothing, Brother Thad. I was just talking to myself.

Belladonna has Thad drop her off two blocks from the bungalow.

—You may go now, Brother Thad. I will take a taxi home. Here is a gratuity.

Thad takes the outrageously large tip.

—Thank you, Sister Belladonna!

—You are very welcome, Brother Thad. I have en-joyed working with you.

Belladonna pulls her sable coat up around her chin and steps outside. All the white-bright glare makes it difficult to see. Her heels scrape and tock against the ice-pithed sidewalk and echo back off the sound barrier. When she turns around to make sure no one is following her, she slips, flails, almost falls, and boffs herself in the head with her purse. O god she must be brave and strong for Flora and Ronette and Sid now. Think of their first joyful moments together.

—Can I hold her? I'll be careful. I promise.

Belladonna is finally presented with the merciful site of the bungalow. Icy footprints climb cement steps otherwise covered with knee-high snow. She grabs the listing railing and is halfway up when it buckles then collapses and sends her sprawling into the snow. Her bag flies sideways and her purse boffs her on the head. The bottle and toy rest atop an un-reachable drift. Staggering to her feet, telling herself not to complain, she decides it was frivolous to bring gifts to an aggrieved family anyway. Yes, this mishap was for the best and the pain in her knees is blessed. She has overcome the first small obstacle.

The front door is obstructed by a savagely pink plastic miniature jungle gym. She squeezes herself between it and the front door. However bursting her heart is with radical love she must prepare herself for the poverty she will face inside and so touches her mouth to make sure it isn't spasming judgmentally—So far so good. She considers the flaking paint, warped walls, sagging foundation, and filthy windows; the total indifference towards upkeep. Yes, this is easily the most rundown bungalow on the block but this is only meaningful insofar as Flora will be facing the additional challenge of living in a crumbling home full of hidden hazards. The unfairness of this wrenches Belladonna in the gut and makes her want to scratch off a massive check for Sid and Ronette. But since a measure of suffering will be unavoidable if her niece is to ever transcend her limitations, Belladonna decides money would only be a false solution, a shortcut through what is necessary. Sighing steam over the jungle gym's lookout deck, she scans the windows of the bungalows across the street hoping someone is spying on her so they can witness how she suffers on behalf of everyone's suffering—O if only everyone could be struck by a bolt of radical love and not only see the other side of their suffering but springboard off that motherbleeper like she has. Belladonna squints up into the feathery snow, feels something like a toothache or a sneeze coming on. . .and suddenly begins to cry. O god it doesn't feel like she remembers, there's nothing redemptive or emptying about it, the feeling of helplessness only doubles and redoubles with each snort and sniffle, and when she tries to stop but cannot she begins moaning and sobbing, thinking she might vomit, holding her hands out to the indifferent bungalows, pounding on the jungle gym's slide, wondering why no one rushes to her in compassion, tries to yell for help but can only manage a low and raspy bellow, then desperately pounds on the door.

—Hello?! *Hello?!*

But it's too late. She is going to drown in her own tears. She is nothing but a lost bitch, an undiscovered island covered by the rapidly rising seas. She isn't even relevant enough to get in anyone's way any-more. All her efforts to *get over herself* had rendered her obscure, neither here nor there. All these long hopeful months trying to bring love into her life had only been the beginning of what she now knew was her final disappearance. Yes, even if she had somehow lucked into being loved by someone she would have only gone plummeting down the soft, warm vortex of the sensation until her voice and all her after-aspects sunk to the bottom and jettisoned the useless husk to the surface for the seagulls to feed on. No, no one would miss that extracted soul, they would only smile at the remainder resembling this zombie of a woman dumbly reaching for the door knob to balance herself but, either out of habit or some unavoidable instinct, also turning and pushing the knob inward and suddenly stumbling forward, at first slowly, distracted as she is by how her sadness and faintness amplify one another, and too intensely maudlin to slow her gradual, tripping descent and feeling pretty damn sanguine about the fall as it gains speed so why not just trip over a baby buggy, swerve, stagger, boff herself in the head with her purse, skate on some baby clothes, kick a bike frame and snort not at the pain but at how foolish she would appear if anyone were watching, collide with the side of the sofa, go oof!, see her mother swirling and snorting as her daughter finally becomes dizzy enough to just give in to the fall yet remaining just enough of a preservation-minded animal that she flails to grab hold of something and pulls several mannequin arms down along with her before the floor separates her left shoulder from her body and whiplashes her head as the arms and secret notes tumble around her and she passes out smelling mold or maybe yeast.

o   o   o   o   o   o   o   o   o

In a white-walled hospital room, wearing an aquamarine gown, her thumb pumping a medication button, shivering from the heat register blowing on her like a grudge, wincing from the white-bright of the buzzing fluorescents, trying not to listen to a cheerful old woman on the other side of the curtain beg information from two reticent children, her shoulder heavily bandaged, feeling the after-effects of heat stroke and minor snow-blindness due to her bellowing census of the bungalows for someone who might help. . .*Is it hours or days since her fall?*. . .Belladonna feels. . .well. . .strangely care-free. Likely it's the meds. Possibly she should wait a bit longer before taking another boost, not wanting to seem like a junkie since the man who had finally opened his bungalow door and quickly closed it again had told the police that Belladonna was. . .*probably a strung out prostitute looking to score*. . .Yes, it's coming back now, she was finally admitted to the man's bungalow when the police arrived and had sat on his sofa spinning and sweating while the earnest men above speculated about what had happened to her. Eventually they had ushered her into the merciful dark of an ambulance where a woman in a crisp white uniform told her to try not to cry so hard since it was bad for her fever. . .*Why didn't anyone answer their door? It's a blizzard, right?*. . .The woman had smiled down and spoken to her like she was addressing a child. . .*Well, now, darlin', maybe they all went to the beach?* . . .Belladonna laughed so hard her arm fell out again and she passed out. She came to surrounded by a team of young nurses in sky blue uniforms and a hand-some doctor purring warm reassurances in her ear. He shone a light in her eyes and asked her to rate her pain with a number while he slid his hand beneath her back and carefully helped her to her feet. He then asked if she had allergies, family they might call, or a mental illness. Was she taking any medications, on her period, aware of how high her blood pressure was? Was she married, did she have children, did she remember what happened? He softly buzzed around her primping the bandages on her knees, hands, and head while she grunted answers through the medication haze. Then she suddenly felt his hand sliding up her hip then deliciously brushing against her breast before wonderfully, O god so wonderfully, cupping the ball of her shoulder while continuing to purr. . .*Mmm-hmm. . .mmm-hmm. . .Yes. . .Yes, I see.* . .up until the bizarre moment when two of the nurses leapt to hug her around the stomach and chest while he. . .*Mmm-hmm. . .Mmm-hmm. . .Ready.* . . commenced to tear her shoulder from her body again and shove it back in. When Belladonna's screams died down she gave every single nurse the finger and asked those aggressively healthy-looking women. . .*Are you happy now?. . .Isn't this what you've always wanted?.* . .just before their powerful arms wrestled her down to administer another shot to put her back to sleep.

Thinking back on the episode, now pleasantly amused by it, tolerably fond of what a psycho she had acted, grateful for everyone's patience, feeling, well, a bit bashful and, okay, admittedly crushed out a bit on that brute of a doctor, wishing he would return to perform a modified version of putting her back together, pulling the Huguenot-tight bed corners up to give herself some play, hiding the pump under the covers, glancing over at the perfectly adorable silhouettes in the curtain and pumping away and pumping away until, ah, oui, she is feeling pretty terrific actually, not just riding the meds-high but open and floaty, happily compelled by some sweet, listless other. What remains of her feels delicate and vulnerable, sweet and cute. Yes, she is ready to believe the old bitch might have finally flown the coop for good this time, such transformations not being unheard of she is guessing, especially when a blow to the head comes into play. But Belladonna doesn't want to think too much or over-remember her former self. What she has experienced and why and where she goes from here seems like the most tedious pile of crap in the entire world when the thumb working the button pressed against her navel is the only thing that matters now. No, she just wants to sit back and groove on this high a while longer, occasionally look over at the curtain, smile approvingly at the shadow puppet play there, the kids waving their arms and whooping, performing some charming skit for grammy maybe, reenacting another adorable little childish foible,

Belladonna hoping the curtain is never pulled back, wanting to remain innocent of these loveable characters' faces, remembering how curtains hid the psychotic little world Sid and Ronette were supposed to be raising a baby in, how she had reeled among all that junk and tried to focus on something and saw the heavily bandaged baby blue sack of flour with a bellowing bull on the front. Was it a piece of artso esoterica . . .*Flour in Box*. . .or another bit of domestic lunacy? Whatever it was she found herself staring at the tough old stud and wishing he would call her a taxi and escort her home to do with her what he wished. He had indicated that this was impossible but had implored her to get up and snortingly cheered her on during her peregrination around the snow-bound bungalows. She remembers thinking that if she ever made it back to the hotel she would have to have someone go pick her up a bag just like him so she could install him as her confidant. But until then why not transport herself back to the bull's starkly lit, shadowless plane for some bluntly functional and bestial doinking? Yes, she is now pumping the button, fighting the sheet and the sling and the pain, feeling limbless and pinioned, doinking and doinking, floating away, wanting to bloom into a fat pink carnation for once, pumping and doinking, desperately clinging to the prettiness she feels inside but slowly losing the trace, tying herself up in the sheet, staring nervously into the over-bright corners of the white-paneled ceiling, feeling perverse, getting nowhere with herself, the bull not responding, hinting he wants to keep things platonic for now, provide her with friendship and solace, this feeling better to Belladonna than any doinking, making her cry happy tears as the floating inclines downward and she starts plummeting, pulling her good arm out from the sheets so the bull can leap through the package with his hooves parted to slam into her belly in an embrace.

  —Oof!

  —Are you alright, ma'am?

Another intensely healthy young nurse materializes.

  —I see your medication limited out. Is the pain very bad, Ms. Maybacy?

  —No. . .but can you bring me my purse, please?

There is an old cache of happy pills in there somewhere and there might be enough to help her hold onto the lingering sweetness in her bones and give her the courage to ask her new bull friend if he will help her locate her wayward soul so they can decide what to do with it—become engaged, basically.

—Of course.

Belladonna watches as the nurse makes an adorable little effortful mouth while lifting the purse onto the bed.

—Goodness. So heavy.

Yes, she can feel it now. By sheer chance, and however implausibly, Belladonna has found someone who will accept her for what she is. . .whatever that might be.

—Could you leave me alone now, please? I need to get some sleep. And thank you.

—Of course.

Anxious to find the pills, Belladonna overturns her purse and pours out the bandaged sack of flour whose logo is a frightened bull wearing a silver ring in his nose.

15.

—I'm going up, X.

Ronette hugs two heavy grocery bags to her chest. The sidewalk is knee-high with snow and she is having a hard time keeping her balance. She does not call out to Exene for help, though, because this is but one of the many small routines she will have to master in preparation for her return to the outside world. Yes, predictable and replicable behaviors. Structure. These were the things which had allowed her and Sid to heal and make bungalow life navigable again. Yes, family life could become just another ruthlessly pursued discipline. But since she was still a novice at balancing everyone's needs it was only natural that there had been some casualties. Sid is frightfully happy but terribly nervous. And Flora—no longer an infant but a stubborn little child—recoils at each new rule, squirms to be put down only to cry for attention, screams that if no one will let her do exactly what she wants she will go find someone who will. . .*Flo go! Flo go! Flo go!.* . .These violent outbursts leaving Ronette no choice but to leave Flora at home this morning while she and Exene shopped. . .*This will give you a chance to think about things, Flora. . .You're becoming a big girl now. . .And a big girl needs to learn how to be alone.* . .Flora had just sat their quietly, pretending not to hear, not making a sound even as

Ronette closed the door. . .*Quick, X, let's go before I change my mind.* . .Yes, Ronette needs to be strong if she is ever going to get back in touch with her general tendencies.

You see, she needs her simple life on the rig back, training with Sid, delivering; all the regular little habits she had installed and which she now realizes constituted stability and happiness—the very things that a child needs in order to feel safe. And while her desperate attempts to get inside her motherhood had taught her a great deal, maybe even accelerated Flora's development on many levels, she had lost track of herself in the process, only realizing how imbalanced her life had become once Sid started leaving those sad, needy notes everywhere. No, Flora, no matter how much she cries about it, needs a well-rounded mother with clearly defined boundaries.

So Ronette had begun detaching, left Flora in the alcove after Sid fixed the leak over the mathematical center, cut back on Wheee! time, slept exclusively with Sid, maintained these disciplines even as Flora wailed in terror during the night, refused kisses in the morning, and went cold at her mother's touch. Ronette would hug and kiss her limp body while whispering that from now on she was going to have to make all Flora's decisions for her and not the other way around. . .*I'm your mother.* . .*I have certain needs.* . .*We all do.* . .*And in a small bungalow like this we have to respect each other's general tendencies.* . .But it is painful to come home and face the ominous silence coming from the alcove; Flora's pouts being of practically operatic proportions these days, the dust motes over the nighty-night box performing a harried dance at the sullen respiration of the sack of flour below, the humidity in the alcove rising with the increase of her stifled tears. Yes, it was all Ronette could do to not drop the bags and run to her instead of staggering to the kitchen with the heavy bags.

One by one she unloads nine brand new five-pound sacks of generic deluxe all-purpose wheat flour and one brand new five-pound sack of organic wheat flour. What a handsome group, each with its own distinct posture and inking, their crisp and unwrinkled sacks smiling back, all so excited to be Flora's new friend—not her brothers and sisters, mind you, just her friends. Yes, when Ronette returns to work her daughter will have this huge group of friends to play with through the long cold bungalow days.

But a slow introduction was necessary. Suddenly surrounding Flora with what resembles an invading force would be emotionally jarring. So this morning she will only introduce her to one of the sacks. . .*Flo-Flo, honey, this is Koko. . .You and Koko are going to become best friends just like you and Alma. . .I've already told her all about you. . .* Then she will introduce her to the babysitter she had been making veiled allusions to for the past few weeks. . .*Flo-Flo, Mama has to go back to work. . .Sometimes Aunty X and Cousin Alma will be able to come over but the rest of the time you're going to need someone to look after you. . .I want you to treat her like she is another member of the family. . .You can—*

—Where should I put you-know-who, Ron?!

Exene has shouted from the sitting room. Ronette tries to remain calm.

—Just put her in the easy chair for now!

But when she hears the dry thud in the other room her stomach drops. Is it really necessary that she pawn her daughter off on some stranger? Are her general tendencies more important than her daughter's happiness? But wait. . .no . . .no. . .that's the old thinking. This is good parenting. This will pay off for *everyone* in the long run.

—Alma got shy on us. She's still in the car. You know how she gets sometimes.

Exene has swung into the kitchen to find Ronette braced against the counter and holding one of the sacks of flour.

—You know I found a bottle of champagne out there?

—Oh?

—Those Coopers just can't stop giving, I guess.

Exene touches Ronette's shoulder.

—It'll be okay, Ron. She'll make it through this.

—Yeah, I know. I'm just a bit nervous.

Exene gives the sack a pat on the head.

—Aw, she'll love Miss Koko here and that other thing will be fine.

—Yeah, you're probably right.

Both women look at the sack of wheat flour.

—Anyway, where's Flora? It's a bit of a mess out there.

—She's in her nighty-night box.

—No she isn't, Ron. I just looked.

They hurry out of the kitchen. Ronette looks in the empty nighty-night box then notices all the mannequin arms and notes scattered around the dresser and then the imprint of a weaving transit over the dented tarps, through all the disturbed junk, and clear to the front door.

So this is what all the future voids will start out feeling like. Hysteria choked down to nausea in the name of remaining calm. Yes, as Flora gets older and becomes more independent, more capable of achieving her stated desire to. . .*Go! Go! Go!* . . .it is inevitable that all the little mile-stones, while joyous, will make her mother feel like she is being left behind. Even if Sid just skipped practice, picked her up, and went some-where with her it is still *possible* Flora managed to climb out of her crib and run away. Yes, a mother's intuition will always contain a great store of potential calamities but as the years pass and she and her daughter wade into the unknown together she will probably develop an almost omniscient power to anticipate approaching danger and these initial slugs of hysteria won't be quite so disorienting and she will become far more effective far more quickly.

—Sid probably skipped practice, came home, and took her somewhere, Ron.

Looking back into the empty nighty-night box then out into the wide white-layered world beyond, Ronette tells herself that if this is the day her daughter has taken her first steps then she should not mourn the loss of closeness that this portends but concentrate on helping her daughter navigate this passage safely. Yes, she will provide her with the encouragement and praise which will spur her to future achievements—even if they rip a piece of her heart out every time. . . *I'll always be proud of you, Flora. . .Nothing can change that* . . .Ronette turns around, surveys The Big Room's knee-high floes, the uncharted chasms and cliffs, the many pitfalls a five-pound sack of wheat flour might encounter while testing the contour and gravity of the unfolding world. If her daughter is only trapped under some debris then she is safe. But if she succeeded in escaping the bungalow and started walking down the snow-strewn street someone might have picked her up, mistaken her for a curiosity and given her to the authorities who, in turn, would have probably pawned her off on the medical experts for a barrage of painfully invasive and traumatic tests before they, in turn, pawned her off on some well-intentioned but ultimately over-burdened facility. Ronette leaps and lunges to the sitting room window and desperately scans the snow for a trail.

—No, this was supposed to be their first day at home together.

An old, horrible feeling swirls into a funnel and plummets down her intestines while, off to the side, The Eel Prince awakens, whispers. . .*This is what you wanted all along*. . .Yes, Sid had been too agreeable. She had terrorized him for months but he kept coming back for more. . .*Why else would you have left her alone?*. . .He knew it was impossible for her to care for both their daughter *and* him without going bonkers so, eventually, he would have to intervene by throwing Flora into the river. All those needy notes he had left in the nighty-night box were nothing but a *threat* of removal. Instinctively, she had tried to stall him, played at the happy family thing, threw him some bones and, admittedly, felt more stable, even more connected to the manipulative jerk. But this had only made her more vulnerable to having the rug pulled out from under her like this. . .*Admit it, you want more than a sack of flour with that big moron*. . .She would now throw herself at his feet and beg to know why he had taken her daughter away and he would say tough love was the only thing that could save her from herself and she would collapse into his arms like some dumb weak woman. Installed as her protector, the only remaining distance between them would be that of owner and possession. Finally, he would have the submissive woman he had wanted all along. And she had to admit that sometimes she *did* want to put herself under his power, abscond from all the hurt and loss that lay ahead, the unending threat of abandoned nighty-night boxes, bondage to this insensitive little being constantly demanding servitude, the slow obliteration of what was left of her general tendencies. . .*And now that Flora's gone you can con him into getting a real one*. . .So why not cop out and let Sid ride lead on their tandem bicycle while she consoled herself by thinking that Flora had at least been spared a traumatic childhood and tenuous future. And, who knows, maybe once she gets her shit together they could try again. . .*I have the perfect name for her.*

Luckily, Ronette has just enough muscle memory to recognize these thoughts for what they are: The beginning of training. Yes, that's right. She is weak and her habits are not well-established yet. Faced with an obstacle she is prone to turning into a sniveling, melodramatic little baby. Lazy compromises, spiritual acquiescence, and hollow achievements lie lurking, waiting to ensnare. If she can just buckle down and embrace the pain and fear she might gain a foothold and gradually establish a routine for facing the challenges ahead. She must remain vigilant, constantly remind herself that however radically flawed and limited she is—as a mother and otherwise—there is still a chance it can be different for her daughter. Yes, a baby's possibilities are limitless. A good example was all that was necessary and Ronette would remain in training for the rest of her life. And perhaps as she travels that winding, precipitous road she will occasionally allow herself to reflect and be able to say she has given her daughter a better childhood than her mother had and a stronger foundation—a stable home, loving parents, and a predictable future. Yes, considering Flora's departure in this light, Ronette decides that only a strong and independent child would have had the courage to throw herself into the deep end like that. She only wishes she could have been there when Flora pulled herself up from the tarp and took those first few steps.

—Let's go find her, Auntie X. She's out there somewhere.

—Shouldn't we leave Sid a note or something?

—No, this family needs to stop relying on notes.

Outside the sitting room window the snow-fringed noise barrier elongates to the north then flattens into a featureless white plane at the horizon until a plow abruptly corners at Evers and comes barreling down the road.

o   o   o   o   o   o   o   o   o

The snow has kept Sid's training partners away so he asks the only other Co-op riders if he can ride some lead-outs for them. But maybe they haven't heard he is doing speed training now or expect him to be at home with his newborn instead because they appear concerned by his request. He explains that mother and baby are out shopping and that this is going to be his last day of training for a while. But the other riders look at him judgmentally, demonstrate by raised eyebrows and lowered heads that they don't think he should be there. Sid then nervously confides to these relative strangers that this is going to be his first afternoon alone with his newborn and that he wants to sweat himself free of distractions so his daughter will have his undivided attention. . .*Seriously, fellas, I know what's best for my little girl, okay?*

After taking the first banking turn, though, Sid knows he will not take another. Maybe the other riders had messed with his mojo. Or, more likely, the hungry tug of gravity held a warning. . .*Next time round, I'm taking you to the bottom like I did Mama. . .*Shaken, he pulls into the infield, hurriedly pulls on some layers, tucks his ponytail into his jersey and heads home.

The ice on the bridge makes it hard to get a good cadence going. Wind and sleet slap and shove, threaten to cast him onto the iron grating. Fortunately, there is no traffic. Everyone is smugly hidden inside the millions upon millions of boxes sprawled and climbing around him, obscured only by the remorseless weather. Only that idiot in his rig is out. Only that low-grade vertigo sufferer would have braved the bridge on a day like today. Only a man terrified to be alone with his daughter would distract himself by putting himself in danger. But wait, a father with responsibilities knows better than to run himself under the bus like this. Yes, he must remain intensely focused, take one careful, steady turn after another until he finds himself coasting down the ramp on the other side. It's slow going and a bit nerve-wracking but absolutely necessary. And while, yes, he has been a little less steady in the saddle lately, this was only because the stakes were inestimably higher now that he and Ronette were really starting to click as parents. . .*I know I've monopolized Flora, Sid. . .I'm trying to be less of a control freak. . .So, yes, it's definitely time you two get more of a chance to bond. . .*And while he worries that he might muck it up somehow he is also excited some breakthrough could occur. Maybe he and Flora will start to connect? Maybe they will begin to understand one another? Maybe mother, father, and daughter will soon be sitting around the dinner table having perfectly normal family conversations?

So when his rig skates and swivels on a patch of black ice he should not be surprised that he experiences one of those flashes of hysteria which shoots up his spine and lodges in his throat. Yes, he is totally getting used to them by now. Terror and joy must coexist like this when a father and a man and a family are just beginning to come into their own.

He sees the railing fallen over in the snow. Jesus, he hopes none of the girls had a spill. He should really get around to shoveling these stairs. Small failures can lead to massive disasters. Yes, after he has had some quality time with daughter he will shovel the stairs and sidewalk, maybe even bundle her up and ask her to supervise.

He pushes through the front door expecting to see Ronette and Exene engaged in one of those inscrutable games they play with their daughters.

—Hello? Hel-loooooo?

He drops his rig in the mathematical center and walks to the nighty-night box.

Empty.

—Ron? X? Flora?

Sid thinks for a moment. Ah. He has beaten them back from grocery shopping. His daughter has not been kidnapped. Everything is fine. Again, it is not unusual for a new parent to have the occasional melodramatic, worst-case-scenario turn of mind like this. Hyper-worry is just another form of love and will likely coalesce into another strength once he gets a few more reps in.

—You're not in here, Ron, right?

When he pushes into the kitchen he sees nine five-pound sacks of all-purpose generic deluxe wheat flour and one organic five-pound sack of wheat flour sitting shoulder-to-shoulder on the counter. His stomach flashes. Sweat spikes his forehead. But wait. . .just wait. This can make sense. . .sure. There was probably a sale and Ronette wanted to stock up what with all the accidents she's been having. God, what a klutz his championship Mama has turned into. The repairs were getting increasingly difficult and soon Flora's package would completely fail and they would have to perform some kind of ritual to transfer her soul into another sack. Anyway, with their solid postures, unwrinkled surfaces, and vivid colors the sacks resemble nothing more than a rank of smart little soldiers. Staring at their auspicious labels and tidy forms he wonders, though, if it might be demoralizing for Flora to see so many reflections of her former self. So he hastily crams the sacks into the cabinet before returning to The Big Room.

—But if they've already shopped, where the heck are they?

He surveys the wastes around him and then sees it. His shoulders are preposterously muscular. The hoop piercing his septum sparkles gold. There is a subtle but unmistakable implication of genitalia. A baby blue 30-pound sack of wheat flour imprinted with the generic deluxe bull is reclining in Sid's easy chair. The titling font is tall, bold and cursive. The bull—as big as Flora's entire sack and two-dimensional—does not flee for the interior of the stark plane he is trapped in but leaps outward with his sharp hooves extended to tear his way out. Next to the sack lies a bottle of unopened champagne. Behind him all the arms in the dresser have been pulled down and their secret notes are scattered everywhere.

—Who the hell are you and what the hell do you think you're doing?

There is something very wrong, Sid thinks. The five-pounders were one thing but this. . .this *monster?* Who the fuck is he? And what the hell is he doing in his easy chair? And where the hell is Ronette? And where the hell is his daughter? And come to think of it, if all those sacks are for future repairs why was only one sack organic like Ronette prefers? No, there was nothing here he could put in *perspective*, nothing to *prioritize*, nothing to wield his precious *nowness* at. No, the presence of the 30-pounder makes him feel like a crumbling edifice, a boneless little sack of nothing. He stares past the sack and up into the cracked and boarded ceiling, frantically searches for an explanation in those savagely subdivided coves, finds none, searches for the briefest strait of uninterrupted sea which he might abstract into in order to calm down, finds none, and then begins to fall apart.

—Ronette?!

This was obviously far more serious than some childish note stuck in his spokes. Yes, this was probably the announcement of some terrifyingly aggressive and final *phase*. Ronette was raising an army and the 30-pounder was the general who would lead the charge to push Sid out for good. He thinks about the sacks he crammed into the cabinet who would already be stirring in rebellion. He looks into the angry eyes of the bull, his sharpened hooves poised to strike. And the bungalow, with all its hulkingly ambivalent matter, begins to close in around him and partition his thinking. . . *They want me out. . .I was never supposed to be here in the first place. . .*He trips and lunges to the bathroom, locks himself in, puts his ear to the door to listen; and the steady drip of melt water falling onto the tarps may as well be the sound of the 30-pounder dragging himself across the room with his foot soldiers bringing up the rear. Yes, the flimsy pillars which have allowed Sid Doe to build tremulously upwards or, more often, sideways in his life, have received a foundational blow. What little faith he has in himself goes tumbling as all the adaptations and compromises under-pinning his identity begin to crumble. And without Ronette or even Flora close by to help him re-gather his thoughts he can no longer distinguish between possibility and probability and so suffers in horrible limbo and in complete isolation as the world as he knows it fractures beneath him—Which is to say that with one undermining stroke he has become completely unmoored from reality.

—Fuck you, bro, okay?! FUCK you!

His tinnitus takes a bizarrely croaking turn and a hectoring voice bubbles up from his diaphragm. . .*Well, I suppose we shouldn't be surprised, my friend. . .I mean what is to be expected from a community college dropout?. . .*He yanks on his ponytail hoping the pain will distract him. . .*The internal muscle was never there, you know. . .There are certain deficiencies no amount of legwork can overcome. . .*The light-bright from the bathroom's flickering halogens activate his vertigo. . .*Now hold on, don't interrupt. . .All I am saying here is that one father's deficiencies don't necessarily explain his son's. . .*He tears his hair out of the rubber band to shield his eyes with it. . .*So if I am going to grant that this hypothetical Sidney Jonathan Dublinski III does exist and that he is the father to a five-pound sack of wheat flour. . .well. . .heh. . . ahem. . .I mean I'm not about to conclude that that's my fault, you know?. . .*Sid shouts as loud as he can. . .*Blah-blah-blah! Blah-blah-blah!. . .*but his father ignores him as usual. . .*Now shut up, SHUT up! Once again you are coddling our* *hypothetical Sidney J. . .Just listen. . .lisss-sen. . .*and he thinks that even if his father just exists in his mind he is still the only one to blame for that. . .*You're point is not lost on me. I agree that such a hypothetical boy. . .er, man. . .should occasionally be granted his premises. .* .just as he will be the only one to blame when he sticks a knife into the abdomen of a 30-pound sack of wheat flour. . .*And if granted his premises, i.e. that a family can be constituted of a hypothetical man, a hypo-thetical woman, and a sack of wheat flour. . .*Yes, this all just proves how shoddy a job he had done of taking control of his life. It now seems likely that his father has been calling the shots in subtle but incalculable ways all along. Blinded by a few paltry personal gains, he had forgotten that family life is a never-ending struggle. . .*then would it be too much of a stretch to say that that stud lounging in his easy chair in there is not only the hypothetical woman's longtime paramour. .* .an ongoing symposium on the many ways we can hurt the ones we are supposed to care for. . .*but ipso facto the hypothetical Sidney J.'s permanent replacement?. . .*He bursts through the bathroom door and stumbles into the kitchen. . .*Now you may find this hard to believe but I do have one regret. .* .then throws all the crap on the counter aside looking for something sharp. . .*I wish I could have warned the kid that for poor hypothetical schmucks like us family life is the worst thing possible. . .*but he has forgotten that Ronette had him curbside all of their knives for fear of accidentally stabbing Flora. . . *You get into it with the best of intentions. . .You genuinely love your wife. . .You want to make her happy. . .You are confused as to why someone would love this hypothetical schmuck you walk around in but, hey, there must be something she sees in you that is real so grab hold of her and don't let go. . .Even a moron like you can pull off marriage, you think. .* .He thinks that in this entire gear-choked house there is not a single object which might aid or console him. . .*And you do it for a while and feel pretty damn proud of yourself until you start to have the old doubts and choose to interpret them as not feeling as turned on by your marriage as you used to and wonder if your life is merely a melodramatic routine you have installed to distract yourself from how insubstantial you feel inside. .* .He has allowed himself to be buried, hopelessly clogged the path back to Ronette with delusions. . .*Yes deep down you have never stopped doubting your our own*

*existence. . .And even if you manage to hang onto the woman
you share the house with and she consents to—either out of
habit or practicality—keep on loving you, you begin to smell
the sham in this. . .Her ongoing tolerance is no different than
changing the vacuum bag or having the tires rotated. . .*What
he had taken for clarity was just a less obstructed view of the
bottom of the trash heap. . .*You're no more vital than a coat
rack or a dishwasher or a dining room chair. . .You think,
well, love didn't save me from all the nothingness inside but
maybe cruelty will. . .Maybe inflicting unrelenting pain on the
one person stupid enough to go on loving you is as close as
you will ever get to feeling alive again. . .*Then he remembers
Woody II, plunges through the piles on the counter and finds
him, breaks him over his knee and lunges out into The Big
Room. . .*And in particularly pathetic cases like mine you
never quite wound your victim severely enough to make them
flee or rise up and kill you like they should because you still
hold out hope that some lightning bolt will strike and you will
be transformed before you can infect her with your hypo-
theticalness. . .*Doomed to an echoing loneliness, his sole coherent impulse is towards violence. . .*So you consent to raise
a family together desperately hoping for that lightning strike
and become increasingly bitter when it never comes, realizing
too late that you have doubled your original mistake. . .*Sid
holds the splintered wood spike over the 30-pounder's midsection. . .*What I'm saying, my friend, is that if Sidney J.
really loves his family he should walk out that door before it's
too late for his wife and daughter. The damage, as they say, is
done, but the die is not necessarily casterooni. My son can
still be a better man than his old man was if he gets out while
the getting's still good. . .*His arms drop to his side. He has
nothing against the 30-pounder. Chances are he will be a
better partner for Ronette, a better father for Flora. Anyway,
with Ronette getting her act together as a mother like she was
and the 30-pounder's far more intuitive understanding of
Flora, Sid was totally expendable now. His loved ones should
not be made to suffer for how insubstantial he is any longer.
He would always be nothing but a garbled gesture, the ellipse
between declarative sentences, neither here nor there; always
at a remove. Yes, he should just get on his rig, head for the
bridge, and take it from there. The sooner he does this the

sooner it will seem as though he was never here in the first place. Maybe just leave a note.

```
        DA-DA GO-GO
        DA-DA GONE-GONE
        BYE-BYE BYE-BYE
```

The car halts, rocks, and seizes in front of a narrow parking spot. Hale bashes against the roof. The spring rains blow sideways. She ratchets the gear shift, pumps the gas, breaks jarringly to a halt, wipes the sweat from her eyes, then desperately starts turning the steering wheel again. Reverse and forward. Angling and re-angling. Trying not to panic. Needing to hurry through this so she can hurry through the next part. Reverse and forward. Seizing. Trying again. But she just won't fit. Finally, she decides to ram her rear bumper into another car and push it back far enough so she can slide forward into the spot.

—Don't tell anyone about that, okay?

She unhooks the seatbelt and wraps the five-pound sack of generic deluxe all-purpose wheat flour inside the poncho and then inside her own raincoat. If they run fast enough the world won't swallow them. Yes, they've proven that this is so.

She slams her door into the one next to her. Hale conks her in the head. Rain catches in her eyes. She is trapped, tangled in the coats, starting to panic. If only she could see better. . .but her new glasses are on the dash and she can't risk being outside much longer. A fury builds inside. She is always unprepared, forgetting things, choosing poorly. She lacks foresight, can barely concentrate, loses track of time. It was no wonder her brothers and sisters kept telling her they would take her daughter away if she didn't start taking better care of herself.

Darnit. Darnit.

She looks around to see if anyone is watching.

—*Fuck!*

After finally squeezing free she makes a run for the complex of buildings at the far end of the parking lot. Her milk-laden breasts bounce painfully up and down inside her shirt and she is winded inside twenty yards. When she finally bursts through the doors the man and woman behind the welcome desk are overjoyed then horrified.

—Sister Ronette! Baby Fauna! Oh god, did you get wet? Fauna, honey, are you okay?

The man hurries around the desk then buckles and gasps when Ronette tosses him the bundle. The woman descends upon her with a towel and starts furiously and tsk-tskingly drying her face and hair. The man glares once at her before hurrying behind the desk to carefully unwrap the raincoat and then the poncho. What he finds inside pleases him.

—It's okay. She's fine. Just *fine.*

The woman tries to usher Ronette towards a locker room.

—Let's get Mama into some dry clothes, huh? She's *soaked.*

She peers up into Ronette's eyes with outlandish de-light and gutturally and exhalingly reiterates her concern.

—*Isn't* she?!

—I'm fine, too.

She must not appear angry. Their counselors say Fauna picks up on things like that. Yes, she must behave like the perfect little Co-op mother. If Fauna is ever going to improve little sacrifices like this will be necessary. But then she has a vague memory of herself, someone who was in firm control of outcomes, capable of dictating pace. Things were so much easier then, she thinks, even if it was all just an illusion.

—Thank you, Sister, but I am anxious to get to the socialization.

—Oh, of course you are. Of *course.*

The woman shoos Ronette away while the man presents her with the sack of wheat flour.

—Now, Sister Ronette, due to a minor flood in the Little Cooper Center we had to move the socialization to The Fun Bubble. You will need to go to the end of this hallway, turn right, and follow the arrows. We'll look after your coats in the meantime. Please hurry.

A bunker of a hallway veers right and abruptly shoves her into a vaulted buzzing darkness. Though there is a long curving path of yellow electric tape arrows flanked by fat and flicker-ing white candles, until her eyes can adjust she may as well be floating through some strange astrological configuration resembling a crescent moon or a bull's horn. Feelingly reaching into this asterisk-spiked night, forcing herself to get further and further away from the light of the hallway behind her, she enters a deep roaring respiration interrupted by little wails and screeches. This could be the exposed ventilation ducts straining against some obstruction or injury or it could just be her imagination—She sees little difference. Either way, the immanence of thick volume and heat which accompanies it tightens around her body then threatens to pull her under. Leaden, desperate to stumble out into the starless dark outside the path and sleep, she clutches herself up to awaken forgetting she is holding Fauna. She gasps at the sound of the sack expanding in her arms and feels sure her daughter is about to explode.

    —Oh no.

    She loosens her grip and holds Fauna close to a candle. She is only misshapen and a little bottom heavy. There is no leak. Even so Fauna will arrive to the socialization looking a mess and this will prove once again that she is an unfit mother and The Co-op will threaten to take her daughter away. But wait, maybe the other parents won't notice, anxious as they always are to descend upon her daughter and press the hands of their inquisitive Little Coopers into her sack, encourage them to ask her questions, suggest games they might play until the bravest of their number sweeps Fauna away and straps her into a swing to recite gibberish soliloquies while pushing her harder and higher while the rest of the children form a perimeter to watch the swing move closer to parallel as Fauna goes on staring into the middle distance as though she might be wailing in horror or screaming in glee. (Ronette now trying to shake and smooth the sack back into shape, walking faster, beginning to feel dizzy.) God, why did they have to keep going through with this? Would it be so terrible if instead they moved to the woods and grunted urges at one another until their lives ran out? Would that be less meaningful than wedging Fauna into a social apparatus so that one day she might scrawl out a legible mother's day card? (Striding, desperate to leave this endless room but afraid what the next might hold.) Were Fauna's mute ways somehow inferior to Flora's moody and rebellious yet more articulate ones? Why not just rely upon sheer presence and proximity for once? Isn't there a beautiful kind of faith in just *hoping* for love or just receiving tolerance or patience from others? Why do we require so many reassurances? Is life somehow better for all our gab? (Kneading her breast, ticking off all the well-intentioned clichés about parenthood between footfalls, not believing them but reflexively putting one foot in front of the other, finally seeing a glowing red EXIT sign.) Why not consign ourselves to, if not silent communications, then at least less invasive ones? (Panting, sweating onto Fauna's sack, leaning her burning forehead against the cold, rusty door, turning around thinking she should go back but seeing that the hallway she entered through is so distant now that it is nothing more than the brightest star at the tip of another crescent moon or bull's horn. Then the door falls away.)

—There you are, Sister Ronette. I was worried.

She stumbles into a small, over-bright room. Shielding her eyes with the sack, she searches out that one sole reassuring voice.

—You were supposed to be here an hour ago.

Warren stands across from her, resting a proprietary hand against another rusty metal door. He knocks twice, takes two quick strides to swallow Ronette in his arms and expertly scoops Fauna away from her.

—Anyway, how is our little niece today?

—Good, Uncle Warren. We're sorry we're late.

She should provide some unit of parental detail.

—We were practicing counting on the way over and got a little lost.

—Excellent! That Little Cooper is really coming along.

Warren foists Fauna into the air in his massive hands then gives her mother a sidelong look.

—Though, she does look a little worn out, Sister Ronette.

—She's fine, Uncle Warren. Maybe just a little nervous.

—Well then what about her mother's new glasses?

He stands away to study her face, wants to be as gentle as possible, but still lets her know with that fiercely caring look of his that he will step in if he has to, especially now that he is the only person in the position to do so.

—I left them in the car, Uncle Warren. Don't worry, I wore them while I was driving.

He doesn't want to overdo it, though, and shifts abruptly. By telltale amplifications of his naturally buoyant spirit—swooping Fauna from side to side now, dancing over the sawdust-strewn concrete floor—he makes it clear that he wants to do a poor job of disguising some secret.

—Ah. Good. Well, in you go then. I have a feeling today's socialization is going to be a real game-changer.

He winks at the bellowing bull and hands the sack back to her.

—Oh and I have a little surprise in there for you, too, Ronnie.

—Great, Warren. Good. Thank you. Uncle Warren, I mean.

Since she cannot disguise how badly she wants to hide in his arms instead of going in The Fun Bubble, he kisses her reassuringly on the forehead, pushes the door open, and nudges her to go inside.

—Remember, Ronette, I'm still proud of you. I still believe in you even if you don't.

As she turns back to him with tears in her eyes a wall of sound crashes down around her.

—There they are!

Hundreds of brothers and sisters dressed in formal blacks press in to touch Fauna. A chant goes up. . .*Faw-nuh! Faw-nuh! Faw-nuh!.* . .which echoes back flat and loud after bouncing off the faceted plastic of the white-yellow Fun Bubble dome. Hands reach out to pin a ∞ pendant to Fauna and she only just pulls her away in time. Stunned and confused, her vision further muddled by sweat and tears, she concludes that this chaos is probably just another innovation to the Little Cooper Socialization Curriculum. But then she wonders why Warren wouldn't have warned her.

—Ronette! Fauna!

Exene materializes to take her by the arm while Virgil clears a path to a small stage where the Co-op children often perform skits and songs. Both are also dressed in formal Co-op blacks. Exene wears the ∞ pendant as a barrette while Virgil has rotated the one on his chest to form an 8. Both are Coopers in good standing again but it is strange to see them here since Alma is afraid of crowds.

—Don't freak out, Ron. You're going to like this.

She shelters over Fauna while Virgil steers them through the sea of outstretched arms. As he helps her onto the stage he shouts into her ear.

—Alma stayed home but she says 'Congratulations!'

Faw-nuh! Faw-nuh! Faw-nuh!

Somehow Warren has skirted the crowds and beat her to the stage and is sitting next to what looks like her repaired bicycle. To his left his fiancée is chatting with Belladonna Mabuse. Both women are holding crisp five-pound sacks of generic deluxe all-purpose wheat flour. Warren's fiancée holds hers stiffly, concentrating more on sitting with good posture than molding her body to the sack. But Belladonna seems practiced and comfortable, gently rocking the sack in the crook of her arm and occasionally giving the bull a little tease or tickle. Ronette squints past them then out into the milling crowd and sees that nearly everyone else is also holding a five pound sack of generic deluxe all-purpose wheat flour. Most hold theirs over their heads and rhythmically shake them at the stage. Some hold children over their shoulders who in turn shake the sacks for them. Many sacks wear a black headband fashioned out of a black racing wristband embossed with a yellow ∞. One little girl dressed in formal blacks pushes a black tricycle with just such a sack strapped to the seat. She pushes her rig as fast as she can until it suddenly tips over. But seeing the sack is uninjured, the child rights the rig and keeps on racing.

—Ronette! *Sister* Ronette! Welcome!

Belladonna Mabuse has kneeled in front of her to shout over the chanting.

—What you see here today, Sister Ronette, would not have been possible without your Little Flora.

Belladonna gives her a meaningful look and then a kiss on the cheek.

—I think I speak for all of us when I say that she has taught us how fragile life is.

Faw-nuh! Faw-nuh! Faw-nuh!

When she sees tears forming in Belladonna's eyes she has the urge to leap from the stage.

—But remember, family, true family, comes in many forms. Just because she is no longer with us doesn't mean we have to *feel* that way or that we can't take steps to make sure she is never forgotten. Just ask your brothers and sisters.

When Belladonna sweeps an arm out over the audience a cheer goes up. Adults are shouting over one another and shaking their sacks. Children are screaming, running amok, and behaving perfectly normally. The child with the sack of flour strapped to the tricycle goes on racing herself. Virgil and Exene, huddled together by the side of the stage, have somberly raised their fists to The Fun Bubble dome.

—And I for one have learned the importance of stretching the definition of 'family.'

When Belladonna gently places her hand on Fauna, Ronette looks away and then down, pauses at Warren's cycling shoes, notices her black bicycle seat now has a yellow ∞ on the saddle, gives Fauna an absent stroke, looks at Virgil and Exene, follows the angle of their upturned arms, briefly searches out the translucencies of the open air for the after-images of the family she has lost, feels thankful they at least have at each other, thinks about the nine still untouched sacks of flour crammed into the bottom shelf of the bungalow's kitchen cabinet, then hurries upward to slowly abstract into the yolky glow of the rain-concussed Fun Bubble dome.

—But that will never be an issue for your Fauna. The manufacturers of the generic deluxe brand have been persuaded to come to an exclusive agreement with The Co-op and Warren has written a bylaw change. I will be teaching the test module of *Flexible Parenthood* and insist that you be my indispensable advisor.

Without her glasses on she can pretend that the thick wire seams binding the plastic panels together are the gullies carved by the streaming sky outside which, instead of inundating or just dampening the souls within, will merely go on relentlessly insisting upon itself.

—We should all be so lucky as to have Fauna's instant popularity.

When Belladonna stands to walk to the podium the cheers spike and then quickly die down as she speaks into the microphone.

—Ladies and gentlemen. Brothers and sisters. I would like to announce the full and permanent endowment of The Flora Okampo Childhood Development Center.

There is a long rousing cheer, more chanting of Fauna's name, more rhythmic shaking of five pound sacks of all-purpose wheat flour. Belladonna looks back and addresses a moony-eyed Ronette.

—Ronette. . .Fauna. . .come say hello to all your nieces and nephews. Your brothers and sisters.

Faw-nuh! Faw-nuh! Faw-nuh!